Women and Words: The Anthology
Les Femmes et les Mots: Une Anthologie

edited by the West Coast Editorial Collective

Harbour Publishing Co. Ltd.
1984

Designed by Penny Goldsmith
Typeset by Claudia Casper and produced at
Baseline Type & Graphics Cooperative
Cover design by Gaye Hammond

Canadian Cataloguing in Publication Data

Main entry under title:

Women and words: the anthology=
Les femmes et les mots: une anthologie
Text in English or French
ISBN 0-920080-53-7

1. Canadian literature—Women authors. 2. Canadian
literature—20th century. I. West Coast
Editorial Collective (British Columbia)
II. Title: Les Femmes et les Mots: Une Anthologie
PS8235.W6W6 1984   C810'.8'09287   C84-091405-9

49,532

Harbour Publishing Co. Ltd.
Box 219, Madeira Park, B.C.
V0N 2H0

Printed and bound in Canada by Friesen Printers

Acknowledgements

The editorial collective would like to thank the staff in the Women and Words office for their untiring passing on of messages and manuscripts, and all of the women who sent us their work.

Remerciements

Le comité éditorial souhaite remercier le personnel du bureau Les femmes et les mots de leur patience et assidiuté dans la transmission des messages et des manuscrits. Nous souhaitons remercier aussi toutes les écrivaines qui ont bien voulu nous envoyer leurs textes.

Table of Contents

Table des Matières

Preface

Women and Words: The Anthology/Les Femmes et les Mots: Une Anthologie is a project of the West Coast Women and Words Society, which also organized "Women and Words/Les femmes et les mots," a bilingual country-wide conference held in Vancouver, British Columbia in 1983, bringing together for the first time over 800 women working with the written word: writers, editors, publishers, translators, critics, printers, librarians and teachers.

An anthology committee was formed while the conference was being organized. Ads, flyers and postcards calling for submissions in French and English were sent across the country. More than 300 writers responded, and the committee began the lengthy task of selecting from approximately 1,000 poems, stories, essays and one-act plays.

One editorial group was formed to read the French manuscripts, another to consider those written in English. The editors of this book range in age from mid-twenties to mid-sixties and represent established writers, editors and professors of literature as well as women whose previous experience had been primarily as readers.

The two editorial groups worked separately for the most part, establishing somewhat different criteria for selection. The English group was committed to making a selection which reflected as fully as possible the cultural and linguistic backgrounds, race, age, sexuality, class and location of the women who submitted their work. The group operated by consensus, although in several cases, differences of opinion resulted in the inclusion of a piece about which the whole group was not in agreement. The French group, which also operated by consensus, received fewer submissions, so they chose to concentrate on variation and innovation of theme and style. The criteria for their choice lay in the authors' success in achieving this variation and innovation.

After selections were made and authors notified, the French and English groups came together to discuss the shape of the final manuscript. We decided not to present the work in thematic sections, preferring to devise an order which emphasized the impressive range of theme and voice. All of the work is previously unpublished in North America.

Victoria Freeman   Alison Hopwood   Ellen Tallman
Penny Goldsmith   Naomi Mitchell   Audrey Thomas
Barbara Herringer   Barbara Pulling

Préface

Les Femmes et les Mots: Une Anthologie/Women and Words: The Anthology est un projet de la Société des femmes et des mots de la côte du Pacifique. Cette société a aussi organisé une conférence nationale bilingue en 1983. Ce colloque, tenu à Vancouver, a ressemblé pour la première fois plus de huit cents femmes travaillant avec l'écriture: écrivaines, éditeurs, rédactrices, traductrices, critiques, imprimeurs, libraires, professeurs.

Lors de la conférence un comité d'anthologie s'est formé. Les textes ont été sollicités partout au Canada et plus de trois cents écrivaines ont répondu à cet appel d'une côte à l'autre du Canada. Un comité anglais et un comité français ont sélectionné les manuscrits. Les membres de ces deux comités varient en âge de vingt-cinq à soixante-cinq ans et représentent plusieurs milieux: écrivaines, rédactrices, professeurs, lectrices chez les éditeurs.

Les deux comités ont travaillé indépendamment selon des critères quelque peu différents. Ce comité anglais s'est soucié d'effectuer une sélection reflétant autant que possible les antécédents culturels et linguistiques des participantes; le comité français, ayant reçu relativement moins de textes a fait sa sélection à partir de critères tenant compte de la variété thématique et de l'originalité d'expression.

Le tri ayant été effectué et les auteurs prévenues, les deux comités ont décidé du format définitif de l'anthologie. Les textes ont été ordonnés non pas pour mettre en relief la variété des thèmes mais pour faire ressortir l'étendue impressionnante de ces voix de femmes.

Silvia Bergersen   Grazia Merler   Thuong Vuong-Riddick
Olga Kempo   Christianne Richards   Jennifer Waelti-Walters
Kathy Mezei

Simultaneous Translation

J'ai essayé et
J S A A   A
   J S A A   A
      J S A A

je ne suis pas capable / j'ai pensé tous les fois
je ne suis pas capable / j'ai pensé toutes les folles
   jeune suivra capable jay pensé toutes les folles
      gêne suivra cap pablum jay pensé toutes les folles
      gêne sweep pa cap pablum jay pensy toutes les folles
   june sweep pa cap pablum jay pensy toot les folles
      june sweep pa cap pablum jay pensy toot lay falls

tant m'échappe mais j'embarque
taunt m'échappe mais j'embarque
   taunt may chap may j'am barque
      taunt may chap may jam bark

car nous sommes toutes traductrices
car nous sommes toutes traductrices
   car new sommes toutes traductrices
      car new some toutes traductrices
      car new some toot traductrices
   car new sum toot trad duke trees
      car new sum too trad ostrich

dans un silence qui ne sait pas s'exprimer au langage masculin
dance un silence qui ne sait pas s'exprimer au langage masculin
dance on silence qui ne sait pas s'exprimer au langage masculin
dance on sill once qui ne sait pas s'exprimer au langage masculin
dance on sill once key ne sait pas s'exprimer au langage masculin
dance on sill once keen say pas s'exprimer au langage masculin
dance on sill once keen say pas s'exprimer au langage mask you lent
dance on sill once keen say pa s'exprimer au langage mask you lent
dance on sill once keen say pa sez primer au langage mask you lent
dance on sill once keen say pa sez primer oh langage mask you lent
dance on sill once keen say pa sez primer oh long age ask you lent
dance on sill once keen say pa sez preen eh oh long age mask you lent

essay on
essayons

Penny Kemp
Women and Words
June 1983

Kristjana Gunnars

Milky Way Vegetation II

[*excerpts*]
(*for Sam*)

2.

between dry stretches
covered with sedges
I have been through carpets of cotton-grass
in the central highlands

between tundra bogs
ridged with gravel and stone
been through grasslands and heaths
scattered with plants

my journeys uncharted, undated
the boundaries unlined
the hours broken
my uncoordinated life

3.

a touch of the wild thyme
and moss campion of very old
mountain-drifted freedom
appears with you

you do not know how
with you the highlands occur
showing again the old sky
approximately as it would look

to the unwarned eye

4.

even while the blue and red summer nights say yes
yes

the black sands follow me
the lowlands extend barren
newly-poured lava flows down the gullet of hope

and there is continuous no on the wings of the gulls

5.

I want nothing more
than beds of moss
dwarf shrubs, birches
rained-on

ravines of ferns and herbs
luxuriant
brilliant red stars at my fingertips

life a glowing object
                          You

6.

if I can live with you
a third of the year

in the warm soil
studded with adder's tongue

the summer a descriptive text
a road map of my dreams

then the star fields of uncertainty
the extensive untouched areas

the barren winter
will not kill

Daphne Marlatt

Vivaldi & you

Come through bright
where i sit tell me
about Vivaldi's
orphan girls disfigured
or simply
girls, girls with angelic
pitch singing
behind a screen
unseen, their tried hearts one
single note, one pitch

imperative:
to rise to it

we screen our flesh
with names & notes, ideas, break/
water of thought & then
desire floods in
your look i meet
am met, flushed, hear
the singing sound of my blood
rising to it: one

urgent note
one pitch identical
in reach, intent
on hearing each
the other, love

Louky Bersianik

Eremo

(extrait de Du Beurre de Plomb dans l'aile, roman inédit)

Le monde était en guerre et toutes les prières qui montaient du couvent étaient destinées à fléchir le ciel en vue de l'obtention de la paix.

Ce n'était pas la première fois que l'esprit de Sylvanie se trouvait agressé par le mot "guerre." Elle se souvenait comment, peu de temps après sa naissance, elle se réjouissait d'être une fille car les filles, lui avait-on assuré, ne vont pas à la guerre.

La "guerre!" C'était là un de ces mots qu'il fallait tenir en respect en le mettant entre guillemets, autrement il vous sautait à la figure et alors la vie n'était plus possible. Et puisqu'il fallait vivre, il valait mieux laisser à l'écart les mots assassins.(. . .)

Au cours d'histoire, Sylvanie mit du temps avant de saisir la différence entre les mots "stratégie" et "tactique," et surtout entre les mots "guerre" et "bataille." On disait la guerre et une bataille.

Sylvanie Penn ne pouvait imaginer que la guerre était la somme d'un nombre incalculable de petites et de grandes batailles. Comment l'aurait-elle su?

L'idée que des êtres s'entretuaient ne pouvait pas se subdiviser. . .

Elle était là, cette idée, toute crue et sanglante, elle était animale, elle n'appartenait à aucune espèce de vivants en particulier, c'était une idée d'un autre monde, une idée qu'on ne pouvait chasser de son esprit, qui était incrustée à jamais au fond de son cerveau archaïque.

Un autre mot que Sylvanie ne comprenait pas, c'était le mot "coalition." Il était toujours employé dans son manuel d'histoire quand il était question de la "guerre." On en parlait à propos de la "conquête" de son pays par un peuple "colonisateur." Encore deux autres mots dont elle ne parvenait pas à saisir le sens. Etait-il physiquement possible qu'un peuple pût en conquérir un autre?

C'était comme si deux fillettes de sa classe se battaient pour avoir, l'une, le bras de l'autre. Le combat serait terrible.

Adélie, celle qui aurait eu l'idée saugrenue de briguer le bras d'Agathe, demanderait l'aide de ses compagnes, il y aurait une "coalition." Cette "coalition" aurait vite raison d'Agathe, laquelle ne se soucierait aucunement du bras d'Adélie mais se verrait dans l'obligation de défendre son bras. Soeur Sado conduirait sa classe sous la tonnelle de chèvrefeuille et agirait en arbitre. A la fin, Agathe serait sur le sol, le bras à moitié arraché. Soeur Sado trancherait la question:

—Adélie est la plus forte. Elle a gagné. Elle a gagné le bras d'Agathe. Elle peut l'emporter.

Et, d'un grand coup de hachette, elle fendrait le bras d'Agathe à la hauteur de l'épaule exactement, et remettrait ce bras à Adélie.

Toutes ses élèves se mettraient à l'applaudir et féliciteraient Adélie. Adélie serait portée en triomphe à travers les longs couloirs du couvent.

Adélie essaierait ensuite d'éduquer le bras d'Agathe pour le faire travailler à son profit, lui donnant à accomplir les tâches les plus ingrates: le bras d'Agathe apprendrait à faire les devoirs d'Adélie, à faire son ménage et son lit. Adélie jouirait d'une grande liberté. Ses propres bras n'auraient à s'occuper que de choses agréables. Parfois, elle prêterait le bras d'Agathe maintenant "colonisé" à ses amies qui avaient formé une "coalition" avec elle et l'avait aidée à gagner cette bataille. Mais le bras d'Agathe demeurerait la propriété exclusive d'Adélie.

Qu'adviendrait-il d'Agathe dans cette histoire invraisemblable?

Agathe serait reléguée à l'infirmerie où elle se mettrait à dépérir nonobstant les cataplasmes, jusqu'à son dernier soupir. Elle serait vite oubliée.

Dans les annales du couvent, on rapporterait l'exploit d'Adélie avec force détails qui tous seraient à son avantage. On lui élèverait une statue à côté de la statue de la Sainte Vierge, dans le tertre central, devant la façade du couvent. La renommée d'Adélie franchirait le couvent et s'étendrait à toute la communauté. On ferait allusion à l'exploit d'Adélie à chaque page des archives de la communauté. On écrirait des livres là-dessus et Adélie serait auréolée d'une gloire napoléonienne.(. . .)

Sylvanie remarquait que le mot "vainqueur" était un mot masculin qu'il était impossible de mettre au féminin... Comment alors qualifier Adélie?

Vainqueur était un mot-couteau. A proscrire de son vocabulaire.

Il valait mieux pour Sylvanie Penn ne pas trop faire attention à la signification de certains mots. C'étaient des traîtres. Ils véhiculaient de la dynamite à travers un circuit inextricable qui les reliait tous les uns aux autres. Dans la réalité, ils n'existaient jamais pour eux-mêmes, beaux et nus comme elle les voyait en rêve. Le mot "paix" ne voulait rien dire, absolument rien, si on ne lui collait aussitôt le mot "guerre" comme une poêle bruyante à la queue d'un chat. A quoi bon faire patte de velours dans ces conditions?

Il n'y avait que les noms de choses à qui l'accolade ne donnait pas de crocs; à la rigueur, les noms de certains êtres vivants comme certaines plantes, mais sous toute réserve.

Mettez par exemple le mot "cornaline" en présence du mot "samare" et l'entente sera parfaite. Ajoutez-y l'innocent "carcajou" et, qui sait si de carnivore ce vocable ne deviendra pas herbivore...

Et même les noms de choses pouvaient être corrosifs ou érosifs. Le mot "eau" était un mot bienfaisant pour tout le monde. Personne n'y trouvait à redire. Mais si vous le laissiez travailler pendant quelques siècles, il vous changeait complètement la face de la terre et même du ciel.

Et que dire de ce mot "eau" quand il était employé en trop grosse quantité. Il était meurtrier, comme les autres. Comme tous les autres mots. Et quand il se trouvait dans la gorge de Sylvanie et d'abord dans ses glandes lacrymales... ce mot se transformait en une chose qui ne tarissait plus! Et pourtant, il fallait la refouler cette chose "eau," lui faire reprendre le chemin de l'aller. Il n'était peut-être pas défendu de pleurer à Erémo, mais il était formellement interdit de le montrer. Il fallait secréter des larmes secrètes. Que Sylvanie se le tienne pour dit.

Le petit Larousse illustré en noir et blanc de la classe était la seule arme dont disposait Sylvanie pour affronter le monde. Sa seule défense. Entre chacun des mots qui s'y trouvait, il y en avait au moins un qui était encore invisible parce que pas encore inventé. Ainsi, sans trop de heurts, elle apprenait noir sur blanc de quoi elle était faite.

Ce gros livre représentait pour elle son seul aliment naturel. Mais il fallait être prudente. Bien connaître les mots, se nourrir de la substance de quelques-uns mais ne pas prendre au sérieux la majorité d'entre eux qui étaient, soit menaçants, soit pleins d'énigmes.

Parfois, elle ne pouvait pas les suivre, non qu'elle manquât de souffle, mais il lui aurait fallu connaître des rudiments de chimie, ou d'astronomie, ou de calcul différenciel, pour comprendre vraiment leur langage. Et même de médecine et de philosophie.

Parfois aussi, ils étaient muets sur l'essentiel et Sylvanie restait perplexe pendant des jours et des jours et autant de nuits.

Ainsi, le mot "eau" dans le dictionnaire ne faisait nullement mention de cette eau qui remplit les yeux si souvent sans qu'on sache vraiment pourquoi. On ne savait pas non plus d'où cette eau provenait. Bien sûr, elle venait du corps, mais le corps était solide en apparence... Et cette eau-là, c'était vraiment de l'eau, ce n'était ni du lait, ni du vin de messe, ni du sang. C'était un "liquide transparent," il n'y avait aucun doute là-dessus; ce liquide était "inodore," ça tombait sous le sens; mais "insipide?" Insipide voulait dire sans saveur comme tout ce qui apparaissait sur la table du réfectoire.

Sylvanie avait déjà remarqué que ses larmes étaient salées. C'était comme si de l'eau de mer était conservée là, derrière le regard des fillettes naufragées. Celles qui avaient échoué sur la terre aride d'Erémo. Mais si l'eau de mer n'était pas insipide, on ne disait pas pour autant qu'elle était faite avec des larmes...

Pour savoir si l'eau des larmes était réellement de l'eau, il aurait fallu que Sylvanie puisse l'analyser. Les larmes avaient-elles deux volumes d'hydrogène pour un d'oxygène? En songeant à ces deux gaz qui se mettaient ensemble pour faire du liquide, Sylvanie les soupçonnait de "coalition"... Elle imaginait que c'était l'oxygène respiré par ses poumons qui ressortait en eau par ses yeux, ayant rencontré par hasard deux volumes d'hydrogène sur son parcours... A la réflexion, ce n'était sûrement pas par hasard: la rencontre avait lieu trop souvent... La "coalition" se produisait à son insu dès que Soeur Sado l'interpellait avec son mépris habituel, ou que ses compagnes lui parlaient un peu rudement. (...) Quand, par miracle, par une circonstance exceptionnelle, elle était appelée au parloir, et ses parents étaient là soudain et demandaient à la voir, la "coalition" provoquait des torrents de joie de cette eau occulte.

Et où allait l'eau des larmes? Elle devait s'évaporer dans son mouchoir. Et où allait la vapeur? Où, ailleurs que dans les nuages? Sylvanie Penn était bien étonnée à la pensée que les larmes de son corps servaient à fabriquer quelques gouttes de pluie, quelques cristaux de neige... Cette pluie allait faire pousser un brin d'herbe où une violette avant de retourner dans les airs et voyager jusqu'à ce que l'hiver arrive, pour devenir glacier, ou iceberg, ou océan... L'avenir des larmes de Sylvanie était inquiétant et plein d'imprévus.

C'était une chose bien étrange que ce don des larmes. Cela passait pour de la pure sensiblerie aux yeux de tout le monde. Mais depuis longtemps Sylvanie avait appris à pleurer en cachette. Et personne, même pas elle, ne soupçonnait la violence de toutes ces "coalitions" intérieures qui se soudaient secrètement au plus profond d'elle-même.

Dans cette vallée de larmes amères et quelquefois douces qui avait nom Erémo, Sylvanie Penn devenait une force de la nature.

Eremo est un mot latin qui signifie désert.

Ayanna Black

A Pretty Baby Girl In A Da Nursery

(To a immigrant women)

Mi 'ave a baby girl
She dah weight six pound two oz
Mi dah com' out a hospital pon thursday
Mi nuh 'ave no place to go
And only a dolla' to mi name

Mi dah call de pickney father
'im sey
Him comin to se mi
Mi nuh se 'im yet

One whole 'ear now
Wi dah go together
Yu no mis
'im left an' go married Doris two mont' now
'ere mi a lay
With only a dolla' to mi name
With only a dolla' to mi name
'nd a pretty baby girl
In a di nursery
'nd a pretty baby girl
In a di nursery

A Pretty Baby Girl In The Nursery (English Translation)

(To an immigrant woman)

I have a baby girl
She weighs six pounds two ozs.
I'm coming out of hospital on thursday
And I have no place to go
And only a dollar to my name

I have called the baby's father
He says
He was coming to see me
I haven't seen him yet

It's one year now
Since we have been dating
You know
He left me and married Doris two months now
Here I am
With only a dollar to my name
With only a dollar to my name
And a pretty baby girl in the nursery
And a pretty baby girl in the nursery

Jeannette Armstrong

World Renewal Song

Nothing was good.
The winds blew
and grasses died.

I thought I was pitied
so I longed
for a Whole Time Song.
I danced for it
in deerskins.

I made thought with paint
in red lines
from little finger to the left shoulder.
I, silent,
listening by dying grasses,
began hearing
at dawn.

A new fire is lighted.
The finished world is here,
formed in mind patches.
It is come,
the song for rain and green
and good.

I sit by talking grasses now,
with nothing more
to make a good world of
than thought paint
and dance talk in lines,
but song colours
pour over my world
and my good time
still goes on.

Candis J. Graham

Nothing Special

"S*top that! Stop that!*

His voice shot through the silence, through the floor between his apartment and mine, with frightening clarity, tearing me from sleep.

"Do that one more time and I'll kill you!"

Jessica crawled into bed with me. "I want a duvet, just like this one, for my bed, for Christmas. Are you awake? One that has a beige cover, like yours."

I sighed and opened my eyes. The Saturday sun was shining, filling my bedroom with light. I had planned to sleep in, waking gently when my body decided it was time.

"Why does he scream at his kids so much?"

"I don't know, Ms MacLeod." I call her Ms MacLeod because it makes her feel eighteen instead of thirteen. I keep meaning to warn her that eighteen isn't all it is cracked up to be, and that thirty-three is much better. "He is, perhaps, a frustrated man."

"Yeah. But why doesn't he do something about it? Steada taking it out on his kids."

"It isn't that simple." Or is it? I am not up to these philosophical discussions first thing in the morning.

The inevitable wail from a child rose up to us, from the apartment below, followed by, *"Shut up! Stop crying!"* It occurred to me, for the nth time, that I have a responsibility to respond seriously to my daughter's questions.

"He's a tense kind of person. Not well suited to having kids. Remember the time he tried to fix our hall light? Such a simple job. He cursed and groaned the whole time, and didn't fix it in the end. He may not be doing what he really wants to do in his life. What do you think?"

"He's a turd!"

"Jessica!"

She laughed, with no hint of apology, as she looked over at me. "What are you doing today?"

"Nothing special. I'm going into work this afternoon."

"Ahhh, Mum!"

"I must, Jess. We need the money. You need a pair of jeans, new boots. I want a perm. This overtime money makes the difference. It'll just be for a couple of hours. What are your plans? Aren't you going somewhere with Freddie?"

"Yeah. Freddie and I are going to the library and her Mum's taking us to her granny's farm this afternoon."

"Sounds like fun. Shall we have pancakes for breakfast, Ms MacLeod?"

We got out of bed and went into the kitchen. It is my favourite room. When we first moved in, Jess and I painted the walls an off-white colour and the cupboards pale yellow. It has two windows, one facing south and the other facing east, and is filled with sun on bright days.

After breakfast we dressed and Jess went off to meet Freddie at the library. I lingered over a third cup of coffee, savouring the peace and solitude, before turning my attention to twenty-four hours of dirty dishes.

I was patiently scrubbing at some cheese sauce which was glued to the rim of a plate, and wondering at the same time if I should dump the dirty dishwater. The phone rang.

I let the plate slide back into the water and grabbed the tea towel from the counter, drying my hands as I walked toward the phone. I lifted the receiver as the second ring started. "Hello."

"Hello! How are you today?"

There was a long moment of silence while I considered the question and the caller. I did not recognize the voice: he spoke with the intimacy of a lover. Or a salesman.

"I'm fine," I ventured, cautiously.

"How would you like an erotic phone call this morning?"

I answered quickly, "No, thank you. I don't have time." And I hung up.

I returned to the dirty dishwater and attacked the dried cheese with a sudden burst of energy. What if he phones right back? I won't answer the phone. Will that call be the beginning of a string of similar calls?

I thanked him. Imagine that. What a dummy. No, what a well-brought-up woman I am, that I thank an obscene caller.

The blob of cheese gave way and dropped into the water. I rinsed the soap from the plate and propped the plate in the rack. As I filled the basin with clean water, I wondered what he would have said if Jess had answered the phone. Everyone told me bringing up a child alone wouldn't be easy. But somedays it seems like there's one thing after another to worry about. How could I protect her from an obscene caller?

I left the apartment at noon after vacuuming the whole place and washing the kitchen floor. While I stood at the bus stop, a carload of boys drove past. They honked and yelled at me and waved and honked, in simulated friendliness. I pretended they did not exist. There must be a better way to handle such a situation, but I don't know what it is.

At work I manipulated the keyboard to produce the required documents, not paying much attention to what I was doing. The obscene phone call haunted me, making me feel vulnerable. He could be someone who knows me; he may have picked my number from the phone book; or, he may have dialed randomly. If he knows my address, that is frightening. Something to worry about. He could extend his violence to a physical assault. We should both take a self-defence course.

All the way home on the bus I kept thinking about Jess. I hate leaving her alone, especially for hours at a time. Usually I am proud of her independence, but the obscene caller made me think about her lack of experience in coping with life.

When I opened the apartment door at 7 pm, I found myself praying to some unknown being that Jess would be there, sheltered and safe from all harshness.

She was stretched out on the chesterfield, eyes closed, looking tired and pale. Freddie was curled up in a chair, watching TV.

"Hi there, Delila," Freddie said to me. Freddie calls everyone Delila.

I had found this disconcerting at first, and questioned Jess about it. "Freddie calls everyone Delila," Jess assured me. "It's just one of her idiosyncrasies." "Idiosyncrasies?" "Yeah, you know, something that's just her." "I know what idiosyncrasies means," I said indignantly. "I'm merely surprised that you do."

"Hi, Delila. Are you okay, Jess?"

"Oh, am I glad to see you. It's started. My period. I think. My stomach hurts." She sounded like a battered child, not the blossoming woman I usually live with.

I felt threads of panic spinning through my body. I am in charge here, I told myself firmly, sternly. "Jessie, how wonderful. When did all this happen?"

"A while ago. When we got home there was blood on my pants, so I changed them. And now my stomach hurts."

I found myself speaking rapidly. "I'll get you one of my pills. You know the bottle of pills I have on my dresser. Motrin. For cramps. You certainly won't have to suffer with cramps. I'll phone Ellen on Monday and make an appointment. I don't suppose you're too young to take this drug. We'll see what Ellen says. I'll go to the store and get some pads. We'll ask her, at the same time, if she thinks you're too young for sponges. Would you like to use sponges instead of tampons? They don't recommend tampons for women under eighteen, but I don't know about sponges. What harm could they do? Use pads, until we see Ellen. And some hot chocolate. I'll make us hot chocolate when I get back from the store." I sat on the chesterfield and hugged her. "It's alright. Are you okay?"

As I hurried down the hall I heard Freddie say, "Sponges? What's that?" Jess chuckled.

I made a quick dash around the apartment, taking *Our Bodies Ourselves* from the bookcase in the kitchen, and returned to the living room. Freddie watched from a solemn face as I handed Jess the Motrin tablet and a glass of milk. I laid the book between them, saying, "Read up on menstruation while I'm gone."

When I returned from the store, they were huddled together with the open book. I put Jess into a hot bath, then showed her how to use the pad. I made hot chocolate for the three of us, and we settled on the chesterfield.

"Are you staying the night, Delila?"

Freddie nodded and giggled.

"Anything else happen today, Ms MacLeod?"

Jess was returning to her former self. "The Portuguese guy was fighting with Jean-Paul's father on the street outside our building."

The Portuguese man lives in the building to the left of ours; Jean-Paul and his father live in the building to the right. "What was it about?"

"Oh, something about the garage the Portuguese guy is building in his backyard, making noise all the time, and not having a building permit. The police came."

"Sounds unpleasant." I worry about this neighbourhood and its influence on Jess. On both of us, for that matter. But housing is hard to find and I can't afford the nicer areas.

"Naw," said Freddie. "It was exciting. What an exciting day."

"Yeah," Jess agreed.

I still have to tell her about the obscene phone call, to warn her. Tomorrow. Enough has happened today.

I got the beige duvet from my bed and spread it over us. Jess sat in the middle, between Freddie and me, and we watched an old movie on TV. It's a black and white, and Jess moans every so often about how *everyone* has a colour TV. I wish I could give her one. I get so tired of saying we can't afford it. And she must get tired of hearing it.

After the movie ended, with the immaculate socialite marrying the dedicated doctor, we prepared for bed. Jess took a second Motrin and changed the pad. Freddie watched with keen interest. Before parting from them, I gave Jess and Freddie a hug and said, "Pleasant dreams. I'm sleeping in tomorrow."

I was dreaming about living in a drafty mansion with ten kids and three dogs. It was a busy dream. Just as we were sitting down to a meal of dandelions, grass and poplar leaves, I heard a police siren. The siren changed to a ringing phone and I was awake.

Jess answered the phone, speaking quiet and indistinct phrases. I left the warm bed, reluctantly, and went into the kitchen. The room looked drab; I could see a cloudy sky through the window beyond Jess' head.

"Good morning, Mum. It's Grandad. She's up now, Grandad. Here she is."

Dad wanted to remind me of the dinner tonight, in honour of their thirty-fifth wedding anniversary. And to let me know that Sears had a sale. Didn't I want a washing machine? Yes, I want a washer, a perm, winter boots for Jess, a colour TV, and a telephone answering machine. He was not amused. "We'll expect you at five," he ordered before hanging up.

I sat beside the phone, regretting my anger. I picked up the receiver and dialed. Dad answered after the first ring.

"Hello, Dad. I'm sorry about my smart mouth. Yesterday was a rough day."

"Never you mind, love. Have a strong cup of coffee. Come over early and I'll take Jessie to the flea market."

I checked on Jess and Freddie—they were watching *Star Trek*—and went back to bed. Just as I was drifting off, his voice roared loud and clear, as if he were beside me rather than in the apartment below. *"Jon-a-than! Look what he's done. Damn him! Jonathan! Jonathan, get in here. Right now!"*

Why does he scream at his kids so much. How dare he inflict his anger on us. I should wear my leather boots and stomp around, banging the hard leather soles on the hardwood floors. Let the loud noise disturb his life. I waited for the crying and a minute later it started. Turning over, with one quick movement, I pulled the duvet around my head.

I woke a second time to the ringing phone. Jess answered it, again, but her muttering quickly became audible. "What? What did you say?"

I threw myself out of bed and down the hall, into the dark kitchen. Jess looked stunned. I grabbed the phone from her.

"Hello."

How are you this morning?"

"You. You're a sick excuse for a person, aren't you. Assaulting a child! *Get help!* See a doctor. Don't phone here again. Never. Or I'll track you down and squeeze the life out of your puny balls. In a garlic press! Do you understand? You're sick, sick, *sick!*"

I hung up and sat down, trembling. Jess stood in the same spot, staring at me. Freddie, in the doorway, looked from Jess to me and back to Jess.

"What did he say?" I felt I was going about this the wrong way. But what would be a better way? Jess looked at Freddie, then back at me. "I'm not angry at you, Jess. I'm furious at him. What did he say?"

"Cut that out! Stop that! Jonathan!"

I moaned and buried my face in my hands. Jess patted my shoulder, saying, "It's alright, Mum. I'll make you some coffee." I heard Freddie seat herself at the table. Damn him to eternal torment. How could he do this to a child. I uncovered my face. Jess was scooping ground coffee and dumping it into the filter. Freddie was watching me. It could be worse. Much worse.

"He said," Jess was facing the window and the overcast sky, "that he wanted to suck my breasts." She turned to face me. Where had this child acquired such strength?

"He phoned yesterday, after you left to meet Freddie at the library. I was going to warn you, today, about him." The child downstairs started bawling, loudly and with gusto. "Let's have some coffee and I'll tell you about it. We'll have to be prepared, in case he dares to phone again." I walked across the room and put my arms around Jess.

"Shut up! Do you hear me? Stop that. Stop crying!"

Freddie cleared her throat. "My mother's had enough. She says we're moving to my granny's farm after Christmas."

"Do you have room for two more?"

Freddie giggled. "I'll ask her."

"Don't be silly, Mum." Jess gave me a stern, grown-up frown. "We're alright here."

"Yes. I suppose we are. Well, what are you two making for breakfast?"

Freddie made toast, Jess made scrambled eggs, and I drank coffee and talked. "I'll buy a whistle and leave it beside the phone. If he phones again, we'll blow the whistle into the receiver and rupture his eardrum."

Freddie leaned on the counter, watching Jess pour orange juice into glasses. She grinned at Jess and said, "What do you think, Delila?"

Jess grinned back. "I hope the turd phones back as soon as we have that whistle." They laughed so hard that Jess knocked over a glass and spilt juice all over the counter.

Milda Danys

Perhaps I Could Imagine You

"A man today requires 3500 to 4000 calories a day if he belongs to a rich country and a privileged class."

Fernand Braudel, *The Structures of Everyday Life.*

V*otre Excellence,* I write
(because generals like to be addressed that way)
J'ai l'honneur d'appeler votre attention sur le cas d'Immaculée

Mukamugema

Yes, it is my honour to write
I am a writer, not well-off
Indeed, very poor: I cannot buy new clothes
Though calories are something I count backwards
Here they swarm like malarial flies

Immaculée Mukamugema
(what a pretty name! it ripples
The nuns sent us out in May
to collect pussy willows and wild flowers
Feast of Mary the Immaculate)
Only Immaculée
condamnée à dix années de prison
cannot be very clean or pure
anymore—rape, you know
and then the *cachot noir*
cell without light
She sits in the dark, alone

more than two years now
no exercise, no visits
They say she's sick and going crazy

I cannot imagine the *cachot noir*
Dark, yes, cold or hot?
stinking of sweat and shit, piss and blood
What does she do about her periods?
but then I'm told you don't have
those when you're starved and sick and beaten a lot
Maybe I will sit in my closet for an hour or two
Only it is too crowded with clothes and shoes

Votre Excellence, I suggest
     a nice cell in the women's block
     a doctor
     a visit from her family
That would be kind for Immaculée
condamnée pour des activités
purement politiques
She passed out pamphlets criticizing her government
There I have something in common
Students all pass out pamphlets or sign protests
Once I marched carrying a placard in Ottawa
in front of the Soviet Embassy
It was hot, stifling
We marched round and round
shouting at the wall
No one stood at a window
No one came to the gate
but a man in black (it was hot)
took careful pictures of each of us
I looked right into the camera's eye: I was not afraid

Cachot means hidden too
Immaculée is in a black box
I am sorry: I write the letter
but I cannot really imagine her

legs folded under her on the dirt or cement floor
She cannot imagine me
with my *grande inquiétude*
which I mis-spell and correct
and then check in the dictionary
to be sure it is feminine
"my great anxiety"
tossed into the mail-box
like a pebble into a puddle
rippling and still and then rippling again
like the name of a woman
hidden away

Gillian Robinson

Flossie

They say
nurses in dark corridors
behind me
that almost everything these days
is made from away,
on the mainland.
Everything.
I heard the other day
that men get drunk with women
and women go to bars alone.
One night I heard through
my door two of them talking
about some women that don't get
married, they live together in
common law they called it.
I started thinking, while I was dreaming,
did I get married for fear? I never
liked men, never liked boys. Never
liked any of them. All those
years in the orphanage they beat me,
made fun of me, laughed at me,
played with me, played against me,
god they called me more names
than I can remember. They pulled
me into dark rooms and pulled my
clothes off. They laughed at me when
I peed my bed. They told on me.
They didn't like me. They never loved me.
Why did I get married?

Must have been my fear of the dark,
all those nights lying in that bed by the window,
shivering. Waiting for morning and one more
day to pass and one more year until I was old
enough to leave. Oh god how I waited to leave.
How I watched from the window, children younger with
their parents, holding their hands, pulling,
knowing the limits.
Why, why couldn't I have parents. Why
was I, Flossie, left alone at age three
in a huge building with one hundred other
children begging for love and getting
nothing but rules and the gospel.
Oh god if I could just once have been
given my mother to explain why she left me. Why
these boys taunted me day and night. Why I
wasn't beautiful and why I was so unlucky.

When I was eighteen he called me into his
long office and asked me what I thought my future
was and what would I do to earn a living?

I shook. I said silently I would find something,
I had lived this long.
I said I would work in the laundry. I would clean
their clothes. I would wait some more.
When I was twenty I was looking at the paper and
found an ad for someone to clean house down
the bay. I moved. He said calmly, you were
a great trial to us. I hope you realize the
investment both us and god have put in you.
I said, yes sir.
When you marry, he said, if, if I repeat, you
ever do, be careful to curb that tongue of yours.
Oh yes, I said trying to be calm.
I went away from all those walls, windows and boys.

Coming down the bay I was hungry. Always hungry and
always laughing. I thought I had finally begun life.

I stayed in that room looking on those hills full
of copper. Bleak. No trees, nothing. Only rock
climbing down into the town. Filling it up and
filling every one there with hunger.
There was thunder when he came to visit. A widower
and hungrier than most. Oh young I looked. Oh
young he wanted. I didn't drink in the bar. I took
tea before bed and read the bible. Never looked at
a newspaper, never asked for anything.

The orphanage was further away. I was less hungry.
He came in with the thunder bringing the rain. I sat
there pressed against the table, knowing another
man. Fear. I bent down and asked
after the cold and he said, You're young.
I didn't know what to say. I just smiled
and said come again.
Two years later he asked me to marry him.
I said no inside and the thunder covered it
and I knew yes.

I didn't know then of the mainland. That I could leave.
That I could drink in bars. I could stay unmarried.
He scared me. He seemed like the walls. Fear.
He said you're scared aren't you and I thought
he loved me.
His name was Robert. His heart was cold. His name was.

He worked one year. Sick, so sick he laid in bed for
a year. I was pregnant and named the baby myself. Sick.
I looked out of the window and all I saw was
the copper cliffs coming down. And the sea
rising through his window.

The second baby came when he went back to work
and slammed the door saying I was a mean old
woman and he should never have married me.

I knew then I would be waiting a long time to live.
Seven years I didn't go out of the bay. The women

never talked to me. They thought I was bad. Bad
to him. They liked him and called him uncommonly good.
Oh I prayed for release. I prayed for someone to love
me just once. Someone to reach out and say, Flossie,
you're beautiful. You are a beautiful woman and I love
you. Oh yes.

An orphan in marriage I bent my life to
stand his names, his beatings, his hate. I stood
there and stood there and waited.

Women work on the mainland. I worked in
a laundry and then I cleaned houses. I cleaned
houses when I got older and when I came home
he would yell at me and ask what was I working
for and thrust at me the geese he had killed
that day and say, Clean.
I stood there until I was old. What was I waiting
for? Nice, they finally called me
and I felt proud.
Then he died. It was raining when I came in the door.

The nurses say I don't try enough. I should be able
to walk at my age and I just won't put my mind to it.
They don't know I'm content to put all my will to
looking at the world. I want to look. I want
to listen. I don't want to walk. There's orphans around
the corners and there's walls I can't see and maybe
he will come at me with names.

I am released by my window and the gentle dark corridors
behind me with the gentle talking nurses brushing past
me and my own gentle hand.

Mona Fertig

For Jean Rhys
Your Sargasso Sea

O cry. Flood the gates. Drink a cup of milk
for luck. Under the orange tree by the nutmeg
pool and the sun shone. Mad she tasted like
honey. Mad she poured another white rum. White
man pulled her into this pool of pain. Drowning
she tore her dress off. The nights so hot she
couldn't breathe. Couldn't even breathe out.
Dispel him. Pain like love racked her body.
Threw her mind out the door and under the pink
heat moon. Soft as a rose she lifted off her
petal dress and sang. Sang for everything the
humidity held. The sea and the grape green
mountains. The lemon tree. Her eyes poured.
Rivers of all the flowers she loved. Thirsty
and wilting. She sang for the sweat on her
body her childhood the wide and distant passion
sea. Sang for this West Indies island. Pushed
all her pain into her room mouth. Stretched
her soul till breaking. Till woman was a spent
dream. A shell on the morning beach. Then he
sent her away. Now she lies in a cold and
English room. Her red dress hanging. Mama.
Sweet milk did her no good. If you visit.
Pick her up. Gently. Carry her into the other
room. Hold this Creole lady. Put your ear to
her lips. Listen. If you cup her right you
can hear the sea. If you cup her just right
the pain may subside. Song loved this woman.
Love her like an island loves the sea.

Michèle Boisvert

Le cri d'Archimède

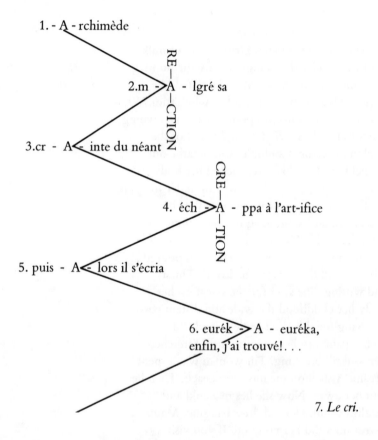

1. - A - rchimède

RE—A—CTION

2.m -> A - lgré sa

3.cr - A -> inte du néant

CRE—A—TION

4. éch -> A - ppa à l'art-ifice

5. puis - A -> lors il s'écria

6. eurék -> A - euréka,
enfin, j'ai trouvé!. . .

7. *Le cri.*

Murmure. Mode d'emploi à l'intérieur. Genèse, ou guide du par-
fait créateur en sept étapes faciles à suivre (. . .)
La vie, en vrac: c'est un chaos de particules en mouvement qui
patiente dans son bouillon de culture. . .
Magnétisme, collision-éclair et fusion des espaces intérieurs.
Lente incubation.
Duplication, mitose ou naissance des frontières. . .
Protection, parois cellulaires,
Choix et progression.
Animation-élévation; la rose sent si bon, et la vie est truf-
fée de recommencements.
Apprendre ou à laisser.

Murmure-récessif, silence-dominant.
Ultimatum et mutation première. 10^{-43} seconde, quantum indi-
visible, dimension subatomique.
CRI.
Et des racines de l'enfance lointaine rejaillissent les
convictions de la conscience primale. Je suis soudain à
quatre dimensions. La dernière est de porcelaine, c'est le
temps.
Hibernation. . .
La vie,   en poudre ou en conserve???

Alors faute d'espace et d'espèce, je garde donc l'espoir
et l'esprit.
Gestation.
Le quark.

Adaptation.
Créer est une réaction.
L'art de l'évolution par la prise de pouvoir, pouvoir de soi.

Grâce à sa crainte du néant, la raison fait le tri, tord,
transpose, transgresse, réduit, rature, traduit, contrôle.
Croiser pour croître et renaître en spirale, de l'enceinte
nébuleuse au coeur de laquelle pointe le trou noir, inima-
ginablement dense, magnifique, en perpétuelle rotation-rétrac-
tion.
Et lorsqu'il m'entraîne, positif du négatif, je n'ai plus
peur d'y tomber... La gravité finit toujours par triompher
du nucléaire; avec l'âge, les liens s'effritent et cassent
comme des cure-dents...Infinis à l'infini...
(si je suis là, le néant n'existe pas)
Créature rétro-cinéraire, je découvre mes lettres en chambre noire, pour développer la clef des sons. Je songe aux
crélations idéales et réanime les sens évanouis.
Je ne suis plus une machine à penser; mosaïque moléculaire,
je suis l'être - chimère en action.

Et puis soudain, contractions.
L'Oeuf cosmique gonfle son ventre comme un ballon et pal-
pite, c'est la valse-invitation.
De son cocon, une aile s'extraie et frappe le vide de plein
fouet. Joissance tacite, implications.
C'est Atlas, sur mes épaules, qui détonne et met le feu aux
poudres.
Toccate et fugue, premier mouvement, écrit en fureur-acalmie.
Intermède d'exaltation.
Inspiration, c'est la mort de l'embryon.
Je ne respire plus par le cordon...
Festin des sens, c'est une avalanche de mots réunis autour
d'une table, c'est la dernière Cène à compléter...
Moi,,,Caryatide???
J'entends l'écho du cor, au loin, qui m'appelle, j'entends la
mer, en torrent, qui se dé-chaîne, j'entends le coeur, le mien,
le sien, le nôtre, qui cogne,

battements, qui s'amplifient,
poussez, encore, et qui m'incitent à, poussez, poussez...
traverser
       traverser
            traverser
                 traverser
                      traverser
                            traverser
                      traverser
                 traverser
            traverser
       traverser
traverser...MACH1 MACH2 MACH3...

1983/03/03
19:57
Montréal.

(c'est une fille)

Susan Andrews

play

she tells me about Pobie Aster
her friend at night
and Pobie's dog Sinchi Paco
and Sinchi's friends Zancu and Cusi

she says they all run fast together
on the road with bumpy stones
not like the pavement in front
of our daytime house
the stones are so smooth she doesn't wear shoes
and it's always safe
it is before cars

lately she tells me Pobie
has been coming in the daytime too

Maureen Leyland

Earth Mother

Laura walked down the road toward the farm. Her strong, tanned feet were filmed with dust. The baby lay heavy and warm against her chest looking up at her with its dark, embryonic eyes; she gazed into its face and felt milk spring in her breasts.

She turned over, her nightdress tangling around her legs like seaweed. On his side of the bed her husband snored fitfully, his eyebrows drawn together in a frown. She adjusted the covers around him and went downstairs like she always did when she had the dream. In the kitchen she leaned against the counter watching water heat in the enamel saucepan. Then she poured scalding water over herb tea leaves and sat at her scrubbed pine table.

She was a big woman with a strong body. She'd consequently worried that physiognomy was destiny and that no one would ever feel romantic about her since she didn't look fragile and in need of protection. When Charles said "I always feel so tender toward big women" during their courtship, she'd been afraid to ask questions. She was anxious to leave his tenderness undisturbed. She'd been grateful for Charles's words; no one else had really chosen her, had thought of her as more than pleasant company. She'd vowed silently that in return she would do her best to make Charles happy—he had a problem being happy; his expectations were so high.

For a while she'd been successful. "This is what I've always needed," he'd said once. "An earth mother."

"Don't be fooled by all this cooking," she'd warned gaily. But of course he had been fooled and so had she. She sipped her tea, wrapping her long fingers around the pottery mug. She looked serene. It was her misfortune, she often thought, to look calm even when she felt frantic. People thought she was strong and told her their troubles. They drank her tea and marched back to their lives feeling comforted. Laura once mentioned this to a friend and had been advised to act weak. "I'm not really as strong as you think I am," she'd said calmly a couple of times—with no effect.

She looked out the window. In the darkness outside her garden was growing. The second crop of peas had already climbed the sturdy lattices she'd placed along their rows. The tomatoes hung red and sweet, their skins translucent; yellow peppers bent the plants. Tomorrow she would dig in the earth and the sun would be warm on her back. She never burned; people said her skin was her best feature.

She and Charles lived in an old farmhouse; it was a perfect place for children, they'd thought. There was a lot of space—a big kitchen, trees to climb outside. Never, she told herself now. Never. The ghost child who wandered through the yard disappeared. The spare room would never become a child's room. "You could adopt though," the doctor said, patting her shoulder. Despite his words she'd felt a burst of hope each time she experienced nausea or dizziness. When she wiped herself and saw blood staining the toilet paper, she wanted to press her legs together to stop the flow. Now she knew the doctor had been right; she would never have a child.

It was ironic. I even write cookbooks, she thought desperately. "Just reading one of your books makes me feel more secure," a woman told Laura once at a party. Her books were filled with comforting anecdotes and hints. Although Charles occasionally hinted that Laura might do something less culinary, more intellectual, Laura preferred the colours, the fragrances, the meditative stirrings and bubblings of the kitchen.

When they bought the house Charles had stood helplessly in their shambles of a living room and predicted disaster, acts of God, and financial ruin. "It'll be okay," she'd soothed and he'd gone doubtfully out the door to work, carrying his attaché case, while she'd scraped and stripped the wood floors and peeled off layers of wallpaper.

"Look at this," she'd cry when she was continuing her work after dinner. A strip of flocked *fleur de lis* would be held up. Charles would stride from his desk holding a book in his hand.

"God!" he'd exclaim. "That's horrible!"

"Can you imagine living with that?" she'd ask, ripping it energetically off the wall to show him that he'd never have to.

"Laura transformed this house singlehandedly," he'd tell people. "She was like an archeologist sifting through all the layers left by people who'd lived here before." Their friends thought he was generous with his praise. He loved the house. In that Laura thought she had succeeded. He sat in his study smoking while he looked out on her lush, fertile garden and told her that he finally felt secure and grounded.

"Really?" she'd ask, pleased, trying to get him to say more.

"You're so insecure," he'd tease.

On weekends he'd lie in the hammock and she'd cry out, "Aren't the peas good this year?" while she weeded and he'd agree, smiling, although they both knew he couldn't tell one green plant from the other.

Charles made the money. In the beginning they'd talked about her contribution. "I have income from royalties," she'd said, looking up at him. It was such a delight to look up; she'd danced with short boys at all the high school dances, feeling gargantuan.

"Well," he'd answered indulgently, "that will pay for the extras." He'd paused and looked at her. "If you take care of the house and grow food," he'd said, "that's income—it all evens out." However, she was never sure. People referred to her as a woman who didn't work.

Laura wished fervently that she could really understand Charles. He had bouts of deep unhappiness during which he'd sit bitter and silent while she laboured to cheer him up. "I'm thirty-six," he'd finally burst out. "Almost thirty-seven! And what have I accomplished?"

She'd hover anxiously. "You have a tenured position in a good university," she'd point out. "You just finished a new article." Inconsolable, he'd remind her that this was certainly not the university of his dreams, that the article was not published in an important journal. She'd find herself scanning the newspaper for cheering news.

"You really know how to comfort me," he'd said when they were first married, and she'd held him against the fresh bosom of her natural fibre Afghan dress and stroked his fair hair. She'd thought it was like a child's hair or an angel's. "You're so wise," he'd said in those days. Lately her bosom and her wisdom were less comforting.

"Just talk to me," she'd beg tearfully. Shifting in his chair he'd look past her and sigh.

"I'll be okay," he'd say hopelessly. "Just leave me alone." Sometimes she'd linger and massage his tense shoulders. She didn't know what else to do. Her throat was choked with unspoken words.

"Well, I guess I'll go to bed," she'd announce helplessly. A long time later she'd hear him come upstairs and she'd know he'd been drinking bourbon and reading mysteries until he could finally sleep.

She thought about it as she delivered snacks to the university daycare centre that gave her feedback on her recipes. She'd been working on a cookbook for young children and their parents. The children clustered around her and called her the cookie lady. She tried to keep herself from looking longingly at the small, curled hands that reached for her baking. As she walked back to the car it struck her that perhaps she could no longer go on. Now she knew what the expression meant. Opening the car door seemed an act beyond her capability. Her fingers felt too heavy to hold the car keys. Just drive, she commanded, encouraging herself by noting the landmarks. Turn left here. There's the supermarket. Keep going. The car pulled into the driveway almost automatically. Howling, she ran stumbling in the gravel to the house. Oh god, she said to herself. Oh god. She sat on the kitchen floor keening. I can't believe it, she said, as if there had been a death.

Every morning when she awakened she would see herself in a hospital bed looking up saying, "I had a baby," in a calm voice. She and Charles had a Saturday night dinner party and as she was serving pumpkin cheesecake she found herself looking at the scene like an outsider. It looked perfect, unreal, like a stage set. She was just maintaining it; without her it would collapse into a clutter of cardboard, paint and dust. She was just being fanciful, she told herself. This was the same table she'd bought at an auction last summer; she'd carried it out to the back yard in triumph.

"You sure have patience," Charles had said. "I'd go crazy if I had to do that." She'd smiled at him as she'd carefully scraped the putty knife across the solvent-softened paint. He'd kissed her neck.

"More," she'd demanded happily. They'd gone into the house.

"We could adopt," she said tentatively one evening.

"I've thought about it," Charles answered, "and I don't think it's such a good idea."

"Why?"

"I only want to have a child with you," he said gently.

She left it for a while and tried again. "Look," she said firmly, gathering herself. "We have to talk about this."

He put down his paper and sighed. "Talk," he said.

"Well," she began stiffly. "We need to talk about what we're going to do about the fact that I can't have a child. There are options." Charles gazed steadfastly at the floor, stretching out his legs restlessly. Laura put her hand on his knee. I don't mean to hurt you, she thought desperately. I don't want you to suffer.

"Okay?" she asked when he said nothing.

Charles got up and stared out the dark window. He stood hunched, his hands in his pockets. When he turned toward her, his face was bitter and drawn. "I'm really angry," he said. "Very angry." His voice shook. "This has been a disappointment. I'd be lying if I said it wasn't. And I'm living with it. But," he said, enunciating his words carefully, "I do not want to be constantly reminded of it. I do not want endless discussions of it."

"You mean we just don't talk about it?" Laura persisted. She felt she had to press on even though she knew it was dangerous. She had failed him. In her imagination she saw him holding a young, fertile woman as tenderly as he once held her.

"Talk!" Charles shouted. "Talk! But not about this!"

"But I can't stand it," Laura said and burst into tears.

"Neither can I," he answered and spent the rest of the evening in his study.

There had been several scenes like this, each one ending with her weeping while Charles patted her helplessly. She told herself that she was alone with her problem and that she'd better pull herself together. The garden fell to seed and she canned the tomatoes and peppers, lining her basement shelves with bright jars.

"We'll never eat it all," Charles said, laughing. Things were not always bad between them.

"Let's look on the bright side," Charles said one night. "We can go to Greece next summer." She knew he meant that now they would not be limited in their movements; unlike their friends they would not have to put off anything until later. But she wanted the limiting. She wanted something to fasten her. She wanted to say again, but what about adoption, what about a surrogate mother, but she knew that if she spoke his hand would stop stroking her and his face would close.

"I hate it when you don't talk," she'd say. Often he wouldn't answer.

She couldn't seem to stop herself from reading the Children's Aid advertisements in the paper. The blurred faces of children stared out at her from the photographs.

"You're such a victim," Charles said one day. He'd come upon her standing in the kitchen weeping into the soup she was stirring.

In the winter she worked on a new cookbook about leftovers. It was to be indexed so that someone staring at a pantry that contained only a cup of leftover rice, a carrot, and an egg, could look up these ingredients and discover some dish in which they could be combined. She even included a yeastless bread and an eggless cake. When it was finished she sent it off to the publishers with relief.

She began to design foods which were highly nutritious but spare. She experimented with a drink which supplied almost all nutrients. "Don't expect me to eat any of this stuff," Charles said, gazing suspiciously at a pale, frothy drink in the blender.

"It's good for you," she murmured, concentrating on her notes.

"What are you trying to prove?" Charles asked. She just smiled. She ate her mixtures alone in the kitchen. Charles began to eat at the faculty club a couple of nights a week. She didn't mind. He brought home folders about Greece. Sometimes she found herself in a kind of trance. Sitting alone in a room, she would suddenly speak. "I did it," she would say. Did what? she worried. After a while she became used to it; she wondered if it was a message.

Dust began to film to golden wood of her furniture. The spring sun shone onto floors that were no longer quite perfect. She wandered through the big house gazing out windows. The ground was not warm enough to begin planting. She told herself stories; her favourite was one in which she saw herself living with a child in an apartment above a store. It would be cheap, she thought dreamily. The child would learn its colours by watching the cars go by in the street. Each time she imagined it she added details; she would buy food each day. Like European shoppers. Everything would be new and fresh. The apartment would be bare so the child could play. While the child slept she would work on her cookbooks.

Charles began to complain about the state of the house. She looked at him with mild surprise, as if he were a stranger. She bought seeds for the garden but when she looked at the ground she was overcome by despair. It was then that she called the woman. She found the number in the telephone book under children. "Yes," the woman said. Yes, it was quite possible. Laura was told to come in. They were always looking for people to foster children.

Laura put down the phone and sat quietly in her chair. Her body felt light. She glanced out the window and saw that the cherry tree was in bud; the old windowpane distorted her view so that the green leaves shimmered in pale sunlight. It looked like a view seen through a kaleidoscope, she thought. One shake and a new pattern would fall into place.

It took her only a few minutes to pack a suitcase. It was surprising how little one really needs, she thought. She felt a pang for Charles because he would never understand. She could see his hurt face. He'd be angry. He'd think that he'd made the best of it by staying with her even though he'd been disappointed. Now he would feel that she hadn't properly appreciated his sacrifice.

"I'm middle-aged," he'd say to the next woman. "I'm middle-aged and I have to start all over again." And she would take him in her arms and comfort him. But perhaps she wouldn't, Laura thought. Perhaps she wouldn't. The thought pleased her.

Murielle Poirier

To Jean the Day After

We spoke in echoes
of beaten women
that we knew
who still breathe
with the fists
that pound their flesh

of Pam who married
because her best friend did
who now
after three girl children
& a two floor bungalow
is left with only her genitals
as a bargain for life

of Myrna with the laughing ears
who latched onto the first man
who lifted her skirt
she never dreamed that
one drunken night
he would carve his initials
in her ass

we spoke in echoes
you & I
in a mist of wine
& tobacco smoke

I never showed you
the bruises on my thighs
or the scratches on my breast

we spoke in echoes
                      of beaten women
                      of bleeding ankles
                      of you & I
and I and I and I and I and I

Sandra Shreve

White Lies

Surely the child's eyes
betrayed the lie—despite
the calm assurance of her words,
delivered precisely the way
her father had earlier
formed them for her,
(just in case we're not home
this is what to say . . .)

But no—the census taker
hastily noted:
father, working—specific location;
number of children—sex, age;
mother, housewife—*does not work*

Then left behind
her friendly smile,
subtle traces of cologne
and a child concealing
the facts of her mother's
typing at home for money:
facts her parents feared
once ingested by any
government agency—*none to be trusted*
would be smuggled through promises
of confidentiality
to income-tax inspectors,

who should not know
of money coming in
unless it's going to be reported
and paid for.

This was the child's
first lesson
in the higher education
of permissible 'little white lies'
from which she learned
one truth about governments,
one falsehood about housewives.

Claire Hélie

Printemps Printemps

Printemps des petites rues
de rumeur d'eau tendre
dans le froissis du noir velours

à la déchirure des fenêtres
tourne tourne tourne
un blanc visage levé

ce soir serpente du doux
carrousel de larmes
un blond vertige

courir dans le blanc
des mains subites et nues
des bouffées de sourires

vert vert d'eau lente
trouble des miroirs
aux ramures d'enfance

Maryse Pellerin

À ma mère

Faisant le ménage   je pense à ta culpabilité
l'épreuve faite de l'indignité   inapte au service domestique
le regard de grand-mère   t'enfonçant   mieux que mille sables
mouvants
dans le mépris de toi   un désordre inquiétant

> (crasse aux encognures   cernes autour
> du col   murs éclaboussés à la sauce
> tomate   indécrottables cabinets
> à la merde   vêtements froissés de
> l'amour propre   une douleur à repasser)

comme preuve de ton incompétence   n'est-ce pas ce que
j'ai pensé longtemps   cru de toi

> (qui nous dicte la haine de la fille
> pour sa mère   la maternité sans
> le choix   la maternité sans l'autonomie
> qui nous cache cette dépossession)

La perte de contrôle de ta vie   en monceaux   petits tas
couches superposées de poussière   quelque part
au lendemain de ton mariage tardif   après ma naissance
au terme d'une troisième césarienne   j'ai ce désir de toucher
du doigt le revirement   à la minute près ta démission ou
ta rébellion

> (au bout de quel tunnel une femme
> intègre-t-elle la honte de ses enfants
> muette ou formulée la réprobation du
> mari   l'insulte)

L'obsession maniaque de la propreté aurait-elle
pour toi rendu le verdict moins sévère   Une vie
à décrasser la soue à cochons   nous innocente-t-elle

Ta bataille pour les tiens   contre la maladie   la pauvreté
singulièrement enfouie au fond de ma mémoire
l'oeil sourd à ton cycle infernal   pourquoi
en faisant le ménage   ma révolte se tournant ailleurs que vers toi

août 1982

Devant le Miroir

Deux femmes se regardent   enlassées debout
    dans le miroir d'une commode

Deux femmes interrogent l'étreinte

Tu me presses dans tes bras ma pareille
    Modeste dans l'insolence

Dis-nous ce que tu vois   Image
    étrange autant qu'insécable

Toi et moi jamais réfléchie
Le miroir jamais traversé

Tu hésites et dévisages
Regarde-nous prendre place

Vois
Nous occupons l'espace poli des évidences

Dis-moi qui s'y mire
Si ce n'est   entre femmes
l'amour en représentation

Regarde-moi   en moi
   quand s'estompe la chair de l'inconnue
à qui un homme faisait l'amour

Ma miroitante vertigineuse

Demain nous marcherons dans les rues
   le jour nous tenant par le bras
De vraies Italiennes
   folles de fous rires folles

Par la main le soir   épaules étroites
   proéminentes

L'image en rien semblable à la veille
dans les yeux des passants

               Nos pas dans la ville
               n'épargnent que les aveugles

novembre, 1982

Makeda Silvera

Breaking the Silence

I want to break the silence then and now, I want words to come easily, I want our common experiences to flow through my pen... but I'm afraid, will I alienate if the words come? We have been divided so much by the world already—*but I want to break my silence*—and breaking *my* silence means taking that chance. It means, speaking about my mother's shame, reaching out to my sisters. On so many occasions the powers that be have pitted us against each other. It means sharing my fears, pain, vulnerability and vision with my daughters. It is hard, and I hesitate... I too, sometimes do not want those words to flow... but they must, because I'm stifling. I am suffocating. I feel like a bird who knows that it is her right to fly, yet, she cannot find her wings, and she will not, cannot rest, until she has those wings. These words... my words... the words of my daughters, sisters, mother: they will *come!*

1962

The first time I became aware of the fact that I wanted to create with words was at the age of seven. It was around this time that I was introduced to words, written words. I became enchanted by the land of fairy tales. *Cinderella, Snow White, Hansel and Gretel* became my life. *Hansel and Gretel* was my favourite book, I read and re-read it many times, perhaps because I could relate well to Gretel and Hansel as working-class kids, lost, with only crumbs and no way home.

Twice a year I waited eagerly for the parcels to come from abroad where my parents had emigrated, because I knew that inside those parcels would be more books about fairy land, and more European clothes. By the age of eight, I knew that I was going to write stories some day. But it was an ambition that I learned soon enough to keep to myself. At an early age, I learned that artists were considered strange people; I found out that working-class kids are rarely encouraged to dream, to have visions. . . to be something that was not "practical."

I remember one day we were all sitting under the mango tree, my cousins, my two aunts and myself. When the subject of what we wanted to be came up, one cousin said she wanted to be a nurse, another a teacher, and another still, a secretary. The adults nodded approvingly. "And what do you want to be?" they asked, all eyes on me. "I want to write stories," I shouted proudly. I was unprepared for what followed. A storm of laughter and scorn.

From my cousins: "You! How can you write stories? You can't even write, nobody can make out your handwriting it's so bad."

From my aunts: "How are you going to live? Do you have some rich husband in mind to go with your occupation?" More laughter. I was devastated. How could they be so cruel to me? That night in bed I cried, and I vowed that I would never let on to anyone ever again what I wanted to be when I grew up. That, I decided, would be my secret. I also decided that from then on, I'd say that I wanted to be a teacher—that seemed safe enough.

The next day, and for months to come, I was to hide myself under my bed, or at the foot of a dried-up coconut tree and write my own fairy tales, then I'd read them to my doll. My beautiful white doll whom I named Elizabeth, after the Queen of England. She enjoyed the stories immensely, because she never stopped smiling. Yes, she enjoyed my stories—replicas of Cinderella and Snow White.

1965

As I grew older, I became acutely aware of my working-class position in the world. I stopped writing Snow White and Cinderella stories. I ceased writing altogether.

I remembered exactly when that happened. It was during my first week at an upper-middle-class preparatory school. My mother had sent my school fees from abroad and my granny had spent months scouting around for a "good" school to enroll me in—a "good" school where I would meet the right people and get a "good" education. I was excited about my new school. It would be very different from the working-class schools that I had attended. I was ready for new excitement. It was one of the cleanest schools that I'd seen. . . no writings on these walls.

There were a lot of new things to be absorbed—a lot of new experiences. It was also to be my first real education in class and colour and what it meant in my country. It was my first real contact with the light and white-skinned minority in my country. My very first day, I had a confrontation with a white Jamaican girl whose desk I was to share. I remember that she was very angry when she realized that we would be sharing the same desk. She was very rude to me but I tried to ignore it. I remembered my granny's warning before I left for my new school that morning: "Please, don't go there and fight. This is not that kind of school, these people are good people not riff-raff." But by the end of the day, I could ignore her no longer, and I was ready to thump her to the ground, when another classmate held me back. My white classmate remarked: "Where are all you people going? Every day more of your kind of people seem to be coming to this school. Why don't you stay where you live and go to school there?" She turned away angrily and ran to the parked chauffeured car waiting outside for her. No one had to explain to me why she was angry. I knew then that in her eyes I was the wrong colour and from the wrong side of town.

That day, as I took the bus home from school, I vowed that the minute I got home, I would tear up all the fairy tales I had written. They were not a part of me any longer. My white classmate had looked too much like Cinderella; her features were too close to that of Snow White. My writing career was over. My writing stopped. What could I write about? She had shattered my love and friendship with Cinderella, Snow White and Gretel. There was nothing left to write about. I did not want to write stories about my life and that of my cousins. Those were not fairy tales—they were only a series of tasks—wash dishes, clean house, iron school clothes, wash socks and panties. I wanted to write fantasies. Soon I stopped thinking about ever becoming a writer; instead I concentrated on becoming the best student in the school. English literature soon became my favourite subject, I came out top in the class for essay writing.

I fell in love with the library shortly after and read every minute that I was not bogged down by household tasks. I cannot remember entirely what the contents of those books were, but I do remember that none of them spoke to my experience or to that of any member of my family. The characters were all white, and all the children in the books led very exciting and leisurely lives. Still I read, it was a route to escape. The dynamics of class and colour were too much to absorb then, and in these books there was no mention of either.

December 1967

At the age of twelve, I came to Canada and met my mother and father for the first time. The next few months were busy ones, getting to know my parents, finding out more about myself and also about the other people who lived in this—my new home—Canada. I was also looking forward to my first day at school. I envisioned new friends—wonderful friends. Everything was new to me, and I was open to learning. English again became my favourite subject. There were so many books to read, so many books that I could take home from the library to read.

I began writing short little stories about animals. I showed them to my classmates and they liked them; they laughed and I felt good. But within a month of my experience in my new school in Canada, I was wishing that I had never set foot in this new land and again my wish of being a writer vanished.

It happened one cold January morning in my English class. My class was introduced to the novel *Huckleberry Finn.* Up to this point, I was just another student in the class—or so I thought. "Now class we will begin reading *Huckleberry Finn,* and I want each student to read a paragraph aloud. Will you begin?" asked my teacher looking straight at me. I was shaking, and I had begun to sweat. Earlier, I had skimmed the page and had seen the word "nigger," "nigger" all through the passages. And this particular paragraph that I was supposed to read had that word. He, my teacher, wanted me to say that word. What should I do? The class stared. "Will you begin to read?" my teacher asked impatiently. I began, then I said it, I said the word "nigger," and I broke down in front of the class and I cried. No one understood. No one said a word. Silence. Then my teacher commanded one of the students to take me to the nurse's office. He felt that I was sick. When the nurse asked what the matter was I cried even more. How could I tell her?

I did not go back to school for the remainder of the week. I told my parents I had a stomach ache. I did not tell them the real reason. I could not relive that experience. I could not call that word.

The next week in school marked a change in my life. I became very withdrawn and spoke only when spoken to. I stopped writing animal stories, and English became my worst class. The next six months seemed like six years.

October 1968

I discovered a new world of words—Black words—beautiful words—proud words. I found James Baldwin, Richard Wright and a whole number of Black American male writers. I was ecstatic, because after my experience with *Huckleberry Finn,* I had stopped reading. It was only by accident that one day I found a novel of Baldwin's on the sidewalk that had accidentally fallen out of someone's bag. Slowly, my dream of being a writer drew strength. Perhaps I could write like them someday, I thought. During the next few months, I talked more to my parents, pushing them to tell me more about their lives—about how I came into the world. I was excited. I discovered I had a past. My parents had experiences I could write about. I could write about them—about us—about a family. I didn't have to live through Gretel, Cinderella or animal stories any longer.

One day, I shared my dream with my parents, I told them I wanted to become a writer, "a famous writer," I said. They were not encouraging, but they were tolerant, no doubt thinking that it would wear off. But as the months went by and my talk increased about wanting to become a writer, my mother became less tolerant.

"Concentrate on your typing, then after you land a good secretarial job, you can think about writing."

1969

"I was born in Kingston, Jamaica, I am 15 years old. My mother was 16 years old when she gave birth. She was not married to my father at the time, so I was born an illegitimate baby. My father left us when I was three years old, he left for the land of opportunity, my mother followed him a year later. I was left in the care of my granny. Now, we're all together again, as a family. My mother and father are now married, I was flower girl at the wedding. I'm happy."

I looked at the page proudly. I was excited. I had created with words. Words about my own family, not Cinderella stories, not animal stories. I felt good about myself; I was beginning to write again. But this happiness was short-lived. Close to me I could feel my mother's warm breath over my shoulders. "Rip this garbage up." "Do you think this is writing?" "What kind of disgrace do you want to call down on us?" "We've forgotten that life, why do you want to remember it?"

I had done something wrong, I had dug up something that she wanted to forget. I sensed her shame as she grabbed the paper and ripped it to pieces.

1971

As I became more engrossed in the lives of Richard Wright, James Baldwin and Claude McKay, I began to plan my departure from home. My mother's shame of her own strength, of her past, drove her to make my life unbearable. She wanted us/me to live up to petty-bourgeois standards which she thought would erase our past. It was as if she were ashamed of me—afraid of the identification—immigrant, working-class. It was as if she were terrified of confronting and defending the strength of those two words.

I wanted an experience of my own, one that my mother could not rip to pieces, one that would be mine, only then could I write—could I create with my own words.

1972

I've been away from home for a long time; I've been to jail, I've been raped, I've stolen. Le Coq D'or, Yonge Street, Club Jamaica, The Silver Dollar, Darcy's in Yorkville, 52 Division and the 24-hour restaurant at the corner of Bathurst and Bloor Streets are no strangers to me—they are in fact familiar haunts. I know the world of the women and men who frequent these places. I want to write about their lives, my experiences, but. . . but. . . .

January 1973

I've decided to go back to school. I don't know what I want to do but I'm tired of the streets. There must be more to life.

September 1973

After much hassle—writing, re-writing application forms. . . essay writing on why I want a chance to continue my education. . . answering questions on my financial state. . . interviews. . . smiling . . . saying the right things. . . smiling. . . . They finally accepted me in the Transitional Year Program at the University of Toronto.

April 1974

I've completed the Transitional Year Program, and I can now apply to any university for admission to first year. But I'm finding this academic experience quite alienating, the people pretentious.. . .

September 1974

I'm working at a Black community newspaper. News reporting isn't the kind of writing I want to do, but it is a start. I'm meeting a lot of new people, and learning new skills. . . paste-up, typesetting.. . .

I want to start a column for Black women, but I'm making no success, my editor wants me to write recipes and a love advice column. I'm tired.

1975

I've become wife and mother. In my spare time I'm writing children's stories. I haven't completed one yet, because a new baby is very demanding.

Fall 1976

I'm totally absorbed in the world of motherhood. My 21-month-old daughter grabs at my dresstail for attention, while my one-month-old baby girl sucks greedily at my breast. I am 21 years old, and my husband is gone. . . a wealth of experience. . . but still the words. . . they won't come.

I wonder if this is how my life will be. It is different and sometimes beautiful but, is this it? Bottles, babies, milk, diapers, cries, fights with my estranged husband. . . scrimping and saving to make ends meet. . . dodging the landlord.. . .

Winter 1976

I've begun to have a disturbing dream. It is a persistent dream. It frightens me. I've begun to sleep with the lights on.

There's pain and I'm pushing, I'm trying desperately hard to rid myself of the pain by pushing. . . I'm giving birth. This time I'm not in a hospital—but in a barren room. I'm alone. . . I'm pushing. . . there's pain. Each time the dream ends the same way, I scream—this breaks the silence.

Spring 1977

I've begun to write again—children's stories and I'm feeling good about myself. I've received a small grant from the Ontario Arts Council through my publisher and friend at Kids Can Press. I've been commissioned to write a children's book. I'm really excited about it. Writing words. . .my dream come true. . .and I'm getting paid in the process. I have new friends too. Friends who also create with words. I have a new life, I'm going to be a writer soon.

Fall 1977

The children's story is incomplete! Time is going. But. . .I can't write. I'm depressed. I'm confused about what's happening to me. This is what I've always wanted to do, always wanted to be. I have the plot all worked out, I know the story that I want to write. It is such a beautiful story. . .not an ugly tale. . .it's like a modern-day fairy tale. . .the characters are Black. . .so why won't the damn words come?

I'm supporting two young children, I'm completing a university degree, I'm holding down a part-time job. . .recovering from a nervous breakdown, and trying, trying desperately to complete this story that just won't come. . .dammit, dammit!

   "Perhaps if I were to write about my own experience, the words might come. . . .no. . .I can't write about that—my mother would be ashamed of me."

I cursed myself. I could not share this with my friends who seemed to create with words so easily. For a simple fantasy I couldn't find the words. I could feel myself turning inward, pulling away from my friends, reluctant to talk about "my" failure.

1978

It is close to my 23rd birthday and I am exploring the world of women writers. I've read Maya Angelou's *I Know Why the Caged Bird Sings,* for the first time this summer. Toni Morrison's *The Bluest Eye,* Paule Marshall's *Brown Girls Brownstones*. . . These stories are familiar, close to me. Memories of my life in Jamaica come back to me as I read these women.

1979

I am deeply into the works of contemporary women writers—Angela Davis, Gayl Jones, Toni Cade Bambara and a number of others, but still it seems as if there is something missing. True their varied experiences are most helpful in me understanding my own life, but their experiences are beginning to seem limited.. . .

I've also begun to explore the short stories and novels of Alice Walker, and the missing shapes are beginning to take form. She is touching on things that no other woman writer has attempted to touch on. It seems to me that Walker has taken her life experience as a source—and transformed it into her writing.

Spring 1980

I'm meeting more women of colour who are writers. Fantastic! Their visionary process is endless. Barbara Smith, Audre Lorde, Maria Campbell, Cheryl Clarke, Hattie Gosset, Gloria Anzaldùa. . . have all become part of my life. I am gaining new strength. They have dared to write with words that break barriers. They do not apologize.

Summer 1980

I'm discovering a number of white women writers whom I have come to respect. I cannot mention them all, and some I'm just beginning to know, but the ones whom I've come to know through their writings are Tillie Olsen, Adrienne Rich, Robin Morgan and Marie-Claire Blais.. . .

I've given up the thought of writing that children's story. I've grown tremendously. I'm slowly beginning to realize that until I begin dealing with my own life—coming to terms with my own pain, my own struggle, my own silence—I will never be able to write. To do this I realized that I had to unlock a few doors, the doors that would open up the lives of my mother, my sisters, my grandmother and my daughters.

Fall 1980

I am playing an active role in the Black and Immigrant women's communities. I am speaking out on issues that affect us. I'm working at the Immigrant Women's Centre in Toronto and becoming deeply involved in the health and welfare of my immigrant sisters.

I'm working closely with domestic workers and have helped to organize a domestic workers' group where domestic workers can come and feel support from other women. I'm beginning to write again about real issues that affect my sisters, my sisters' children and myself.

Winter 1980

I've begun to write children's stories about real children and issues that affect them... working-class children whose families are on welfare... immigrant kids who are having difficulties with the way English is taught in the public school... racism in the schools... friendships among children from different cultures... but... but... I can't keep up with the rejection letters.

"Dear Makeda:

These are very interesting stories but we already have our quota of children's stories for the year.

We wish you luck in finding a publisher."

Spring 1981

rejection letters... rejection letters... . rejection letters... rejection letters... rejection letters... rejection letters... rejection letters... rejection letters... rejection letters...

Summer 1981

I'm continuing my work with the Black and Immigrant women's communities and with domestic workers. We are making progress and we have formed a bond among ourselves.

I'm also meeting with other women of colour who are writers. We are talking at length about forming a writers' group... forming a press... getting our work out there. We are finding that it is very difficult; we lack the material resources.

Fall 1981

I've sent out some more short stories to publishers but I'm slowly losing confidence, not sure of my judgement, wondering what I'm doing wrong.

Spring 1982

I have not written anything for a long time. What's the sense?

Who is going to publish it?

Maybe I should start writing things that everyone will like, stories that the publishers can relate to . . . stories that do not challenge the status quo . . . maybe I should write those kinds of stories if I want to be published.

Winter 1982

I'm beginning to trust myself . . . beginning to understand and trust my judgements. I'm learning quickly to out-talk the little timid "me" who says: "You can't write *that*, everyone will know about you. They'll ostracize you." I'm beginning to laugh at all that; for as I begin to create with my own words out of my experiences and those of my mother, grandmother and working-class sisters, a feeling of power comes up in me. There's no room for doubt.

My words will not always be about beautiful things; they will also be about the violence that has come down on my people, which includes people from my race, class and sex.

My words will challenge and offend some, but I cannot think of the consequences. I cannot turn back . . . not now . . . the process has begun. It has been a long hard struggle, and I can no more choose to divorce myself from words than I can from being woman.

Lorna Crozier

Myths

There is a story of a swan.
See the birthmark at the back of my neck
under my hair. That is where the great bird
pinched me in her beak, snatching me from the sea
and carrying my wet, salty body to the shore.
This is a story I could believe.
Sometimes the wings of a bird beat against
my skull. Feathers fill my mouth and eyes
with a whiteness like winter.

Or I was carried on a dolphin's back.
She pushed me to shore with her soft nose
then turned and disappeared under the waves,
the notes of her song hovering above the water
like seabirds. In the blue light of evening,
alone in the house I float through the rooms,
my sides sleek and slippery.

I waited for a long time on the other side
before the swan or dolphin carried me across.
I, too, was the first.

I was not made from a thin, dry rib,
white and bare as if chewed and sucked
by a small dog. These breasts did not come
from a man's side, this round belly, this hollow
at the centre. We dreamed each other
at the same time and we dreamed a garden.
When we awoke there was wind in the leaves
above us apples glowing like red moons
as we turned to one another in the sweet green air.

Jan Hopaklyissumqwa Gould

A West Coast Woman

"**Y**ou will not bury him at Saqwiss. He lost the right." My Grandfather was shouting, his face was twisted up, he was that mad. "He lost it all."

"But you're his Grandfather," shrieked Sadie. "I'm his sister. Did you forget?"

"I tell you he lost it all. When he went to work for that Jensen Logging, he lost it all. Take him away. Throw him in the Pass. Let the seals get a bite. That's what he's worth."

And then they both started shouting. All their words got mixed up together. Yes, Sadie, little Sadie, she was in some white boat that guy at Tahsis let her have to carry the coffin down the Inlet. Yes, they were shouting so loud that even the ravens took off.

I never saw Sadie like that before. No, she was like that pool — the sacred pool, the one our Grandfather went to before he was old . . . when he took his thoughts to the Maker. Yes, that pool was where my Great Uncle Joe got his spirit power. You had to clean yourself real good, had to rub the fir and cedar boughs up and down your bones and then you got into that cold, cold pool.

We went up there once when I was twelve, all my brothers and Sadie. We went with my Grandfather. It was some ride. We went in his fishboat, the Twin Sisters, yes. Right down the Inlet and to the Point, past Tahanees Rock and into Cook Bay and through the woods. Then we had to go up that mountain. I was so tired. Oh, I was tired. And I was so thirsty. There was yukkma, yes, that's what you white people call salal. That was there, lots of berries so I ate those. But my legs hurt. It was so far. And we went up and up and up. Then we came to this wood with the stream running through it and then hit big pool. It was so big — but I was little and I could have dived right into it because I was so tired. It was beautiful. Like a huge mirror. And we sat around it and my Grandfather talked a lot about the old ways. I looked down into it and I thought I would see myself there. Only what I saw was Sadie. Yes, little Sadie, it was her eyes looking back at me. She was like the pool—still, always at peace.

Yes, Sadie, she was like the pool. Always like that. Not Mark, he was real steamed up, like that little hotsprings near Cook Cove. Sure—only he didn't let it last long. Like that time he was deckhand with that Norwegian guy and they got into some fight at a party and sliced each other up a bit. The RCMP came, they went to court but the magistrate, he just shook his head. They told him they didn't know why they were fighting. They didn't remember and they were good friends. That magistrate, he shook his head a lot and then he fined them both.

Mark was smart. He went to the University for a year. People wanted him to become a lawyer or maybe to work at the Museum. Only he got back fishing, then he went logging and he said he liked it where he was, thank you all. But he got busy and made some of those big logging companies clean up the streams, made them pay damages to us sometimes. And he went over to Jensen Logging to talk about all this and Jensen hired him. Hired a lot of Indians. And he had a good camp with Tee-Vees and a cook came from some place like Paris and they had mobile homes. My brother Simon, he went there, too. But then the Government Project got going and it was all Indian. My other brothers, they went there and Simon's wife kept making noises so he quit Jensen's and went to the Government Project. And suddenly there was all this fighting. Some of the Reserve people said everyone should leave Jensen Logging and work for the Government Project because it was all Indian. Mark, he refused. He said Jensen was fair and good. And he said the Government Project wasn't going to last long. And it didn't have no good mechanic like Jensen did—they had Johnny Amos.

So there we were. . . divided. Half of the people wanted everyone working for the Government Project and half for Jensen Logging. Then people got mad and we had fights a lot. Some of the men working for Jensen were married into families who were working for the Government Project and things got real bad. The Government Camp had this accident. Stephen Smith got killed. It was the last log being loaded onto one of the trucks and it came down and crushed him. He was sixteen. They buried him in a new suit and some special fancy shirt with lace. And it got worse on the Reserve with no mahmuckmee—none of you white people—coming here. Oh the priest did, but not those guys from Tahsis not even Peter Buckington who's married to the Chief's daughter.

There was just Mark and Damien Callicum working for Jensen when Mark got killed in some rockslide when he was falling with one of Jensen's sons. Oh that was bad. Real bad. They said you couldn't recognize the Jensen boy he was just bits and pieces in the rock but Mark they knew, by his hair. And they had this real big funeral at Zeballos. I went, my great-aunt came from Queen's Cove, my great-uncle came from Alberni. And all my cousins came from Ahousat but my Grandfather, no he wouldn't come. My brothers didn't come. Sadie, she gave this real good speech about Mark. She said he always wanted what was right for everyone. Mr. Jensen, he tried to talk, but he was too sad. But they took that Jensen boy's coffin some place before they all went to some coffee party. Sadie she kept Mark's coffin in that hall we used. She said she would stay with it all night in case her Grandfather came over. Only, I know he would not. He was too mad because Mark worked for Jensen.

It was the next day Sadie came to the Reserve.

"I want his camera," she said, "to put on the grave."

Mark used to take pictures of our Elders, he had two books full of them in my Grandfather's house.

"You don't need his camera. He's not Indian any more—he's nothing. He shoulda worked for the Project," stormed my Grand-father and suddenly his voice softened. "Sadie . . . little Sadie, just get on your way."

Sadie sat down then in the prow of the boat. Her voice was like those little waves that pat the beach before the big wash from some freighter comes in. "I will bury him where he belongs. He never stopped being Indian. He was proud of it."

And then my Grandfather started shouting and so did she so I ran between the boat and my Grandfather, standing on the dock while all the kids came running out. I told them about the spawning stream that got all choked up with wood chips and how the trees near that stream acted. It was the story my Grandfather told us when we were real young. The trees that bent to that floor, they lived and grew strong. The ones that didn't bend at all, they were broke off and carried away.

"Stop fighting, Mark cannot hear you now," I said. And for a minute, my Grandfather looked upset. He walked away. I told Sadie to bury Mark at Zeballos for the time being. That later, everything would quieten down.

"Later?" she said. "Later, Martha? We are his sisters. It must be done now.. . ." And she left.

I walked over to where my Grandfather stood, bent a little, his bad leg bothering him some, his scarred old fisherman's hands curled up like hooks. He stared at Magic Island where the old stands of yellow cedar are and didn't speak. I could see the white boat getting smaller and smaller. Then it was real quiet and it was cold on the Reserve. Like when the fog comes in and say someone's sick and the planes can't get in or out, that's how it was, like a bad, bad fog covering the Reserve.

It was real fog we had the next day so my Grandfather and Norma Amos put off going to Saqwiss. They talked of keeping Sadie out, making sure that she didn't take Mark there. And the fog rolled in. I wondered where Sadie was. I thought of her as she sat in the boat, like a Nootka Princess, calm at first. Real pretty, too. Sure, she was wearing jeans and boots, yes, and one of those thick shirts. She's a West Coast woman. Who's going to wear high heels and those Department Store dresses up here when you're going over docks and log booms? There's no roads here on the Reserves, no Tee-Vee. Sadie's not gonna wear high heels or sit in some fancy car.

The fog lifted a bit and some of our men came in from the Project in the tribal boat. They heard that Mark's coffin was still in the white boat someplace and that Sadie had found the old rifle, the hunting gun my Grandfather gave Mark. And they said Sadie was sitting in some coffee shop talking and crying a lot with some of the guys who worked for Jensen.

It was a real light night with the full moon and I heard later that Sadie and two guys from Jensen's camp went over to Saqwiss before more fog rolled in. Sadie told them she wanted to stay one night, that it was the Indian way so they left her there, then they had to wait a full day to go get her and they couldn't find her so they came over here and Simon went with them.

They found Mark's coffin which had been carved by the men over at the Jensen camp and they said it was really something. They had carved out a whaling canoe on the lid. And the old hunting gun wasn't there but there were some pieces of red cedar bark which Mark used when he was dancing at Potlatches and his watch, that was on the coffin. Yes, that's our way. My Grandmother, when she was buried there, we put her sewing machine on the grave.

Simon tracked through the long grass into the woods and he found Sadie, little Sadie, by one of the cedars with the gun by her side. She must have made some deal with someone because there were three new bullets left in the pocket of her flannel shirt. She had had to do it two times. Yes, two times. And Simon carried her into the tribal boat and brought her here and I cleaned her up. We had the funeral right here with one of the priests who used to come and play crib with my Grandfather, only my Grandfather didn't come. He took off to the woods. For two days. He came back stiff with a real bad cold, too.

But all those people came to that funeral and we had all the boats, fishing boats, the tribal boat, the little boats, all of them made a procession when we took Sadie to Saqwiss.

And even Jensen came and his wife and some men from that boat came. And Jensen cried and cried, yes, he's got his big belly and no hair and he's a tough guy—but he cried.

My Grandfather, he went to bed when he came out of those woods. He's there a lot. He doesn't play crib with the priest and he doesn't talk much. Simon says he has lost his power and some of his brains. And the Indian Project ended when the Government ran out of money so all our men were sitting on the Reserve all day, getting bored.

The last time I took the kids over to Saqwiss they asked me why it all happened. I told them the old story about the stream being jammed and the flood and then the trees bending and some not bending and dying. That Grandfather and Sadie were like those trees that didn't bend. The kids thought about this but then Josie, that's my big girl, she saw this otter floating on its back so all the kids forgot about the graves. They went running and running through that tall grass and right down to the sea.

Dawn Star Fire

Letting Go

Funny how you never
   really give up on your dreams,
      and yet they seem to move farther away,
         with every passing year.

It's kind of like
   burning your nose on the toaster,
      because you have cigarettes, but no matches,
   and yet, when you finally remember
      to buy the matches,
         you can't afford the cigarettes.

It's all a matter of timing,
   like waiting twenty-two months
      for you to come home,
         and then leaving,
            when you arrive. . .

Kate Lushington

Griefkit

Good evening. My name is Veronica Mandel, and I've come to talk to you tonight about the psychiatric effects of nuclear war, or what can be done for mental health after the Bomb has dropped.

American psychiatrist Robert Jay Lifton has identified one of the major problem areas as "psychic numbing:" a profound blandness, insensitivity, and inability to experience grief—or indeed to feel anything at all. This will be detrimental to our continued development as whole human beings inside the bomb shelter, and may seriously limit our capacity to form co operating groups in the new world outside.

The natural mourning process, which could alleviate the severer symptoms of "psychic numbing," will be inhibited in many cases, or made very difficult, by the absence of bodies to bury—through vaporization, incineration, or other forms of corporeal annihilation. It is hard to bury a shadow on the wall. Another problem with nuclear devastation is its scale. Try to imagine one hundred million dead. Try it. And of those of us left, how many will be therapists? On a more individual level, it is unlikely that we will survive together with anyone close to us, or even be anywhere near our loved ones at the moment of impact. In the aftermath, the process of grieving and saying goodbye to those we have lost may assume supreme importance.

It is vital—and I use the word in its original sense of "essential to life"—that we are all prepared, in the event of nuclear attack, to be our own therapists. There are self-help books now available: *Good Life, Good Death,* by Dr. Christian Barnard; *Positive Thinking at a Time Like This,* by Norman Vincent Peale; *How To Be Awake And Alive,* by Mildred Newman and Bernard Berkowitz. These are no longer enough. Researching into more appropriate ways to meet an imminent need, psychologists have devised a "griefkit," to keep always by you in a safe, accessible place. It is very simple, consisting of ordinary household items:

—a box, with a well-fitting lid—clearly marked with your name
—a cushion or pillow
—photographs of the people you love
—a safety pin
—some kitty litter.

In the coming emergency, we believe that grief and mourning must have their place: the dead, as well as the living, need space. To this end there will be racks made available for griefboxes in every government shelter, but it is up to the individual to be responsible for his or her own kit. So, when the warning sounds, be sure to bring yours with you. Your future sanity could depend upon it.

Now, how to use your griefkit:
Place the pillow directly in front of you. Take the photographs one by one and name them, give them a name, their name:
Grandad
Suzy and Michelle
Bill
Jimmy
Anita.
Visualize them. See them smile. Hear them breathe. Now, take a safety pin and pin your loved ones to the griefpillow. Say to yourself: "This is me. I am here and I am alive. These are the people I love. They had their own individual existence, and now they are dead." Take the pillow and hold it to you for a moment. (Pause) Now, bury them: place the pillow in the griefbox, take some kitty litter, a handful should be enough, and sprinkle it over the ones you love, repeating:
"Death is random, death is not fair,
death is random, death is not fair,
death is random . . ."

When you are ready to say goodbye, close the lid firmly and put your box away alongside the others, making sure you can find it again handily should the need arise.

Remember, when the nuclear warning is given, if you bring nothing else, bring this. It may mean the difference to your emotional well- being, after the Bomb has dropped. Thank you.

Jacqueline Pelletier

liens de sang

Je suis ma mère soeur
rivée à la lourde toile de l'Ontarie
sombre
lente
triste
au delà des épinettes et des lacs
qui nous séparent
comme fantômes arrogants
languissants

toile dont je voudrais m'arracher
pour fuir le long hiver douloureux
qui engloutit ma race
engourdie de gel

toile qui me berce
et me cause au creux de l'oreille
l'histoire des mille bouches ridées
de nos mères
géantes
stoïques
dont l'écho survole les forêts morbides
pour atteindre les plus éloignées
de la dispersion

lasses de guérillas
de leurs banals secrets elles parlent
plus vives qu'à Toronto
leur parole s'épelle de montagnes de canapés
de fines courtepointes

usées, leurs beautés
et leurs doigts
à recueillir les sous de la survie

tissées à même la dernière catalogne
les révoltes du passé

lourde
lourde histoire . . .

on a cloué la Mère à la virginité de sa fille
mère contre fille
corps à corps
garde corps
crucifiée
bras en croix

infibulation
par l'oeil terrible regard laser
de la Mère

on l'a cousue au clitoris de sa fille
langue liée
monte la garde
sentinelle
veille au corps
implacable
silencieuse

ectopie de la parole

forcée
la Mère tisse de sa langue liée
une toile de mensonges
sur la vulve de sa fille

caryatide de l'hymen
vertu
des chairs gonflées
qui n'appartiendront qu'à l'étranger

pas à la fille

massectomie
la mère condamnée à la contradiction
à la confusion

mère contre fille
matronne contre détenue

c'est là que tout commence
entre les cuisses
où tout a commencé
où nait la mutinerie
où devait naître la solidarité
dans la morbide veillée au corps d'Eve
condamnée à expier son innocence

toutes les mères de l'univers expient
par le corps de leurs filles
privé
nié
puis livré à l'homme
pour le rituel

la merrouge ouverte pour laisser passer le peuple
la descendance
la prochaine génération
la prochaine violation

désapprouvées
celles qui ont nié le ventre

mortifiées
qui ont refusé de tisser le cordon ombilical
          refusé l'extrême onction

que la mère a pu sauver
secrètement
discrètement
dans le silence
les échappées de Berlin de Prague De Beyrouth. . .
ambiguïté. . .

          la mère
          qui a caressé
          ouaté
          oint ce clitoris
          ne veut plus
          ne sait plus
          titube de contradiction
          désespère d'empêcher
          sauver
          caresser
          lesbianiser le corps de sa fille
          protéger

          ne peut rien à part monter la garde
          programmée
          en silence
          sans avouer son affreux effroi aux touristes qui rient
          et prennent des photos
          en attendant.

          infibulation de la cervelle de la mère et de la fille par la
          Mère
          inventée

rompue la mère
complice de l'ordre
qui se vomit par sa bouche

elle avait tout refoulé
comme un vieux lainage
dont on ne veut pourtant pas se séparer

gorge contractée en contractions d'une immense boule
de feu
qui pousse et repousse pour enfin faire crever les larmes
la mère éclate en récits lointains et déliants
délirants

il fallait une rupture finale
trop courbée, l'échine bondit
la gestation ne peut durer
le stress, ultime
d'un trait
mutation
soudaine
le OUI

dans la gorge enflammée d'une mère
s'est tu le silence
à tout jamais

tôt ou tard
la nef des bouches millénaires conclave des mères déliées
s'est mise à résonner
de toute la vérité

elle coule à flots!

nous n'écrirons plus de larmes transparentes

de bouches en oreilles
la parole retrouve sa place

fin de la contradiction

naît le calme respect d'une mère
qui de tendresse complice
ouvre sa fille à la liberté
au choix
à elle-même

Vous étiez au front
armées de colères
d'amères déceptions
armées d'une fauve volonté de naître
belles et fortes artisanes
de la renaissance

l'humanité avait tout à gagner
l'ardeur de votre cri lui a fait parcourir
les millions de lieues lumières qu'il fallait
pour atteindre une pointe d'horizon

un soleil levant verse sa rosée sur vos larmes

pourquoi ce silence qui hurle entre vos reins
pourquoi cette solitude me lance-t-elle son affreux regard
pourquoi cette nostalgie alors que tant de femmes
sont nées de vous
la fête pour vous
serait-elle déjà terminée?

Betty
Beth
Elizabeth
vous avez semé les roses de l'avenir

Précursoeurs

Vous me faites tendresse
Betty
Beth
Elisabeth

pionnières
précursoeurs
éclaireures

vous me faites humble
dousoeurs

une tempête s'érige
du fond de ma mémoire
un souvenir jaillit
comme laser
impitoyable jet d'espoir
monolithe
aux mille inscriptions taillées
à coup de ruptures
de lettres d'avocats

chaque jour sera jour de souvenance
à l'aube je déposerai
devant votre moment historique
les roses les plus vives de la gratitude

En moi je suis femme
en moi je suis française
franco
ontario
femme.
ontaroise

deux têtes valent mieux qu'une
mais c'est lourd à porter
deux têtes en lutte
qui ne s'écoutent pas

l'une entend
"Sauve la langue
crie fort tes droits"

l'autre entend
"Le silence est d'or
tais-toi"

alors ma parole de femme
si vivante et audacieuse
si vibrante
n'en finit pas de mourir
dans ma bouche
française
j'en ai mal au ventre
à la francophonie
à l'avenir

Minotaure!
ma tête de femme est forte
son regard ne baisse jamais les yeux

De minorité sclérosée
ma tête française veut m'assimiler
menacée
méfiante
elle a appris l'hypocrisie
à la patente
dans les coulisses des subventions
àgenouxàtoronto
à elle seule
elle a deux faces

deux têtes
trois faces
lourd à porter

Ma femme parle
ouvertement

de défis
d'égalité
de souffrance
de vulve et de détresse
d'espoir et de frustration
d'inconnu d'orgasme de carrière

ma française écoute
tremble
feint la solidarité

dès que ma femme se tourne
elle lui plante son mépris dans le dos

des armée

la réalité me glisse entre les sens
napalm qui fond
et confond de terreur
j'ai douleur
d'un nuage parasite qui tue d'absurdité

tout est brouillard

d'opulence ma tête déborde
d'informations
étouffantes déformations
je paralyse
agressée jusque dans la peau de statistiques
chimiques
qui déchargent au creux de moi
leur plein de mensonges venimeux

respiration artificielle
je suis minutée
la planète gigote morbide dans mon ventre
en crise
coeur empalé, cris de mots vidés à sec
aseptiques.
verbiage inutile de spécialistes braqués au microscope
trop tard

myopie d'où émane la destruction

Civilisation!

j'ai froid de cette peur
mortel pesticide qui détruit ma résistance
soeur, taisons-nous

que dire de gorges étranglées
où confluent tant d'horreurs

je cherche pour dire parfaitement la paix
faute de mots
faute de maux
faute de temps
parler n'est que mentir
détruire

ne me laisse pas abandonner
comprends le geste qui s'échappe silencieusement
de mes lèvres
et t'enveloppe
muette
de tendresse

écoute mon silence d'espoir

rapt

ils ont homologué la langue
code stratégique du pouvoir
grimoire du patriarcat
l'hégémonie
par la syntaxe
par coeur
inconScience

affirmer l'UNiversel
le reste n'est que [différence]
[exception]
superflu[es]

comme il faut
puisqu'il le faut
ainsi soit-il

nous sommes expulsé[es]
entre [parenthèses]
notre paradis terrestre
déporté[es]
à la sueur de nos silences
réduit[es]
à l'état de dialecte
assimilé

quidame dans ma propre bouche
je n'existe pas!

langue hara kiri
ultime chef d'oeuvre
le coup du maître

l'appropriation
par la voix du code
bien appris
répétezrépétezrépétezrépétezrépétez
jusqu'à bouli

silence languissant

ne pas plier ou perforer
sous peine d'amende.

ordinatrice

circuit instantané
la machine assume le temps
l'espace
la connaissance
tout est révolution
actualisation

éclaté
le sens exige
la folie
ou la synthèse

d'urgence

émiettement de la vision partielle
vulnérable
le laboratoire réclame la relation
pose la totalité

dire les rapports
exprimer les influences
le reste est mensonge

intensément stressé le langage
langue liée
incapable de dire ses propres découvertes
bouche bée
poussé au seuil de l'intégration

cri chaotique devant l'abîme

> départ zéro
> comme l'ordinatrice
> qui dit tout
> et donc métamorphose
>
> affolée
> à bout de mots
> la parole cherche...

Emmasculé[e]
[maconsciencecomprimé[e]enun[e]exceptionàlarègle]
j'étouffe!
de pression
langue d'oppression
de compression
langue de confusion
trou noir
langue homophone
cherchez en vain 10,000 femmes
car un homme assemblé fait le poids
langue violente
notre litham
tissé des litanies paralysantes du masculin
qui l'emporte

langue de censure

Smaro Kamboureli

from *in the second person*

february 6/81

my language.
my greek rusty. my awareness of making mistakes when i use english.
my language that tortures me every time i dare use it.
my language that refuses to flow from the pen onto the page.
my language locked within my body.
my astonishment when i realized i was dreaming in english.

i gaze at my greek typewriter with despair. with shame. after
my olson translation not a single word. not a single word

i've got no language that defines me now. only my accent is a
reminder of my geography. the accent i can't hear. my voice
deluding me. i never thought i was going to be troubled by this
form of exile. will i remain an outsider forever?

february 8/81

i want you to die
any form of death will do

you treasure every dead moment of your life. memory is the
saving grace of the emptiness that fills you.

i don't exempt myself. i changed language. i grew a second skin,
wrapped around my self another self. i've become a metonymy of
my past. my image of myself these days is that of a fractured
bone. a fractured bone that heals itself.

i think of aquin and suicide all the time. is this only an intellectual exercise? a fantasy that affirms the improbability of suicide? a fallacious gesture? what do i have to kill, metaphorically speaking?

blackout: "I am the anamorphosis of my own death, and of boredom."

february 13/81

fall to learn
cupidinous knowledge

february 26/81

hubert aquin, i'm your reader . . . i was lost for hours in the long letter i composed for aquin. i was so conscious of my silent reading gradually rising outside my self, becoming my double. reverie graphs. and myself an anonym musing on the transformation. reveling in the mutation. the letter is all written, ready to be delivered. i want to deliver it personally. but there is a hole in my memory. can't remember where he lives.

july   banff

i walk around
hands in
pockets full of greek time

                    (are cocks ever claustrophobic?)

the road today was a continuous sentence. since coming back from greece i have stopped hearing lines. voices come to me in sentences.

december 25/81   lantzville

had a terrible night. we woke up at 4:00 a.m. (robert worked on the novel for a while. i read.)

french toast for breakfast. talked about the chapter that takes place in greece. very badly written right now but it has enormous possibilities. we plan a short trip to gabriola. nanoose bay full of seaweed today. the sea unrippled. a mauve sky. no wind or rain. robert is taking a nap on the livingroom floor. i'm looking at the sea. virginia woolf appears. she's walking on the water. she's coming in my direction but is not looking at me. i pass through the glass wall. i'm naked and as i approach her my figure gradually fades. we both disappear. no traces left. except me, writing in my journal. and her name. the cats need to be fed. i have to wake up robert.

Kathleen McHale

five & dime
jump-rope rhyme
jump in time
streetcar line
line broke
monkey choke
hit the pavement
one more time
summer sun
almost gone
feet together
jump in rhyme
hit the sidewalk
one more time

Leslie Hall Pinder

June Brides

Part I

She pulled, separating the two large sides of the barn door and then stepped backwards, with the warm ring handle in her fingers. The door gave its dark soft creak, her boots sinking into the mud that was always in front of the barn, no matter what the weather. The steamy air of the barn was pulled out into the hot sun of the day, like a shadow. She walked inside, sucking sounds in the earth.

No one called her from the house.

Her eyes adjusted. The dark forms moved heavily. A pigeon high in the rafters snapped its wings like broken twigs. She had heard that sound a hundred times. More. She paused, then went to the first stall, untied the smooth worn rope from the pole, and led out the red chestnut horse. Its black eyes, wider it seemed than her fist, took in all of the light and all of the shapes, indiscriminating, blank, absorbing even her.

She was startled at the brightness of the day.

She held the horse still, turned her back on the wide veranda of the white house, put her left hand on the mane, and with a slight groan, flung herself onto the bare back of the horse, touched her heels into its sides and moved away. She passed the numerous outbuildings, the house for the hired hands, passed the bright old tractor and combine and onto the short lush grass. Faces appeared at the window and disappeared.

She bent her head as they moved under the low leaves of the maple tree on the upswing of the hill, but held up her hand, just at the end, to the outer branches, grasped a branch that moved with them for a space and snapped back. Her hands were full of leaves. She pinched off two of the leaves from the twigs and let go of the rest. They lay bunched on the ground behind her. She took the leaves and placed one carefully between herself and the horse, beneath each knee. She lifted her heels, creased them into the flanks of the horse; her neck cracked as they broke into a gallop. She was away.

Inside her mother and sister were spreading out the veil, arranging flowers, counting the plates and the glasses. There were many telephone calls back and forth between her house, which was all white and the light swung nicely around and through the glasses set on the table, and his house: rather dark—black suit and hat and the bottles of red wine he would bring.

Over the hill the trees began to thicken until the wide path on which the hooves beat disappeared under the latticework of light through leaves.

It was such easy motion. She could feel her centre of gravity descending from somewhere about her head and neck, lower and lower, through her back, along her thighs, connecting her to the leaves that touched the flanks.

She was two miles away from them now. She looked back. The threshold of her space lay behind her for twenty yards into the woods, and boundlessly in front. Boundless limits. A mathematical idea: that you can get as close to the limit as you want, you can get infinitesimally close, but cannot touch it. Always halving the distance between yourself and the impossible. And it's all boundless the other way. Idea. She rode on. "Without duty or pity," she thought; you must ride very fast to keep up the nerve of that line; stop once and they descend with gravity.

Her long black hair whipped back and forth across her eyes and face. She brushed it back with her hand. The breeze kept her face cool.

She hadn't been out riding for a long time, not since leaving her home three years earlier and returning now for her nuptial ride which she had wrested from her women, mother, grandmother, two sisters, the women helpers, in the most childish way. She had walked out. They would think she was upset. She had turned and turned herself in the mirror, for days it seemed, being revolved by their kindly, helpful hands, putting on and taking off the veil, on and off the wedding dress, the shoes, all the women and their many arms touching, readjusting, moving the cloth—then consulting one another over her shoulders and breast, and then stopping and checking their work in the mirror, where although everyone was reflected in the long light, all the women in their coloured work clothes, only she was seen. They checked her appearance against some idea they had, more real than the image she projected: as though they were trying to match two colours. At first, too, she looked in at herself with interest. Everyone was preparing her as a present. But it became tiresome. As the hours passed the present became more and more perfected, and she became dull, listless almost, the gravity caught up around her head and neck.

He was somewhere else, she supposed, being tendered in front of his men. And although this thought urged a certain amount of sympathy towards him, there was not quite enough to actually bridge the enforced distance between them, the dozen miles to his father's house. Her sympathy didn't find him in those rooms, but played outside his house, like a dog in the long grass. Odd; it wasn't his fault, all of this absurd preparation. He didn't want it any more than she. They were both doing it for the elders, and had joined in submitting themselves to their fussy fingers and their commotion, out of which the air was to become crisp with their union. These were the rational thoughts; she had to work her way over her situation, like someone climbing over rocks, in order to escape the blame she placed on him. Perhaps it was partly the presence of his representative there, his mother, fingering her veil and her hair, that made him blameworthy now. It was unbearable.

"When it's done properly, when the thought is perfect, the hunter and the hunted are one. There is a deer in the empty field. It sees you with your gun. You stand there for a long time, staring. You wait. If you moved quickly to raise the gun to your shoulder you would have it. But you do not move, and the deer doesn't move. It's not as though you are giving it a chance to escape, or that it is giving you a chance to shoot. Both of you are simply recognizing that there is no division between you. There is no victim. The hunter and the hunted are one. And then it's over. It falls." She recalled her father's words, spoken to her when she was a very small child, and in various altered ways since then. The first time he knew what he meant, and so did she. Later he merely repeated the words that once held the idea.

They had slowed to a walk. She had been absorbed in her thoughts and her will had stopped pressing them on and on. She had no idea how long they had been moving at this slow pace. The forest was two miles deep. Her eyes pulled at the stumps and mossy fallen trees, trying to recognize where she was, the way she had pulled with the ring on the door of the barn, trying to release the scene into a familiar place. She thought she had it, murmured an "ah, yes," but passing a similar log further on there was another "oh, now I know" and she was less certain with every assurance. She was not really disturbed; it had been so long ago that these woods were part of her life. "I have forgotten everything, at least twice," she thought.

How far away from them she was now, from all that clattering whiteness. The only purpose, the real purpose of the light was to make these greens revealed. Still moisture on the leaves. She touched the green beneath her legs. The leaves were there.

And the dark red of the neck of her horse, deep with sweat. He fumed now and then, snorted and sighed through his tight back.

Now that she was alone she knew her real isolation. She felt billowed out like a wide white sail, or a sheet. She was perfectly vulnerable. Anything could touch her now.

He had come to her the night before, although it wasn't allowed. He had tapped on her window, a light tap and a whisper of her name. They had to behave as thieves. She had been asleep. She awoke quietly, dreaming of the star sounds. He was at the window. She let him in like a thief. She should have been delighted that he had risked this visit and was, at first. But then it all seemed so silly because they had lived together for a year. Now because of a decision which was mutual and conclusive, they had to assume this foreignness, for the benefit of the witnesses. And again, perversely, she blamed him, and took no pleasure in his breach of the rules. He felt it immediately. And although they both knew he was not blame-worthy, everything that he said seemed inculpatory. "I feel conspic-uous, uncomfortable," he finally said. And then he said he would leave. She didn't want anyone to be blamed, and mostly herself for her treatment of him. But she let him go, back out through the window. Their situation was absurd, and she did not want that absurdity to cling to either one of them. And yet that was the result; his crawling back out through the window attached to him and not to anything they shared.

Her hand-maidens, her mother and mother-in-law, had stood looking at their daughter in the mirror, each holding up one side of her veil.·

She touched the flanks of her horse. They flew.

Billowed out like a wide white sail, she thought. Sweat from the mane touched her cheek. She leaned low over him and they both leaned into the corner. Up ahead there was a long log across the path that hid a fault in the earth. She had jumped it a hundred times, with the same impossible anticipation of wings. She crouched lower. She felt the familiar kick, the inexplicable smoothness which followed, and then the harsh impact of landing. But she was in motion separate from her horse, her limbs were let go, and her body's lightness became a crazy tangle in the air, and her head involved, split by the stopped ground. Two leaves fell from the sky.

How awful. She pressed closer to the ground in an effort of stillness. She took account of her bones. She felt their wholeness, but above them handfuls of bruise. And then slow swelling of blood down her forehead and into her eyes. She rolled back, and slowly moved her hand to clear away the liquid, follow it to its source, to her hair. The bride is dead, long live the bride. She pulled out her shirt tail, put it in her mouth, and tore off a strip of cloth. She twirled this into a bandana and tied it around her head. The chestnut stood, stiff and still, a little ways down the path.

They shaved away a patch of her hair, and implanted five stitches. A wig was set over her skull, on top of the black hair, knotted at the back. Then came the veil.

She walked down the long aisle, the way she had been taught, slowly, pausing with each step: pause but don't seem to hesitate her mother had told her. You must look straight ahead. She did this, approaching the stiff and still back of her husband. Someone whispered "beautiful." She did look beautiful, camouflaged. What a long way it was down the aisle. The hairs on the back of his neck seemed to bristle with her approach. Closer. Finally she stood beside him. He turned his head, his eyes pulled inadvertently up to the crown of her head, then to her eyes. They both faced the minister. He, too, thought "very nice, yes, I like to marry beautiful brides." She could feel the tight skin like a crease in her brain. And what the Lord had joined together, let no man . . . I went out riding the day before my wedding, bareback, with leaves beneath my knees.

Part II

I went to my mother's wedding. There was something wrong: that a child, my father, should die before his parents, and his parents live for twenty years longer. That shouldn't happen, but it did. And my mother remarried.

The reception took place in the house where I was born. The house had been transformed for the occasion. It was painted from its old yellow to a dark brown. I had watched the progress of the painters from the house across the street where I played: every day more was accomplished, from the roof downwards, like an eye closing, until it was done and secure. Or water filling a lock.

It's very odd to go to your mother's wedding. My brother and sister were there. Someone held my sister because she was two years old. My mother wore a blue dress and was afraid my brother would faint. He was white.

My brother has, all my life, had the strange ability to act out the perceptions which I did not have, except perceiving them in him, and then he would go away, shucking his feelings; he had forgotten them, and buoyant, brilliant me, I sink, remembering what he cannot say. That wedding was our divorce; nothing was the same afterwards. We seemed to watch one another from separate households joined together.

My father asked me whether or not he could marry my mother. He said that he wanted to and would I consent. I did. Find a ring, and it goes round round round. He had a handsome face. Perhaps he loved my mother as much as I did.

My mother wasn't a virgin when she got married.

They decided it wouldn't be a very large wedding; only the people who would be related to one another after the wedding would be there. We filled the little chapel off of the main church, which I had, until then, only known as the changing room for the choir. I didn't know that it could be part of the church. I knew that the oak panelled walls were, in fact, the cupboards for the choir gowns. As I sat in the chapel with the rest of the people, waiting for my mother, I looked at those walls and saw behind them the rows and rows of heavy black cloth hanging on the coathangers, some slipping off the metal shoulders, some bumped up against others, creasing, empty hangers here and there and mostly at the ends of the rows. Only I could see them.

It was Saturday afternoon. I knew my choir master would not come to the change room. I couldn't see my gown behind the wall after a while.

My father used to sing in the choir. My real father who was dead. He sang "The Lord is My Shepherd I Shall Not Want." I asked him what it meant. He said even though I need Him, I pretend that I don't, but He knows the truth and makes me lie down so that I will be quiet and listen. Sometimes he would sing that hymn to everyone in the real church. His breath was sweet, but when he sang or laughed I could see that his teeth were a bit crooked just near the front. He was a doctor and not a dentist and so he didn't have a friend who could fix his teeth for free. He did have a friend who listened to his heart when it began to slow down. The friend listened but couldn't hear anything except my father's heart beating, the way it should, like a peg-leg walking. Then his heart stopped and he was dead and everyone was surprised, especially his friend who didn't even come to my mother's wedding.

I started off as a happy child. I took a bright blue ribbon in my hand and held it between my fingers and started to run beside the place where the ribbon was strung, the silk moving smoothly and wonderfully in my hand, but at the end of the ribbon the blue was cold.

Find a ring, and it goes round round round.

We waited for my mother. It was Saturday afternoon. The light which came through the coloured glass of Jesus's head and hands was smoky, as was the light from the candles in the room. Dust descends.

The people sidled into the chapel and took their places. They didn't speak to me when I looked at them but seemed mute and shy, full of half-dimmed recognition. They nodded and put it out.

My mother came down the aisle. She didn't look at me as she passed by, and I could have reached up and touched her blue dress. She passed by me, like a Queen in a crowd: everyone recognized her and she recognized no one.

My other father was waiting for her at the front. I hadn't noticed him there until he stood up. I wanted to shout "there she is" but everyone knew, of course. I wondered if she would say hello after it was done.

Then the marrying began.

"After I say these words, these two will become one."

There were three candles on the altar. One was out. The minister told my mother and my other father that they had to lift their separate candles and light the one in the middle. I held my breath, afraid I would blow a cold wind in their direction. Three candles were lit from the two that were one.

The minister told the two to look at one another. They did. He read a long poem. And their eyes slipped off one another's faces as he read, wandered in a small space. I thought of flies trying to land. They chose a place between the brows. The candles flickered.

"And do you, Elizabeth Margaret, take this man, David Raymond. . . . And do you David Raymond take this woman, Elizabeth Margaret. . . ." A long time ago their names were blue haloes sounding round and round, Elizabeth Margaret said twice, said over and over.

"I now pronounce you man and wife."

Da da da da da da da dum dum dum dum dum dum da da da tralalalalalalala da da da da dum dum dum. They drove off in a yellow convertible. Then I was married to all my cousins called Tom, Dick and Gerry. It would be less sad if it were less true. All of the cousins were put into a taxi, eight of us piled on top of another, like an oyster bar. We were sent to the movies. On the way we passed a yellow convertible, speeding, spacious, travelling the opposite direction. The blinds were drawn. I saw it from beneath the armpit of my cousin Bonnie. Three weeks later they returned.

I went to my mother's wedding on the day she was married. My brother didn't faint. My sister didn't cry.

Nelia Tierney

Tintinnabulations

Once there was
the red rip
the silent wet scream
of the placenta.

Once there was
the white wet
of mute milk.

There is a dryness now
and resonance
of stone and wood
of iron and dessicated wounds.

Now we grind each other
in the hollow of our stone days
taking turns being
the millet and the pestle.

I am a tight drum
you rap on my wooden walls
with your knuckles
and beat
with the palms of your hands
on the skin
of my stretched roof.
Inside
I am tossed about
in a storm of reverberations.

You are the iron gong
that strikes
inside my flared metal skirt
the neighbours hear
the tintinnabulations.

Now you tell me
you wear my touch
like the thin white crust
of salt
left behind
when the ocean withdraws.

Rose-Marie Tremblay

Dialogue

Cette parole que je possède
qui m'obsède
que j'oppose au patriarcat
depuis le moment
où j'ai rencontré le père
sur le champ de l'égalité

C'est pour la forme
que j'ai recours au passé
Quelle importance
de repenser mes
vieilles histoires
de reformuler ces
actions médiocres
et incolores

Juxtaposition de personnalités
de gestes qui reviennent
toujours au même
Aucune évolution
le piège de ma formation
Parlant je me recrée
je m'accorde une puissance
mythique

Pauvre sotte
imbibée de paroles
dansantes et enivrantes
qui te poussent à refaire le monde
selon tes exigences

Tu ne pardonnes pas la pluie
qui limite ta croissance
et cette pluie
qui te tombe
dessus
n'a jamais produit de fleurs

Danielle Thaler

Acte de contri"tion"

Levant délicatement la narine
ils parlent de pollution
de saturation
d'épuration
de nutrition
et les "tion"
à l'infini
font tous la ronde
dans un monde
où l'on s'inonde
de mots accrochés
dans la toile des humeurs
de ceux qui les salivent
pour mieux les recracher
avec un ton courtois
le sourcil haut levé
engagés dans la bataille épique
des pronoms surchargés

Germaine Beaulieu

Je m'arrête,
reprends mon souffle, mon mot
me monte une échéance dans la pensée où les circuits
doivent produire dans la mémoire du temps.
Je suis la maîtresse des circuits, dominée par
l'imaginaire. Je pose dans l'arène du corps
jonglant le sens et trahissant l'origine sous
les yeux arcés des preneurs de mots.
J'imagine mal la fuite.

Carole Itter

The Blues Singer

When he and I walked into the room early in the evening, there were about eight people sitting on chairs. I noticed one woman right away, she had her back against the wall, sitting at a table. Something about her face caught me right away, maybe that we'd met before; we were introduced, I heard her name then repeated it as I said hello and had we met before, I thought maybe we had. There was almost no response from her so I left it awkwardly at that, sat down not far from her, an empty chair and a friendly face next to me, soon talking about labour unions or some such thing. She may have been watching us or listening, I couldn't say, and very shortly didn't think too much about it. It was the beginning of a great party, a three-day weekend and a good friend's anniversary.

Soon enough, good music from the next room drew me there, a few dancing and I joined, wiggling what I could, loosening up. He was enjoying himself, his marvelous laughter easily heard from here or there. She moved towards me, asked if I minded that she join, how formal I thought, we usually just get up and dance on these occasions, no need to invite yourself but I watched how she moved her young body, nothing really exceptional except for her astoundingly good looks. She danced over to me and said, *do you know that man?* referring to him, his laughter, and I was immediately tongue-tied. Over the loud music and the crowding of people what could I reply and how far, was she asking for an introduction or was her only way to relate to me through the man I came to the party with, was I supposed to make some sort of claim right then? I answered an innocuous *yes,* wondering if this was how we were to meet. She replied so excitedly, her grey eyes flashing, *boy, is he ever a treat,* moved quickly away from me, moved back to him. The music took it from there, a number still loud but not easy to dance to so I sat it out, seeing them across the room, now talking, she insisting again

and again that he'd met her before, teasing him and teasing him as to
where, repeating her name again and again, surely he remembered
the meeting, after all her name was the same as that great blues
singer's and he remembered that, didn't he; she, pale, white, frail, a
tiny young woman with an astounding face, her voice—ahh, high,
light, shrill almost, carrying over the music, demanding, she insisting
that he'd met her before.

He picked her up off her feet, raised her into the air, hugged her
closely and slowly lowered her down, leaned her against the wall,
propped his right arm on the wall behind her and he was flirting
too, even yelling, yes, over the music that he did, of course, remember
because she was the one with the same name as the great blues
singer. Their laughter carried above the sound system and the few
who'd been dancing withdrew. How well I knew that mercurial
laughter, this time laughing and teasing this beautiful young woman,
possibly half his age, so spunky, outspoken and very aggressively
holding his attention. He put his hand on her head and curved it
around her closely-cropped hair, withdrew it gently and just a touch
too slowly. His next step was perfectly executed, one small pace
backward, allowing her the space to move forward to him which
she manouvered in mid-sentence without hesitation. There was no
stopping it, the dance of two people meeting and the inexpressible
dynamics of wholehearted attraction.

I sat there numb, meditating the choices I had. Two. I could
adjust my pretend blinders on the sides of my face, straighten up my
fake velour jacket with my hands while actually checking that my
housekeys were still in the pocket, find the host and thank him for
the lovely party and go home. Home wasn't far and beckoning by
its silence, fresh air and solitude. The second choice was to walk
over to them, imagining I was going to his rescue when I knew very
well it was my own rescue I was going to and attempt to join them,
stand beside him and meet her. And I did, leaned to his ear and said
under the music, *I'm splitting.* He put an arm casually around me and
said affectionately, *not yet.*

She directs some of her talking to me but how apparent that it's he
who holds her interest, I'm familiar enough standing in that so I
continue to listen and she introduces herself, same name as the great
blues singer, did I know that singer and I reply *no* and she looks

most incredulously at me as I return her gaze and finally I say *what do you do?* She says *I'm a heavy equipment operator.* She goes on to say she is driving buses now, trolley buses specifically and that she doesn't have the mobility that's required to work in those isolated places where dams are built or new highways are cut through mountains because she is raising a daughter who is now thirteen. Both he and I interrupt her in amazement asking just how old is she because she looks about twenty-five or younger and I ask, far too flippantly, *did you get knocked up at fourteen?* but she doesn't laugh says *nineteen* and that the son-of-a-bitch never stayed around to help raise the kid, that she'd done it all alone, that he just buggered off and never once took an interest in the child.

His marvelous laughter stops. While he was standing between her and me, now he's quickly lost interest and suddenly slipped away gracefully into the party. Now I am the sole focus of her attention and she continues, that he, that bugger, got *his* university education, got *him*self a PhD in economics but she had to quit of course to raise this kid and *can you believe it,* he works for the federal government and has never given her one red cent, the slob, towards the education of this kid and he's a big important man making over fifty thou' a year but can't even take the time to think about this kid.

Every so often she says *end of story* which makes me think she doesn't want to talk any more about it but she starts again with little variation, that slob, that son-of-a-bitch, after he left, she fell in love with a woman, lived with her for two years and then he came back, fell in love with the woman too, took her away and married her and they've been married for eight years, still living in eastern Canada.

This summer, she says, she's gonna take the kid and drive right across the country, the whole three thousand miles, dump the kid on them, boy, let them meet each other, let him see what it takes to raise a kid and feed a kid, that slob, he met her once when she was five and that was it, no letters, no gifts, no help, no nothing, doesn't know a thing about kids, doesn't even know how to talk to a kid, scared the wits out of her when she was five, what a bastard, end of story.

Well, I'm listening and trying not to look at her face which so attracts me, or her trim haircut that I'd noticed as I came into the room and wondered if that was how I should get my hair cut, our faces seemed similarly shaped, perhaps I'd suit a short cut like that.

Earlier I wondered if I'd get to know her well enough during that evening to ask her where she got her hair cut but it seemed hardly likely that our conversation, if you could call it that, was going to move on to such a mundane level. Meanwhile she repeats her story, end of story, once around again and by not looking at her clear young face nor seeing those flashing grey eyes, I hear especially the voice—high-pitched, angry, becoming almost hysterical. I decide cautiously that maybe she's very drunk or verging on a breakdown and my best bet is to take care and simply listen but I can't take much more of the awful anger she carries, this isn't the story *he* listened to when *they* were standing so close, this story's been reserved for me. What it gets down to, I think, is money, that's the raw edge, money it is that's bugging her, what he didn't even give, end of story.

Her voice becomes higher and sharper still and I wonder why I continue standing there. The dimly-lit room is filled with Rolling Stones badass music but few are dancing and I sense quite a few are watching, her story's harsh and her voice shrill. I don't know the blues singer but if she does, then I wonder why she doesn't modulate her voice after the singer's. But with that sort of face, that clear clear skin stretched smoothly over exquisite bones, maybe it's never struck her that anything more was needed, perhaps she's always had all the attention she's ever asked for and I stand there too, waiting for the end of the story which she punctuates so frequently with the phrase end of story and lashes out at that slob again, that son-of-a-bitch, gave her a baby, married the woman she loved, disappeared, never helped out with the kid, but this summer she is just gonna drive right up to his house and lay the kid on him and he could see what it was like.

I shifted feet a few times, I'd already said to him that I was splitting and that's mostly what I wanted to do but now he's split and I am meeting this same young beauty that so enamoured him, yet it is excruciating to have to listen and listen to this mountain of resentment, did I deserve it, I wondered that maybe I did. Maybe I should mention that I have a daughter too, soon as I have a chance to say something, I mean I should say something about myself just to be polite, tell something about myself but I can sense my story wouldn't interest her for long. There is a general large shift of people through the room, a group is standing up and leaving, above the music coats go on, goodbyes are said and she pauses. It seems appropriate now, so I say *I have a daughter too and she's eight.* She inquires *does she see her father?* and I reply *oh yes, it's very important that she know him, she spends a great deal of time with him.* She says something like that is very good, that I am very lucky because the son-of-a-bitch who got her pregnant had never shown the least interest in her child.

I wonder why I continue standing so close but I know it's because her face is so incredibly beautiful to look at but when I look at the floor and hear only the story, it's a tale of the blues and I could walk away, leave her, easy enough to do at a crowded party. I turn around to reach for my drink and when I face her again, she is gone.

Susan Yeates

Frozen

Impossible
The wind moves in circles,
Whirling, cold layers,
Light,
Red, orange, blue,
Banded together
Impossible.
The Yukon.

On the floor of my house
Where the
Sourdough
Sat beside the stove,
It froze
against the ground
And a puppy did the same.
We still get our water out
of the river,
All the dogs have dug
holes to sleep in
Impossible.

My ears ring
with the
Deafening
Silence.

Deborah Foulks

The Three of Us

Your voice on the phone
begs me to forget
that you have not called
in over a year
that the times we have
unavoidably collided
in some public place
we've exchanged a
shifty, casual pleasantry
and passed

Would I like to come over?
You have something
for me
How can I refuse the nostalgia
in your voice, repentant
the way it was when as a child
you called in truce after a fight
when you were the culprit and
knew it

I am walking into a copy
of the house
I walked into the day I
first met you
only this time I am entering
from the front,
as a grownup
And instead of bloodless
salmon tones

austere parlour furniture
even a grandfather clock
the room breathes
Green sprouts from
every corner
drenches the study
the bay window
shades the bedroom
and breakfast nook
Fire darts from the living
room couches
flames shoot from the rug
Paintings you did as a girl
(remember the struggle, the
first shapes taking form on
your basement floor?)
line the walls
grace the piano
you finally won and
carried from your parents'
home like a trophy—
You the composer
I the voice
destined to electrify
the world
I stopped singing
years ago
too busy, too tired
too unhappy
Churned the dead sounds
onto paper
in the early morning
struggling to escape
convention
the way a magician
struggles to break
free of his own knots
dropping out of school
my own expectations

You still working towards
the degree we promised
ourselves by thirty
beginning a thesis in
art history
Herculean imagery on
Roman tombs I think you
said it was
But you have stopped
painting
You are married now
but late, not until
the eve of your
thirtieth year
You kept your own name
which makes me proud
and for a moment when I enter
the tidy convenience of domestic life
I am seized with envy
wish to be taken into this promise
of final security
the easy locking of eyes
the fussing over arrangements
of the house
as if it were a child
(Which will come next? --
Not for a while you whisper
evasively, trying to avoid
your husband's eyes)
I am almost hooked by the
smell of cupboards ripe with
connubial scent
until I am shown the basement,
which, as always, panics me
like a glimpse into some
ancient catacomb
This is where it
finishes
the boxes, books, furniture

and bodies
You briskly brush the dust
from the old couch
you're planning to refurbish
when there's time,
time, busy with so much canning,
preserving
You reach into a stone alcove and
pull out mason jars
ply me
fill my arms with jars as if
they were fresh fruit
from the trees
Plum preserves, fresh spiced
plum jam
Some, you say, as we tramp across
the tiny frosted yard, from the tree
your husband is pruning
"And we've built our own
drainage system," you announce
in your mother's voice
But the eye for the exotic has
defeated the years of
canned salmon and boiled potatoes
tea and matrimonial bars
After homemade antipasto and
Donini wine
we sit, the three of us,
balancing our plates on our laps
in the room that has profited
from all the frustrations of
your imagination
that struts your eye for colour,
form
Your feeling for music jammed now
into canning,
plugged into this
man with warm eyes
features similar,

yet a face so different from
your father's craggy Scottish cliffs
and punitive eyes that taught you to
lie and deceive
This man's eyes welcome
everything about you
applaud your achievements
His soft cheeks are absolved
of deception
"His mother died two years ago"
you say, as if to justify
his adoration
Though we manage to
fuel the conversation
I am shy
almost afraid of
this man who shares
the confidences
once mine
We avoid each other's
eyes
each afraid of the
knowledge
of the piece of you
the other holds
I with the
first possession
the first knowledge of
your mind
your body.. . .
the greed and temper
the white skin blue marbled
the birth mark on
your left shoulder
the dreams you built
your expressions around
In a sense we are rivals,
two kinds of lovers
Each in our way

betrayed
Neither of us knowing
the same person,
so unable, really,
to know each other,
to exchange more than
superficialities
grant mild concessions
When I answer questions about
what I'm doing, how I'm feeling
with whom I'm living
you do not really hear me
and if you did you
would not really
believe
any more than I can believe
the sentences you offer now
as neatly and politely as
cookies on a tray: lies
that have left me thin,
that have dulled the
gold flecks in
your eyes
Let us not dig too deeply
Let us only pretend,
sit in your blazing furniture
in front of the fire
built by your husband
drink wine and tell stories
about the
      old
        days

Annick Perrot-Bishop
Flux et Reflux

Je m'étends à même le sol, les jambes et les bras écartés, les paumes tournées vers le ciel et ferme les paupières. Des deux mains, qui s'ouvrent et se ferment avec la lenteur d'une anémone de mer, j'aspire l'air qui s'engouffre, qui coule le long de mes bras jusqu'à mon thorax en une ondulation lumineuse, puis jaillit par les narines en un long soupir incandescent. L'air s'infiltre ensuite par la plante des pieds, là où la concavité est la plus forte; il monte le long des chevilles, des mollets, des cuisses, pour enfin traverser le ventre et la poitrine jusqu'à sa complète libération. Je vois avancer la femme aux cheveux gris sur le chemin qui longe la clairière. Elle marche avec une lenteur surprenante, les yeux mi-clos; un sourire affleure à ses lèvres lorsqu'elle m'aperçoit, accentuant la cicatrice qui marque sa joue droite. Puis la silhouette disparaît dans les pins odorants.

Le lendemain, je prends ma bicyclette et me laisse glisser dans la brise vers la calanque, vers l'eau qui se précipite sur les rocs fauves dans une explosion de mousse. Le chemin de terre battue qui longe la mer est bordé de maisons plus ou moins luxueuses. Soudain, la femme surgit sur le chemin. Je freine et c'est la chute. Elle m'aide à me relever et m'invite à venir chez elle panser mon genou qui saigne. Nous arrivons devant une maison qui paraît plus modeste que les autres. Elle est petite, avec des volets verts, entourée d'un jardin en friche. L'intérieur est garni de meubles rustiques. La femme m'invite à m'asseoir et me laisse seule. Je m'approche du feu qui brûle dans la cheminée: les flammes ont la mouvance de la mer; à chaque crépitement leurs crêtes jaillissent en écume blanche. Au dehors, le vent se fait de plus en plus violent, les pins se balancent au rythme des vagues qui agitent le feu, le soulèvent, le gonflent dans un mugissement qui fait écho à l'incessante invite de la mer. "Voilà, j'ai trouvé. Venez vous asseoir, vous serez mieux." Sa voix me fait sursauter; elle est pourtant douce, avec un léger accent chantant. La femme me soigne avec des gestes lents, conscients. Je jette un coup d'oeil à travers la vitre, pensant à la nuit qui va tomber; mais je n'ai pas envie de partir. Des bourrasques malmènent les volets et font violemment vibrer les chambranles des fenêtres. Je m'installe confortablement sur mon fauteuil, allonge les jambes, laisse reposer mes mains sur mes cuisses. La femme s'est assise en face de moi et me fixe avec un sourire. Bientôt, je n'ai plus la force de maintenir ma tête; elle penche d'un côté puis de l'autre, dans un balancement qui petit à petit s'intensifie, semble dépasser les limites de mon corps pour aller, toujours plus loin, rejoindre un autre corps, plus subtil, plus diaphane. Puis ce corps même, d'un rose pâle, s'estompe, se dissout dans l'espace pour se reformer tout à coup, devenir plus dense, chaque molécule se rapprochant, se liant les unes aux autres pour prendre la fluidité d'un liquide jaune-or, puis rouge. Les ondes se rapprochent, m'enserrent, une chaleur intense m'oppresse, je suffoque et pousse un cri. J'ouvre les yeux: la femme est près de moi et me caresse les cheveux en un geste affectueux.

La semaine suivante, je reprends le chemin qui mène à la maison près de la calanque. Je cale ma bicyclette contre un arbre et frappe à la porte. Elle s'ouvre presque immédiatement, laissant apparaître le visage souriant de la femme qui m'invite à entrer. Toute la luminosité s'est concentrée aux abords des fenêtres; elle filtre à travers les particules de poussière et s'étire jusqu'aux contours des meubles. La femme me désigne un siège et s'éloigne pour faire du thé. Je ferme les yeux, envahie par une profonde lassitude. Au fond de moi, un souvenir s'éveille: la mer se retire doucement de la plage et découvre une surface lisse et nacrée par un soleil finissant. Je m'allonge sur la sable encore imbibé de chaleur et la mer revient plusieurs fois vers moi, m'appelle dans son langage fluide. Je m'élance à la rencontre de l'eau, dans un désir d'annihiler ce qui nous sépare, molécules si différentes qui nous limitent. La mer me regarde, je me vois avec ses yeux dans un pan de brouillard liquide: mes cheveux sont gris. Puis l'image se perd dans le gouffre de ma mémoire.

La femme revient, un plateau à la main. "Vous paraissez bien fatiguée. Ça va vous remonter." Elle me tend une assiette de biscuits puis verse le thé fumant dans des tasses de terre cuite. A un moment donné, elle se penche pour ramasser une serviette tombée à terre. Un médaillon se détache de son cou, captant dans sa trajectoire un rayon de lumière. Je reconnais le profil de femme découpé dans une pièce de monnaie mexicaine par mon frère, quelques années auparavant. La femme voit ma surprise et se met à sourire d'un air énigmatique. "Plus tard vous le retrouverez; il est au fond d'un tiroir . . ."

Je dépasse la calanque et continue mon chemin vers la plage solitaire située en contrebas. Je m'étends au contact du sable encore humide de la nuit, j'ouvre mes mains pour capter l'énergie de l'air, le souffle du soleil. Mes narines s'emplissent de l'haleine violacée de la mer qui gonfle mes poumons d'un monde phosphorescent que traversent d'horizontales ombres. Puis les arbres s'immiscent dans les fonds marins, l'eau devient forêt, arborescence de trembles géants, de chênes et de bouleaux, qui se courbent et se mêlent en une voûte feuillue tachetée de petits soleils mouvants. Dans l'allée, j'aperçois une femme aux cheveux gris qui avance vers moi: dans l'obscurité de ses yeux, je retrouve mon regard; dans le sourire qu'elle me donne, la forme de ma bouche. La silhouette se rapproche, grossit, s'enfle jusqu'à prendre des proportions gigantesques; les contours s'estompent, les couleurs pâlissent, se perdent dans un flou en expansion qui vient à ma rencontre, m'enveloppe dans un brouillard, puis se dissipe derrière moi. Une vague plus puissante que les autres se fracasse contre l'image fragile, l'éparpille dans l'air soudain embaumé de pins. J'ouvre les yeux et aperçois la mer qui s'agite sous les rafales de vent. La brise a fraîchi et je frissonne. Il est temps de me diriger vers la maison aux volets verts. La femme m'y attend pour le déjeuner.

La porte est entrouverte, je la pousse et pénètre à l'intérieur. L'hôtesse ne semble pas être chez elle et j'hésite un instant avant de m'installer dans le fauteuil près de la cheminée. Soudain, j'entends un léger bruit derrière moi. Je me retourne: l'animal est là qui me dévisage de ses yeux verts. "Attention au chat!" Il bondit et avant que j'aie pu faire un geste me laboure la joue droite de ses griffes, puis disparaît aussitôt par la porte entrouverte. La femme se précipite puis s'arrête à quelques pas de moi pour me dévisager. Ses yeux ont une drôle d'expression; j'y lis un mélange de crainte et d'amertume. Nous nous regardons pendant un très long moment. Indifférente au sang qui coule sur mon visage, je fixe sa joue où s'étale la cicatrice.

La lumière s'est adoucie. Seuls quelques rayons filtrent encore à travers l'épaisseur de l'eau. Les oiseaux nocturnes s'élancent, criant leur liberté, ivres de l'odeur secrète des algues. Je l'aperçois sur le sable spongieux; elle entre dans l'eau froide maintenant, dans un élan à la fois joyeux et désespéré. Puis elle s'éloigne de la berge en nageant et disparaît dans l'obscurité. Mes doigts effleurent le sillon encore douloureux qui creuse ma joue. Je pense au monde d'où elle est venue et qui m'appartiendra un jour. Une mouette flotte quelques instants sur les vagues, à l'endroit même où elle a disparu, puis s'envole en cercles, tourbillonnant au dessus de l'eau dans une explosion de cris rauques.

Maxine Gadd

some of the celebrations

april 8, 1982
              which was the first day of Passover and the day before
                    Good Freya day
                          some friends come by
                                marth miller and cheryl syrx
                                      with a bottle of wine to celebrate
                                            martha's birthday

       AND
       I
       REMEMBER
      ANNA PERENNA
    THE DRINKING GODDESS
          REELING IN THE YEAR

                                          we
                                                want
                                    four cups of wine on
                                          Passover
                                                      we
                                                      have

                hummingbirds
                      seafire
                and water tribes gliding in

april 12   fourth
Easter Moon day   day of Passover

              annaperenna and some friends drop thru
                    red currant bushes

                                          twittering
                                                "a
                                                ha
                                          courant rouge"

                    DEADLY RED TIDE
          OR THE FLOW OF OUR BLOOD
          OR THE THUNDER OF RED SHOES
                RUNNING ON THE ROOF OF THE WORLD

Anne McLean

Firestorm

He promised to return to her
At eastertime in April
She wove a wreath around the door
Of lavender and maple

She drew the last drop from the well
The middle of October
She saw a storm come gathering
She hoped it would blow over

She pulled the wreath down from the door
All whitened in November
But he came knocking in the night
And calling out in anger

"Oh put away your wedding dress
And all its fine embroidery
Was I no better than the rest
To see you so betray me

"And put away your wedding veil
So dark and stained with tears
You never learned to die for me
In all these many years"

She said "I caught my death of cold
I caught my death of fever
I died for you so many times
I cannot count them over"

"Then count the times my bonnie bride
And count them well, my darling
And when you're done go count the stars
That are in heaven falling

"And when you're done go count the stones
That lie below the ocean
And you will know how love is lost
And promises are broken

"I was the blackbird at the door
When the wind blew angry
I was the red corn in the field
When all the world went hungry"

"Now you are frozen cold," she said
"And bleak as any weather
And leave me with an unborn child
That will not know a father"

She's taken and torn her wedding dress
She's torn her wedding veil
And never was a woman seen
To shine so cold and pale

She's taken the white horse from the barn
And tied it to the wagon
The moon swings like a blade between
The Lady and the Dragon

And now she calls the firestorm
That burns in secret places
And all men stand away from her
And cover up their faces.

Veronica Ross

Stinky Penny

The night they took Stinky Penny's children, she howled like an animal. The moon was full and snow covered the ground. The windows in her house were broken. People turned their televisions up. They did not want to hear those eerie cries which sounded like they came from deep in the woods.

It was three days before they saw her again. She was wearing a blue coat they had never seen before. It was buttoned right up to her neck. Her hair was combed and held back by a white nylon band. Her face was pale. She did not talk to anyone on Forest Lane.

In the town, she wandered the streets, looking for her children. She felt hollow. It had never really occurred to her that the children could just not be there. Sometimes they had been lots of trouble and nuisance. But. Her children. They were hers, had come from her body. How could they be taken?

It was far worse than losing a guy. She had lost lots of guys. They came and went. The pain then was not without sweetness because there were nice things to remember, things you could think about when you were in the dumps, things you could talk about after a few drinks.

She did not have to think about the kids to remember them. They were in her bones and hair, blood and guts. The world seemed silent, distorted. She was sure that if she opened her mouth to speak, only screams would come out. Or maybe there would be no sound at all.

Or maybe she would scream and no one would hear. It seemed as if everyone sort of moved away from her. That was bad, bad, bad, losing your kids. It was the worst thing that could happen to a woman. There was nothing lower than that.

She had to get them back. She would fight for them, kill even. No one would ever take them away from her again, even if she had to run away and hide.

Up and down the streets she went, up and down, until it was dark and she was down by the ocean, standing before the Lighthouse Tavern. People were coming and going, laughing and talking.

Her ears burned from the cold. She had no gloves. How could she have been so happy once and not realized it?

She drifted into the tavern.

Dougie was playing pool. He was bending over the table and did not see her. His shirt was sticking out of his pants. He had left her three weeks before after a big fight. They were drinking red wine. He called her a pig and she threw a chair at him. He pushed her out of the door. She sat screaming and cursing in the snow until everyone was looking to see what the ruckus was about. She took a piece of firewood and broke a window and climbed in. In the morning, he said, "You're a crazy woman, you know that?" So they had another fight and he went away because she told him to get out. But then she felt so bad she gave Roy next door five dollars to drive her to the liquor store.

Dougie glanced over his shoulder, saw her, and went back to his game. His new girl, Donna, was sitting there, watching him play.

Penny wanted to do something crazy. Hit him, maybe. Cause a scene. She had caused scenes here, before. But now she couldn't. Why?

Old Reggie Tinker from the Lane was sitting at a table. Toothless old Reggie was always at the tavern. He was a dirty old man who always tried to get at the young girls. Suddenly Penny felt sorry for him. He was smiling at her. He wasn't against her like everyone else on the Lane.

She sank down at his table.

"Cold enough t' freeze your bum," he mumbled.

Her eyes filled with tears.

"You wanna beer, Stinky?"

Sometimes people called her that. A nickname.

He pushed a glass in front of her. Even though he knew about her kids.

After a while, the beer made the hollowness go away. She looked across the smoke-filled room at Dougie and knew that soon she would be able to say something to him. Like, You went away and I

had no money and there was no food and how could I go on? I felt
so bad I had to get out nights, to forget. I saw that Donna in your
car too. So I got drunk. What was I going to do? And then I got
home and they took my kids. If you hadn'ta left, if you hadn'ta
called me a pig, if you hadn'ta pushed me out there in the snow, I'd
still have my kids, you know that? Bastard, that's what you are. Just
like everyone else. Stinky Penny, good old Stinky Penny. Anyone
can screw Stinky Penny. You think I got no feelings?

"Wanna go out some time?" Reggie drooled. "Have a party, hey?"

He pushed more beer towards her. "Cutie," he said. His hand
touched her knee.

Penny let his hand do what it liked. What did it matter? What was
one hand more or less? All she wanted now was to get drunk.

Donna had her arm around Dougie. Donna with her stupid face
and buggy eyes and stringy blonde hair.

Showing off, Penny thought. I'd like to show her, the bitch.
Smash her right in the teeth. Kick her guts in. Dougie wouldn't kiss
her if she had no teeth. Let 'em go try and put me in jail, let 'em go
ahead and try. Fuck 'em. I'll show them, the bastards. That bitch.
Show her how it feels.

He's mine, mine, Penny thought. He even said he'd _marry_ me.

Dougie's hair curling over his neck. What did he know? It wasn't
his fault he was taken in by Donna, the slut. Wiggling her skinny ass
in his face.

Penny knew now what she had to do. Beat Donna up and then
Dougie would be hers again. They'd go to bed and screw, not
caring about the cold house because they were so glad to be back
together again. But in the morning, he'd get glass and fix the
windows. Buy firewood, food. She'd ride in his car again, sit right
next to him. Maybe Donna would follow them around until Dougie
put a stop to it.

Then he'd go with her to get the kids back. He would be their
father if he was her husband. He liked the kids anyway. All the guys
hadn't liked her kids. Some didn't want them around. But Dougie
bought them treats, chips and candy. And he didn't have to 'cause he
wasn't their father.

He'd said they'd get married at the tavern, but Penny knew that
was a joke. She wanted a nice wedding, a white wedding in church.
It was her dream. Dougie could borrow a suit.

"Heh heh." Reggie's hand was on her thigh.

Donna looked over at her and stuck her tongue out.

Penny stalked over to Donna then.

"You bitch, you bitch! You slut! You keep your fucking hands offa him!"

Donna's eyes popped out.

Penny grabbed her hair.

"Nothing but a slut," Penny was screaming. "That's all you are, a good-for-nothing slut!"

Donna wrenched away, grabbing Penny's arm. "Oh I'm the slut, am I? Me? You're the whore, everyone knows it. You wanna fight?"

The waiters were coming over.

"I'll fight," Penny cried. "Come on outside and I'll show you who's the slut."

Someone grabbed Penny's arm. Dougie. He motioned with his head to the waiters.

"I'll go outside, sure," Donna was saying.

"Cool it," Dougie ordered her and pulled Penny out of the tavern.

It was so cold out there.

"Listen," Dougie said.

His eyes, his nice eyes. Blue eyes. She thought of him with the baby on his lap, there in her kitchen, while she was frying hamburgers for their supper. It had been so nice.

"They took my kids Dougie they took my kids." Blubbering now, crying.

"Yeah, I heard."

He kicked at the snow with his shoe.

"What am I gonna do? What am I gonna do, Dougie? You gotta help me Dougie. Oh Dougie oh Dougie."

He had his head down.

"I got no one else," she sobbed.

The tavern door flew open. Donna came for her. "I'll kill you!"

"You get back in there," Dougie ordered. She went.

"Oh Dougie.... Nothin' like this ever happened to me before."

"Yeah. Well." He sounded sad. He had his hands in his pockets. "Gee. I don't know."

Penny cried.

"Listen. Here. Go ahead, take it."

He put a twenty dollar bill in her hand, shook his head and went back into the tavern.

Penny screamed and screamed against the closed door.

She put the money in her pocket.

She began to walk along the railroad tracks.

The wind was coming off the water. She turned the collar of her new coat up around her ears. A woman from the authorities had given it to her. She had said such things as You have to get your life in order. You have to have strength.

Footsteps behind her.

"Thought you skipped out on old Reggie, did you hon? Can't get away that easy, heh heh."

There by the railroad tracks they rutted, the old man and the woman not yet twenty-five.

It was starting to snow.

Hilda Kirkwood

Waterscape

I lie on the bottom of the lily pond
a soft dark blanket of silt
up to my chin.
Through the Venetian blinds of sunlight and shadow
see the green twistings of the lily stems
rubber hoses fuzzy with bubbles
springing from the palms of my hands,
blossoming on the still surface.

Turtles paddle upward
sniff the watery morning.
Fish flutter, whispering.

I do not ask to know how I have become
one of the moving parts
of an underwaterscape,
only how the sun will filter through
the blue and white ice above me
when winter comes to the bay.

Jan E. Conn

Blue Forks of Light

for Roo Borson

in a room in a corner
she kneels
holds the huge blue square
of sky tilting it this way
and that, heavy, awkward,
rocking from heel to toe
and back.

it entered the slanted window
at night, thin and black,
lay cold and bundled
with strings of clouds.

then it was suddenly
a balloon, a pyramid, a sail
of blue in the morning
and she thought
what if she could never
put it down: a lifetime
keeping it precariously balanced
on one shoulder, then
the other.

she walked bowed down, a column
of cobalt air flickering
above her head
like a solid metal bar

or ten thousand blue bricks
stacked to the stars.

she moved to the Arctic Circle
one winter, blessed the
long safe darkness,
put the sky in a box.

one night the Northern Lights
hummed and crackled:
the seam stitching the clouds
to scraps of trees outside
ripped. the box rattled & shook.
blue forks of light
broke against her chest,
exploded in her heart.

Nicole Brossard

La Page du Livre

Sappho Djuna Barnes Gertrude Stein Jane Rule Michèle Causse
Adrienne Rich Jeanne d'Arc Jutras Betsy Warland Nathalie Barney
Jovette Marchessault Mary Daly Monique Wittig Marie Lafleur
Anne-Marie Alonzo Kate Millett Rita Mae Brown Sylvia Beach
Hilda Doolittle Renée Vivien Alice Toklas Vita Sackville-West Marie-
Claire Blais Jane Bowles Bryher Liane de Pougy Geneviève Pastre
Marilyn Hacker Barbara Deming Mireille Best Mary Meigs Lucie
Delarue-Mardrus Radclyffe Hall Jill Johnston Maryvonne Lapouge-
Pettorelli Virginia Woolf Colette Sappho Djuna Barnes Gertrude
Stein Michèle Causse Jane Rule Adrienne Rich Mary Daly Monique
Wittig Mary Meigs. . . . .
. . . .
. . . .
. . . .

A priori, ce n'est pas tout le monde qui écrit et toutes les femmes
ne sont pas lesbiennes. Nous avons donc ici affaire à deux modes
existentiels qui s'inscrivent l'un et l'autre en marge du cours normal-
normatif de la langue et de l'imaginaire et conséquemment en marge
de la réalité et de la fiction.

Mais avant d'aller plus loin, je voudrais tout d'abord poser la
question à savoir: que faut-il donc pour écrire? Je pourrais certes
poser la question: qu'est-ce qu'écrire? Mais il me semble plus pertinent,
étant donné notre sujet, d'essayer de répondre à la première question
et ce dans la mesure où écriture et lesbianisme concerne l'identité des
lesbiennes qui écrivent.

D'une manière globale, je dirais que pour écrire, il faut: a) savoir
qu'on existe, b) avoir de soi une image captivante et positive, c)
répondre à la nécessité intérieure, et ceci même à son corps défendant,
d'inscrire dans la langue sa perception et sa vision du monde. En
d'autres termes, il faut vouloir consciemment ou non, signifier son

être au monde, c'est-à-dire, manifester sa présence au monde, d) ressentir une profonde insatisfaction devant le discours majoritaire et englobant qui nie les différences et qui sclérose la pensée.

En résumé, il faut pour écrire, être un sujet en mouvement et en recherche. Pour écrire, il faut d'abord s'appartenir ou être sur le point de s'appartenir.

On aura donc compris que l'écriture, du point de vue de sa pratique, est un sujet qui concerne avant tout l'individu. Mais comme le dit avec justesse Jean Piaget: "qui n'a jamais eu l'idée d'une pluralité possible n'a aucunement conscience de son individualité." Cela veut dire que pour avoir la conscience de soi en tant qu'individu, c'est-à-dire, en tant qu'être unique au monde, il faut tout d'abord reconnaître son appartenance à un groupe ou à une collectivité. Quelles que soient nos origines ethniques ou religieuses, nous appartenons toutes visiblement à la catégorie "femmes." Or ce qui caractérise le groupe femmes c'est d'être un groupe colonisé. Etre colonisé, cela veut dire, ne pas penser par soi-même, penser en fonction de l'autre, mettre ses émotions au service de l'autre, bref ne pas exister et surtout ne pas pouvoir trouver dans son groupe d'appartenance les sources d'inspiration et de motivation essentielles à toute production artistique. Il est essentiel de trouver dans son groupe d'appartenance des images captivantes qui puissent nous nourrir spirituellement, intellectuellement et émotivement. Quoi et qui donc inspirent les femmes? Quoi et qui donc inspirent les lesbiennes et ce d'une manière intégrale et non partielle? En fait, il faudrait peut-être ici distinguer entre ce qui nous motive et ce qui nous inspire. Ainsi, je pourrais dire par exemple que les femmes me motivent car en tant que femme et féministe je trouve en moi parmi les femmes une motivation profonde à changer la vie, la langue, la société; et je pourrais dire aussi que les lesbiennes m'inspirent en ce sens que nous sommes un défi pour l'imaginaire et en un certain sens pour nous-mêmes dans la mesure où nous nous mettons au monde. Et ce n'est qu'en nous mettant littéralement au monde que nous pouvons signifier notre être au monde et que nous pouvons dès lors manifester notre présence dans l'ordre du réel et du symbolique.

Lorsque je dis que nous nous mettons littéralement au monde, je veux bel et bien dire littéralement. *Littéral* veut dire qui est représenté par des lettres. C'est ce qui est pris à la lettre. Or nous prenons à la lettre ce que sont nos corps, nos peaux, la sueur, le plaisir, la sensualité, la jouissance. Ce sont ces premières lettres qui forment le début de nos textes. Nous prenons aussi à la lettre notre énergie et notre adresse, rendant ainsi notre désir comme une spirale pouvant nous mettre les unes les autres en mouvement vers le sens. Un sens dont nous sommes à l'origine et non pas un contre-sens dont nous serions à la remorque comme de petites étoiles filantes dans le gros cosmos patriarcal. Symboliquement et réellement, je crois que seulement les femmes et les lesbiennes pourront légitimer notre trajectoire vers l'origine et le futur du sens que nous faisons et ferons advenir dans la langue.

Etre à l'origine du sens signifie que ce que nous projetons de nous dans le monde ressemble à ce que nous sommes et découvrons de nous et non pas à la version patentée que le marketing patriarcal a fait de nous en personne et en poster géant.

Ecrire pour une lesbienne, c'est apprendre à enlever les posters patriarcaux de sa chambre. C'est apprendre à vivre un certain temps avec des murs blancs. C'est apprendre à ne pas avoir peur des fantômes qui prennent la couleur du mur blanc. C'est en termes plus littéraires, renouveller les comparaisons, établir de nouvelles analogies, risquer certaines tautologies, certains paradoxes; c'est mille fois recommencer sa première phrase: "a rose is a rose is a rose" ou penser comme Djuna Barnes "qu'une image est une halte que fait l'esprit entre deux incertitudes." C'est prendre le risque d'en avoir trop à dire et pas assez. C'est risquer de ne pas trouver les bons mots pour dire avec précision ce que nous sommes *les seules* à pouvoir *imaginer.* C'est risquer le tout pour le tout entre des mots qui, sans cette passion que nous avons pour l'autre femme, resteraient lettres mortes.

Je crois que l'amour fou entre deux femmes est tellement inconcevable pour l'esprit que pour en parler ou pour écrire *cela* dans toutes ses dimensions, il faut presque repenser le monde pour comprendre ce qu'il nous arrive. Et nous ne pouvons repenser le monde qu'avec des mots. L'amour lesbien me semble donc intrinsèquement être un amour qui dépasse largement le cadre de l'amour. Ce qui est en nous et qui nous dépasse, voilà bien une des énigmes qui concerne l'écriture, la fiction, et surtout la poésie.

Ceci dit, il me semble que pour aller au-devant de ce qu'elles sont, les lesbiennes ont tout à la fois besoin d'un lit, d'une table de travail et d'un livre. Un livre que nous devons lire et écrire en même temps. Ce livre est inédit mais on lui connaît déjà une longue préface dans laquelle on retrouve les noms de Sappho, de Gertrude Stein, de Djuna Barnes, d'Adrienne Rich, de Mary Daly, de Monique Wittig, etc. De plus cette préface contient un certain nombre d'annotations biographiques qui racontent la culpabilité, l'humiliation, le mépris, le désespoir, la joie, le courage, la révolte et l'érotisme des lesbiennes de tout temps.

Le livre est blanc, la préface fait rêver.

Je sais que les lesbiennes ne regardent pas au plafond quand elles font l'amour, mais un jour, j'ai regardé et m'est apparue la plus belle fresque qu'il m'ait été donné de voir, de mémoire de femme, parole d'honneur de lesbienne, c'était une fresque absolument réelle au bas de laquelle était écrit: une lesbienne qui ne réinvente pas le monde est une lebienne en voie de disparition.

Dorothy Livesay

The Lovable Woman

Everything you do
is because you love to do
everything for these

is because
you love to please
are joyous
when they receive
joyously

Everything you do
is twisted his way
her way
girl's way   boy's way
you plan and pray
to find a middle way
out of the muddle
a clear straight path
your way
a flying prayer
that all may be resolved
one fine day

> But O my dear
> your own self shrivels
> where?
> cigarettes   coffee
> midnight TV
> frantic dreams

Suniti Namjoshi

Three Angel Poems

i Familiar Angel

Angel sitting on my shoulder
        is cackling loudly.
I tell her, "This is not wise,
        one might surmise
        that some bawdy bird
        had thus given way
        to absurd mirth."
Angel shrieks. She claps apart
    her two black wings.
                She leans
    over backwards.
                She loses
    her perch. Then
        she digs her claws in.
            She chortles and shrieks.
I mumble, "My shoulder hurts."
And Angel croons. She croons in my ear,
        "Poor thing. Oh what a poor, poor,
                very poor thing."
I mutter, "That's not what I mean."
Angel smirks. "O happy Angel. Smug Angel.
        Beautiful, Delightful and Delighted Angel,"
Angel sings. Angel grins. Angel fluffs out her feathers
and preens.
        And a voice declares,
"Game and set and match to Angel."
                Angel wins.

ii Visiting Angel

Angel, crow, sparrow, sitting on my shoulder and shitting when you please, who are you, Bird? And why have you come to haunt me thus? My left eye brushes feathers. And you're leaning over sideways to nibble my ears. Sometimes I think you like me, Bird. Let us examine the matter. Let us examine this woman wearing this bird. Don't you care how you look? You look unkempt. You look like a most ruffianly bird. And I? Look shy, a little tousled. But we shall have to explain when we meet other people that I am me and we are us. "How nice," they will say. "Do come along and bring your bird." O Bird, what a team we should make! You and I shall become famous. Can't you envision it? —The Incredible Woman and Her Invisible Bird!

iii Unfallen Angel

There are those who have muses that are kind
and gentle, come when called, are glad to be of use.
And they leave when asked; they don't seem to mind.
There are times when poets don't want a muse.
And, unlike Angel, their clothes are pressed,
their manner polite, their gait graceful.
And while it's true that Angel is seldom dressed,
if she were, she would undoubtedly look disgraceful.
Those others never shriek. As for biting,
kicking and fighting, they would think it rude.
Indeed, the only task they really delight in
is making pure poetry out of crude.
And yet, by heav'n, though Angel struts and Angel grins,
she's Angel still. Then who shall say that Angel sins?

Pauline Butling

"A Birth Account" Re Viewed

Gladys Hindmarch's *A Birth Account* is literally what the title says—a record—of her body sensations, thoughts and feelings in the course of a pregnancy, miscarriage, second pregnancy, and birth. She records her states of consciousness at particular points in the process, without attempting to synthesize or interpret the experience. By this method, she succeeds in creating the living breathing presence of that experience, because it is in the concrete particulars that we can share in the event, and come to feel its emotional depths and thematic contours as well. And, given the fact that birth is one of life's most deeply felt experiences, it is certainly worth recording. Since it has for the most part gone unrecorded in literature the account may at first seem strange, the focus on body sensations excessive. But it is a *physical* experience, and cannot otherwise be presented.

It is not a continuous record, though, except for her account of the actual labour and birth. The method is pointillistic. As in the French impressionist Seurat's paintings, at close range you see individual dots of colour; stand back and it takes shape into a continuum of colours and objects in a total composition. But the artist's attention is to each particular dot, not to making a tree, or an apple, or an overall design. Likewise, in Hindmarch's account of pregnancy and birth, she doesn't attempt to synthesize the experience into larger units such as person/place, or self/world. She simply records the sights, sounds, voices, smells, tastes, textures, moods, body sensations, feelings, thoughts, questions, and answers—the equivalent in writing of Seurat's dots of colour in painting.

These "pointillistic" particles, in turn, blend together by means of recurrences, correspondences, contrasts and counterpoints, giving design and shape to the experience and bringing in emotional and thematic resonance.

First to note are the mood contrasts (and accompanying rhythmic shifts). In the first pregnancy, there is a gradual build-up of excitement and energy through the first cluster (nine sketches), then a shift to uncertainty and confusion about whether or not the foetus is alive, and finally, three tense, taut pieces recording the twin deaths of their much-loved dog in a street accident, and of the foetus, through miscarriage, while a death-like atmosphere also invades the outside world in the form of tear gas bombs which are being exploded in an attempt to quell anti-war demonstrations. (She and her husband are living in Madison, Wisconsin, during the first pregnancy.)

The writing here becomes tight and tense in contrast to the looseness and gaiety of the opening pieces. The grief that can't be expressed is felt in the stark details: the dog dying in her lap on the way to vet's, or being buried in the hole he largely dug himself just a few days before, or the simple statement "I know now Shinwa [the foetus] is dead." (p. 27) The final sketch of the first pregnancy ends on a more positive note, as she focusses on her husband and their love while drifting off into an anaesthetic-induced sleep, just before her womb is to be scraped to remove the dead foetus. At least love has survived.

Part II (the second pregnancy) forms a counterpoint to Part I; it goes in contrary motion from sadness and depression to elation. The first few pieces are tight clusters of details, reflecting emotions withheld, herself held in. The opening two dream/nightmares of plants growing and dying out of her body, of herself simultaneously flying and falling show her anxiety and fear. She "feels wretched," but "won't go to a doctor to see if I'm pregnant."(37) Food is repulsive: "the rice looks like rain-covered pinworms."(39) There is "Worry. Worry. Worry. Worry." that "It's not growing."(39)

Then there is a gradual shift to positive feelings, beginning with the doctor's reassurances: "he talked with me and the nightmare stopped,"(42) and fostered by her husband's love reaching out to her and to the growing baby: "When he kissed my belly I felt he was kissing both me and you, little one, inside, his love to you direct. That instant I thought you moved to him and I felt you there for the first time."(43)

That moment of feeling life marks the beginning of the largest section of the book, the sketches written during the middle months where she sits at the edge of herself, so to speak, looking both inward (recording her body sensations and feelings as the baby grows) and outward (recording the objects, people, movements and scenes in the world around her). Rhythmically this section is loose and flowing. There are mood shifts, of course, but an undercurrent of love, warmth, growth, and gradually increasing excitement about the growing baby remains constant.

She sees growth and movement everywhere: ripening apples on the tree in the back yard, birds singing, the azalea growing new buds, boats going by in the bay, rectangles of light sliding down the wall of a building across the street. Even on a cold winter day, she sees warmth and growth: "our dining room feels like a warm ice-palace: a comfy brown-gold place to be in, looking out, surrounded by thick icicles which grow longer and fatter."(50) Even icicles grow! And she herself feels warm and glowing: "I'm a big round chestnut."(46) Inner and outer worlds seem to flow together, harmonizing or echoing each other. While she is *walking* down Granville Street, she feels the baby's first *kicks*. While swimming she notes there are "two salt-waters, the one you're in, and the one I'm in."(58) Inner and outer worlds do finally merge in the last piece of the middle cluster of sketches: "The birds flew into my breast this morning as I brushed my teeth. The new leaves of my azalea reached out to me as I lay in bed."(59)

The field of consciousness expands at this moment so that all the particles—the azalea growing, birds singing in the trees outside the house, her body rhythms and movements—become contained in the larger circle of the life/growth force. It overrides everything. (There is a striking contrast, too, with the opening, nightmarish image of sinister-looking plants growing out of her body. There her fear of death dominated, now the life/growth force takes over.)

In the last dozen or so sketches, the rhythm and mood shift again. The pieces are shorter and tighter; excitement builds as the birth approaches. Gone are the long looping sentences circling out and in. She focusses more on just the physical sensations in her body, as the body draws everything to itself, gathering energy for the coming birth. In describing a "plump red ladybug" in a sketch near the start of this last section, she is also describing herself: "She is happy, has no thoughts, is just bodyfeeling as much as can be."(61)

The last few sketches of Part II focus on that "bodyfeeling." Her senses are heightened: she recalls "tastes of chocolate cake and mocha icing"(69); sounds become louder, her moods more intense: "At times I'm giggly," at other times "I'm weepy." (67) She feels herself slowing down in relation to the outside world: "Doing anything is longer, elongated."(70) She is increasingly absorbed by her womb/world and the imminent birth. "Will today be the day?" she repeats several times. "Within a week, within a week."(73)

As well as rhythmic clusters which reflect the emotional contours of the experience, there are recurring images—image rhymes—which serve to highlight the inner dynamics. The chief ones are redness, roundness and water. Red, the colour of life (blood/heart) and of love (red valentines, red roses, red hearts), comes in only at certain key points, highlighting the underlying but central position of love, and the undercurrent of life-blood that forms the base line of the whole experience. Just before she feels the baby alive for the first time, for instance, she notices tomatoes and apples turning red in the back yard and "A girl goes down the alley on her bicycle, red, I love red."(40) Three sketches later, her husband places a "red heart made of a breadloaf tie"(44) on her typewriter. At this point she starts to open out to feeling and love again, and simultaneously feels life in her womb for the first time—"I felt you there reaching up to him, you little four-incher, red cells growing oxygen blood ears organs hands feet."(44) All linked by redness.

From then on, roundness, too, is a recurring image. "I love red, and roundness,"(40) she exclaims. She experiences her world as a series of circles within circles, from the baby in the circle of the womb, to the circle of herself and her husband, to the larger circle of the household of five people where she lives, to her circle of vision as she looks out her window at the "outside" world. Her inner condition (pregnancy) determines not only *what* she sees—life and growth everywhere—but also *how* she sees it—everything is womb-shaped. Her world like her womb is round and full. Even the form of the writing is circular, circling out to the scene in front of her (from the foreground at her desk, say, to boats in the distance, then back to the foreground). Or looping inward through assorted feelings and sensations, and then returning to the starting point.

The life/growth forces highlighted by the recurring images come into full play during the final section of the book in which she records her experience of labour and birth. The womb (now at an extreme of roundness and fullness) becomes the centre of everyone's attention, and demands all her energy and concentration: "My womb's a heart which pulls us all in."(106) Her "red face" reflects the intense effort required "to center my energy onto the outer edges of the ball."(103)

Water, both as image, and as physical element, is also important here. She herself feels submerged in the body/womb as though in water: "I come up to my mouth to let out/pull in air"(110) or: "Guts, me, my head (down there) comes in, floats up, to push."(108) Water, the element which surrounds the baby in the womb, has been a recurring physical element in her world throughout the pregnancy: the ocean, the rain, the swimming pool. And now at birth, the baby, whose "pool" is broken at the start of labour, makes swimming motions as his first movement. Water is at once physical element and image of the life force which brings the baby into being. The physical reality blends into images which reflect all dimensions of the birth process. Simultaneously we experience the sensate details, the emotional ambience of confusion, excitement, weariness and final release, and the "idea" of life being created.

The book ends, appropriately, with the baby's entry into a new physical element: air, which is also, of course, his entry into that generality we call life. While suspended in air, he takes his first breath. Again, emotional and thematic dimensions are present in the immediate particulars: "A cry. So light. Arms swim gracefully in air upside down."(112) These final sentences describing the baby's first phsycial acts also suggest the emotional release that takes place at birth, the literal airiness of the baby's new element, and the "wonder" of it all.

A Birth Account by Gladys Hindmarch.
Vancouver: New Star Books, 1976

Jennifer Alley

Grandmother

She is marooned on a high bed
and her limbs have turned to water
          Only the mind
is active, flying and dipping
from the grey shore day
to the coral deep memory
like a crying sea bird

Her mind brings up fragments
like broken sea shells;
we arrange them as best we can

the Nurse says it's a pity, but
what does she know?
Anything, anything is better
than to have her awaken
and see her world shrunken
to this grey corpse of a day
and the thins ribs of this bed.

Betsy Warland

this was not a dream

this was not a dream
we had driven all day desire threading us through mountains
snake movement a single-minded seductiveness
on either side we rode each one penetrating eye
that night arrived at dark lake enclosed
a noose of mountains seemed no way out
in net of night rain we walked cold boardwalk saw no one
yet felt watched
came upon concrete steps descending opalescent into water i wanted
    to go
but knew i would not come back knew no bottom no point of return
this was not a dream though i had been there but could not remember
months later on the first step into your eyes i know

Robin Endres

Ghost Dance

(an excerpt)

Ghost Dance is about feminism, victimization, Canadian history, political consciousness. There are five fragmented voices (not characters), scraps of fantasies, obsessions and griefs. One voice tells a story about meeting an old man on the subway, about fighting with the devil. Another mourns the end of an idyllic love affair with another woman. The pregnant one only rants and curses. The political one is in love with and sometimes portrays a bizarre version of Gabriel Dumont. The fifth voice speaks only in gibberish until halfway through the piece when she becomes Louis Riel—the religious fanatic side of Riel.

The women then symbolically re-enact the Métis rebellion; through re-experiencing both the failure of the Métis which is a correlative of their own failure, and the revolutionary inspiration of that struggle, they begin to transform themselves from objects to subjects.

The central metaphor is the many-coloured woven sashes worn by the Métis. The voices of the women are five colours woven together until the verbal motifs form one speech in the Ghost Dance. At the other side of the dance the pregnant woman gives birth to a 20-foot long sash, which the women use for a skipping rope. They have achieved a kind of childhood form of unity and revolutionary consciousness.

This excerpt begins with Loretta's transformation from the Gibberish Lady to Riel and takes us through the re-enactment of the first Métis rebellion.

ROSA: When the Sioux came to Saskatchewan, they told us of a new religion among the Plains Indians. The Dreamer Religion. The Dreamers believed that during the ritual Ghost Dance all the dead warriors would come to life and help them overthrow their oppressors. It was the priests who betrayed us. As for the rest. As for his visions...would we have risked our lives without them? I remember falling from my horse onto the snow, red blood coming out of my head, melting the snow, my men faltering, calling out to me . . . somewhere I found the words, I heard myself calling in the fog, through the pain of the bullet wound in my head: "Courage! As long as you haven't lost your head, you're not dead!"

FOURTH WOMAN: Spent too much fucking time on my back, that's all. Too much time lying on my goddamn back with my fucking knees in the air.

LORETTA: *(Slowly turns around when these speeches are over. She is holding a large wooden cross)* In the name of Jesus Christ, in the name of the Immaculate Virgin, in the name of Saint Joseph, and in the name of the angel the Blessed Saint John, let the Métis Nation rise up and ride to victory! When I close my eyes I see a light brighter than the light of the sun.
(The other four women begin to canter slowly around the playing area, shooting in slow motion at Middleton's troops. Loretta should be elevated. She continues to brandish her cross and pray for and exhort the Métis to victory. The cantering grows faster, becomes a gallop. Sounds of the wild west — war whoops and so on)

FOURTH WOMAN: *Bullshit! It's bullshit!* We spend too much time with our feet in the fucking stirrups as it is. Famous riders — lying on our goddamn backs! We should enter the Vaginal Olympics, the way we ride those stirrups. I say, *Out of the stirrups, on to our feet!* *(She begins to chant this. The others pick it up; all march on the spot in a row facing out. The Fourth Woman breaks away)* Ladies and Gentlemen! Pree-senting —

The Duck Lake Ballet!

(The women act out the Battle of Duck Lake as if it were a ballet. The Fourth Woman plays Middleton. Loretta joins the dance. All five women alternate and repeat the following two lines)

ALL: Courage! As long as you haven't lost your head,
    you're not dead.
When I close my eyes I see a light brighter than
    the light of the sun.
(Eventually they all die. In dying, they revert to their earlier personal suicides.)

FIRST WOMAN: Valium will do it, especially if you mix it with some sleeping pills. But it only works for some. Women almost always do it with pills—everything else is too messy. We don't like to make others clean up after us. Someone I know called up the Heritage Society and paid for her own funeral the day before she did it. Next favourite, that's my thing, is cutting. There's a difference between committing suicide and being suicidal, although sometimes suicidals make a mistake and die for it. You can't go wrong with aspirin. I heard of a girl took a thousand aspirins. She knew they'd pump out her stomach. Got her back in the hospital, which in her books was more fun than welfare, food's a little better than at the juvenile home. She was fourteen years old at the time.

FOURTH WOMAN: *(Laboriously gets up and goes over to First Woman)* The friendly ones are the real bastards. The ones that smile at ya. They're the ones you better make sure you don't trust. Coming at you with their fucking handouts, you're supposed to feel grateful, for what? Making them feel good? Cocksuckers. They should rot in hell. They should have the flesh picked from their bones. Vultures. Feeding off my misery. Someday I'm gonna get my revenge and those scumbags are gonna be sorry.

ROSA: *(Sits up)* Where are your other children?

FOURTH WOMAN: *(Leaps at Rosa, hitting wildly at her)* Shut up, you fucking bitch! Shut your goddamn trap, see. You wanna get hurt? You wanna get your face messed up real good? Then just keep talking!

LORETTA: *(Painfully gets up, holding her cross in one hand)* My people quarrel among themselves, Lord, I pray to thee for guidance, for deliverance for my people and for myself.
(The telephone rings. Virginia goes over to it, picks up the outside line. It keeps ringing. She picks up the inside line. Taped sound of a train, then a train whistle.)

VIRGINIA: They're coming after me! They're coming to get me. The army's coming by train.

FIRST WOMAN: *(Goes over to her)* No. They're coming to take us away from here. To the bright lights of the big city.
(The train whistle sounds from time to time through this next scene—up to the Lonely Girls *song)*

ROSA: They built that track so they could ship the army out to kill us. We were outnumbered ten to one. Still we beat them in two out of three battles. Fish Creek. Duck Lake. Would have won Batoche if it weren't for the lying priests. It was only when they knew there were only a handful of us Métis sharpshooters that Middleton's boys stopping running backwards. It was the priests gave them that information.

VIRGINIA: Because they wanted the Métis to believe that hell would last forever.

FOURTH WOMAN: Sure seems that way sometimes.

FIRST WOMAN: *(Puts on a coolie hat)* I'm one of the Chinese coolies they imported to build that railroad through one million miles of muskeg. They had to do a rush job so they could defeat the last revolutionary movement we had in this country. One Chinese died for every mile of track.

VIRGINIA: *(Puts on a hardhat)* I'm one of the three hundred con-struction workers out in B.C. striking against the CPR. We didn't know why they wanted the speedup, the extra long hours and the seven-day work week. They kept us in the dark. If we'd known we had common cause with the Métis we might have done more than just strike. After all, eight mounties were holding us. Just eight of them.

FIRST WOMAN: My children and my children's children lived out on the coast. The city let them use a few yards of railroad land for their little garden plots. Right where the tracks went through a nice white suburban neighbourhood. The little kids still follow them around shouting 'Chinky chinky China-man! Chinky chinky China-man!'

FOURTH WOMAN: I'm one of the boys from the backwoods of Ontario, sent out to put down those half-breed bastards who killed our friend Thomas Scott. Well, what the hell. I'd been outta work for two years. There wasn't much else to do. Saw two of my buddies go belly up at Batoche, though.
(The coolie, the striker and the soldier chant. Louis-Loretta and Gabriel-Rosa, arm in arm, do a little soft shoe as they watch.)
   Duck Lake, Fish Creek, the Battle of Batoche

Last chance we had
To build a little SOSH-
alism right here at home!
(Sound of the train whistle is heard coming from the phone. All freeze.)

ROSA: *(Calls out)* Gabriel! Gabriel Dumont! Avenging angel! Prince
of the prairies!

VIRGINIA: Victoria?

LORETTA: *(Sings Ian and Sylvia's song,* Lonely Girls*)*
Light there is golden in the evening
Blue shadows forty feet and more
When night comes rushing fast
Cross the flatland you see
Lonely girls linger by the door
Lonely girls linger by the door
Linger and listen by the doorway
Lookin' down the long fence post line
To the highway beyond
Where the headlights roll on
Followed by that low diesel whine
Followed by that low diesel whine
Diesel siren song of the prairies
The strong pull that never lets go
Diesel sing of bright spots where colours run wild
Follow me where the evenings overflow

ROSA: The evening before the last day of the last battle. Riel calls
the people together and makes a prophecy.

LORETTA: Brothers and sisters, the Lord has appeared to me in all
his glory and wisdom. The Lord has decreed that if the sun shines on
our endeavour we shall be victorious. But if it rains, the Métis cause
will be lost.
*(Virginia and the First Woman take off their hats, put on sunglasses, as
does the Fourth Woman. They bask in the sunshine on the beach.)*

VIRGINIA: Mmm, this feels good. Your tan's really coming along.

FIRST WOMAN: Pass me the coconut oil.

FOURTH WOMAN: Anyone for a swim?

VIRGINIA: *(Holds out her hand)* Oh-oh.

FIRST WOMAN: What's the matter?

VIRGINIA: Think it's starting to rain.

FOURTH WOMAN: Aw gee, just when we get here! *(Holds out her hand)* Shit, you're right.

FIRST WOMAN: Damn—what rotten luck. Story of my life.

VIRGINIA: Story of all our lives.
(They are all trying to shield themselves from the rain.)

FIRST WOMAN: Whoops! Double bad luck. Anyone got any Tampax?

FOURTH WOMAN: You've got to be kidding.

VIRGINIA: Nope—sorry. Here. Let's use this. *(She pulls out a British flag. They begin to cut it up into little strips)* Just like our mothers used to do!

FIRST WOMAN: *(Irish accent)* Sure and it's only a liddle pleasure we Fenians have for ourselves when we're comin' across the border to make our liddle point to the Queen there.

FOURTH WOMAN: *(French-Canadian accent)* Tabernac! I lak to give dis flag a good lecon, uh? La Reine she is makin' it ver' difficile for the Canayen!
(The First and Fourth Women continue to cut up the flag and roll up little rags for Tampax. Rosa and Virginia do a dance with Gabriel's coloured sash as Loretta sings the first few verses of Un Canadien Errant. *She moves down stage again as she is singing, then stands perfectly still looking out into space. The others freeze.)*

LORETTA: We were standing there in the pouring rain, O'Donoghue and I, waiting for Wolseley's troops to come and take Fort Garry. It was the first rebellion. O'Donoghue the mad Fenian.

ROSA: *(As O'Donoghue)* I begged that guy to let me put up a little fight, believe me. First we had a fight about the British flag. I wanted it torn down. He thought the Queen could be trusted. We compromised, finally and flew the Fleur de Lis, the Shamrock *and* the Union Jack.

LORETTA: Because I am an honest man I believe that the leaders of other people are honest.

VIRGINIA: *(Puts on a headband, goes up to O'Donoghue)* Sir. The Indians up river have informed us that the troops are coming. Let us release logs into the river and the first ones will die. The rest will go back to Ontario where they belong.

LORETTA: I am the leader of a legal provisional government, recognized in theory by international law. We are gentlemen. Our adversaries will respect our position. I have their assurances.

FIRST WOMAN: *(Takes the sash, winds it around her waist, goes up to O'Donoghue)* Sir. The Métis have received word from the Indians. The troops are on the way. Authorize me to use a few of our best marksmen. We'll pick off the first ones and the rest will go running back to Ontario like scared mice.

LORETTA: I wish to hand over the reins of government formally. I have written my speech. We have achieved our goal—responsible government and provincial status for the new province of Manitoba. I have assurances.

ROSA: Riel! The army is approaching and they're carrying guns.

VIRGINIA: Two men waiting in the rain at the deserted Fort. Two men fleeing in the rain to the river. They are fleeing because one of them ran away.

FOURTH WOMAN: They took off their many-coloured woven sashes and lashed fence posts together to make a raft. They sailed across the river.

FIRST WOMAN: On the other side of the river they met an old man who recognized Riel.

VIRGINIA: *(As old man)* M'sieu le president—take my small offering. Not much, a little bread and some fish.

LORETTA: *(Still staring straight out, standing downstage)* Go. Tell my people that he who ruled in Fort Garry only yesterday is now a homeless wanderer with nothing to eat but two dried fish.

FOURTH WOMAN: Who are the leaders following when they don't listen to the people?

Marlene Philip

Cyclamen Girl

The Catechist

The confirmation dress crinolined stiff
around early blooming brown legs
skinny and satin cotton in their sheen
was all the rage those days.

Black girl in white dress
—photograph circa 1960—
stiff petalled like a hot housed cyclamen
on green stalks of ignorance.

Does my finger now trace the negative
outline of the white dress
or the positive form of the black girl
in that photograph circa 1960?

Where those sudden edges meet
cannistered images blur and bleed into each other
—as if the fixer didn't quite work—
maybe it was the heat that caused the leak.

Nothing could be counted on in those days
most of all not cyclamen girls
early bloomers in the heat of it all
with the lurking smell of early pregnancy.

So there circa 1960 she stands
black and white in frozen fluidity
aging photograph of the cyclamen girl
caught between blurred images of massa and master.

Eucharistic contradictions

Cyclamen girl
with a speech spliced an' spiced
into a variety of life an' lies
sow bread host in we own ole mass of
double imaged
doubly imagined
dubbed dumb
can't get the focus right reality
of mulatto dougla nigger an' coolie
that escapes the so called truth of the shutter
and confirms contradictions of church, god doubt and dogma.
Cyclamen girl in the yellowed confirmation dress
—photograph circa 1960—
curls like copra left to dry in the glare
of unanswered questions
away from the brittle matrix of her coconut cocoon.

Catechism

The preparation more complex than learning about sin
she swung a skilled trapezist
no net below
no one to catch her
between the code of Victoria
—no sex before marriage, no love after-
and the code of mama
—now you a young lady you can press yuh hair—
blood and deceit
would always then be twinned cities.

Vows

Satin white ribbons
cotton white sox
Bata white shoes
prayer white book
satin white cotton confirmation dress
white milk soul
the cyclamen girl stood
ready to promise the triple lie
she who believed in the 'triune majesty'
of sunshine, black skin and doubt—in that order.

Transfiguration

The cyclamen girl would answer to her name
in the ceremony of White
would give rote answers about promises of the godfathers
remembering all the time
when first the drums then the women called out her name
her other name that is
when she whirled into the circle of grief
for her fleeting childhood
that passed like the blood of her first menses
quick and painful
when mahogany tipped breast caught the glare
of the fires
and women of the moon feasted and fasted
and feasted again
about her newly arrived wound

The communicant

This his blood
is my badge of fertility
shed red

is my badge of futility
month by red month
red is the badge is the blood.

With moon-caked madness
the waiting mouth crushes the body
broken for all cyclamen girls
or so they've been told.

Epiphany

In a land of shadows and herring boned memories
the great stone-bird mother
drops her daughters from her open beak
like pebbles
pebbles of blood and stone
the cyclamen girl comes into her own
cyclamen girl
cyclamen girl
—photograph circa 1960—

Kathleen McDonnell

After Birth

Pat looked down at the baby on her breast. It was a quarter past ten. Leueen had been sucking for over three-quarters of an hour. Finally she fell away from the nipple, throwing her little head back in a last gasp of fatigue and satiation. Pat fingered the nipple. It felt raw, but it was only slightly red, nothing like the cracked bleeding sore it had been in the beginning. She thought of the cartoon she'd seen in a feminist magazine of a woman grimacing in agony, a voracious, almost montrous-looking baby clamped on to her breast. Underneath was a quote from a medical textbook:

"Breastfeeding gives mothers a fierce joy."

She handed the baby out to Fred, who was sitting at the other end of the bed, reading the paper.

"Take her," she said. "I've had it."

Sometimes when she thought about the birth now she became sad. The details were becoming hazier in her mind all the time. She wished they'd taken pictures, that she'd written it all down right afterwards. A few things she still remembered vividly. How she'd roared deep down in her throat as she pushed, like an old cow. The intense burning of the head crowning. (Someone told her later that there was a folk term for it—the "ring of fire." Yes, exactly.) Phyllis, the midwife, telling her to breathe fast and shallow. "Pant, like a dog." The burning suddenly ending and the head emerging, then the whole body—greyish, wet, much larger than she imagined possible. Looking in the baby's eye, the only one she could see— wide open, serious, amazed. Later, when the baby had "become" Leueen, Pat saw that look in her eyes again and again. It was her way of greeting the world, then and now: scrutinizing, taking it all in—fearlessly, it seemed.

"I hear you had quite an easy birth." It was Alison, the sociology professor, speaking. Her baby was due in less than a week.

Pat laughed to hide her annoyance.

"It was fast, but I wouldn't call it easy."

Word had gotten around the clinic that she'd had an "easy" birth because her labour was so short, and because she hadn't torn, not even slightly. At first she joked about it herself. "I never missed a meal, a night's sleep, or the morning paper." Now she was starting to find it not so funny. She wanted to tell people that it hurt like hell, that getting that baby out was the hardest thing she'd ever done in her life. She dreaded the whole story losing its power, becoming another "cute" birth tale like the ones her family told.

These long, long nights, she wrote in the second week. *Leueen is testy, restless, doesn't want to sleep. We try everything. Walking her. Singing. Stroking her back. Giving her a soother, a finger to suck. Sometimes one thing works, sometimes another. Sometimes nothing works.*

Fred's mother had come, "to help out." Dolores was a folder, a stacker. All the sleepers and gowns were arranged in neat rows on the shelf underneath the changing table where Pat had earlier thrown them in a heap. Now Dolores was working her way through the rest of the boxes full of baby paraphernalia that friends had sent over — bonnets, booties, bunting bags. She was surprised, she commented pointedly to Pat, that it hadn't all been sorted and organized well before the birth.

"You know the baby was over two weeks early," Pat replied.

Later, in the bedroom with Fred, she blew off steam.

"I can't help it. Dolores is driving me bananas. I'm in a constant state of fury around her."

"Oh, Pat, she's only trying to help. How can you get mad at someone who's so meek and mild?"

"Meek, my ass." It was precisely Dolores' cloying niceness that was so grating to Pat. It's so classic, she thought to herself. The angry daughter-in-law. The doting, interfering grandmother. She wanted to rise above such petty goings-on, but she was stuck right in it. And Fred was driving her to distraction. He'd been so strong and solid right after the birth. Now, with his mother around, he was passive, listless. Pat had to repeat things to him constantly.

She started awake and looked at the clock. Only a quarter to two. She thought she'd been talking to Nick, one of the men in the prenatal class. He was always asking complicated questions about medical procedures. In the dream they'd had a long, convoluted discussion, she couldn't remember what about.

She lay back down with the sinking feeling that sleep would not return. She tried to imagine a peaceful scene to relax herself. The cottage on Bear Lake last summer. The water lapping at the side of the canoe. But the obsession with time kept pressing itself on her. What time was it now? How soon would Leueen wake up to nurse? Three-thirty? Four? Could she get in another two or three hours' sleep before Fred had to leave?

She couldn't hold the cottage scene in her mind. Her whole body felt jangled, restless. She breathed deeply, telling her toes, her feet, her calves and thighs to relax. By the time she got to her abdomen she knew it wasn't working, not this time.

Dolores was up in the middle bedroom, stoically packing her bag. Pat and Fred were in the kitchen, with Leueen in her infant seat on the table, peering curiously at her mother, who was crying.

"I'm sorry I did it. I'm sorry I yelled at her." She lowered her voice to a hiss. "But I don't want her to stay."

Dolores has started in again about the discharge in Leueen's eye. Pat had told her, as she had several times before, that the doctor had said it would clear up on its own.

"But the poor child looks terrible. Isn't there some kind of ointment or something?"

Pat suddenly felt an overwhelming urge to slug Dolores. Instead she slammed her fist on the table, startling the baby.

"Goddamn it, Dolores. Stay out of it!"

Dolores retreated immediately and wordlessly to the bedroom. Now the three of them sat, listening to the back and forth movement of her feet overhead, and the emphatic clicking of the latch on her suitcase.

Fred looked at Pat wearily. She shook her head.

"I said I was sorry. But I'm not going to ask her to stay."

He let out a long, low whistle, resigning himself to the task of facing his mother. Pat knew he would be just as happy to see Dolores go himself. But he was thinking about the rest of his family.

"Let them call me a bitch," she told him. "I don't care. They already think so."

He went upstairs.

"Mother. . . ."

"It's all right, dear. I thought I might be of some help, that's all."

"There's a later bus, after dinner."

"This one will get me to St. Catharines before nine. I'd rather not arrive late."

"I'll drive you to the station."

Dolores stopped to hold the baby for a few minutes at the door. When she kissed Leueen goodbye Pat was flooded with regret. Grandmother, granddaughter. The generations together. That was the way she believed it should be.

"Dolores, I'm sorry. I truly am."

Dolores looked right through her.

"That's all right, Patricia. Perhaps if your own mother were still alive you would be different."

She turned and walked stiffly out to the car.

Some of the mornings were lovely. She would laze around with Leueen, feeding her, talking to her, playing with her. One morning she told her, "When you were born, the whole world had to move over and make room for you. Imagine that. The whole world making room for Leueen."

The baby looked at her with a wide-eyed stare, as if she, too, was awed by the thought of this cosmic upheaval. Pat bent forward and kissed her on the lips, and Leueen responded with her tongue. Sometimes it was so lush, so sensual between them it felt to Pat like they were lovers. Fred teased her about it but he felt the same way. When he was changing her diaper he would spend long stretches of time stroking her naked little body, especially her genitals, which made her coo softly.

I still don't feel like a mother, she wrote in the fourth week. *It's as if someone left her on the doorstep. I say I'm her mother, she's my daughter, but the words feel strange, they stick in my throat. How could she ever feel that way about me? That fierceness, that longing, that adoration?*

For the sixth time that morning the phone rang. Pat pried her nipple from the baby's lips and got up to get it.

It was Nancy.

"Listen, Pat. My agent just told me she's scheduled an audition for this aft. Can we put off our lunch?"

"Sure. Till when?" She put Leueen on her lap, propped her head up with a pillow, and offered her breast again.

"I don't know. I have temp work lined up for the rest of the week. I'm really sorry, Pat. I'm dying to come over but I can't afford to miss this audition."

"I know that, Nan. I don't expect you to. Hold on, will you?"

The doorbell was ringing. She withdrew the nipple again and this time Leueen shrieked with anger. She looked out the front window. It was the man from the diaper service. She'd forgotten again.

"Nan, look. The diaper man is here and Leueen's freaking out."

"I've got ears. You poor kid. I'll call you back tonight."

"Okay. Bye."

She ran upstairs, dragged the diaper bag back down the stairs with Leueen on her shoulder, still screaming. At the door he took the bag and set another one full of fresh diapers inside the doorway.

"Thanks," she called after him.

She slumped back into the chair again, this time remembering to bring the phone over next to the rocker in case anyone else called. A heaviness began to creep over her. She realized how deeply disappointed she was about Nancy. She'd tried to set things up so that she wouldn't be alone with Leueen all day.

She sat rocking back and forth, looking out the window. A garbageman was emptying a trashcan onto the back of a truck. An older woman walked by, in hat and gloves, probably on her way downtown to shop. It seemed to Pat like the business of life was going on at its usual rhythm, and that she was inexorably cut off from it.

She turned on the television. There was a soap opera on. She'd watched it a couple of times last week, then felt disgusted with herself. Oh no, she thought. Don't you get sucked in again. She leaned forward to change the channel and Leueen again lost the nipple and cried out. Pat felt a surge of anger.

"Give me a break, will you?"

She tried putting the nipple back in the baby's mouth but this time she would have none of it, and kept on crying. Pat put her back on her shoulder and patted her back, making soothing noises. Finally she felt Leueen go soft and limp in her arms, and she stood up gingerly and carried her to the bedroom.

She came back downstairs and began to tidy up. As she was running water over the morning's dishes she thought she heard a whimper from upstairs. She turned off the tap. Nothing. She turned on the water again. This time there was a longer, drawn-out wail. Unmistakable. Pat looked at the clock. Five minutes. Couldn't that kid sleep for more than five goddamn minutes? She turned on the water again. I won't listen, she thought. I won't hear her. I'll let her cry herself back to sleep.

She began putting dishes away, clattering them in order to create more noise, to drown out the insistent cries. Suddenly she took a glass plate, Fred's eggs still hardened on it, and flung it across the room, shattering it against the base of the sink.

"Shut up!" she screamed. "You little vulture! I wish you'd never been born!"

This cycle, she wrote in the fifth week. *I must sleep, but I can't sleep. Her slightest sound or movement wakes me. When I do sleep it's dark, heavy. I wake up suddenly, terrified. I don't know what of.*

I feel mired in a terrible chaos. There's no time for anything but sheer survival. They keep telling me she'll change, it'll get easier. When, oh lord, when?

The phone rang one morning just as Fred was getting ready to leave for work. Pat answered it, cradling Leueen in one arm. It was Sue, her old editor at *Canada Journal.* Was she interested in taking on any assignments?

Pat hesitated. "I'm not sure." She covered the receiver and looked at Fred, who was mouthing words at her, urging her to say yes.

"I suppose I could. Something I could do mostly over the phone, maybe."

"I understand perfectly," Sue laughed. "Babies can be a slight hindrance at interviews. Look, I've got a couple of ideas floating around but I have to go to a meeting right now. I'll call you back tomorrow and run them past you, okay?"

Fred grinned as she put down the receiver.

"See, the world hasn't forgotten you."

After he left she felt a knot of panic in her stomach. How can I possibly balance it all? she thought. The baby, interviews, writing? What if I can't come through?

Dream: she wrote in the eighth week. *My typewriter has collapsed into a soft heap—grotesque looking, like skin and organs. I tell Fred we must buy a new one, but how can we afford it?*

Pat sat at her desk, gulping tea, staring at the notes in front of her. *Anorexia on the increase?* she had written. *Why?* The story was about eating disorders. There was a psychologist at the university she was supposed to phone, a woman who was writing a book on the subject.

Her hand was on the receiver but she could not bring herself to pick it up and dial. She scanned the list of questions she had prepared, but still she felt she had no handle on it, that she would fumble around, botch up the interview.

She'd slept poorly the night before, restlessly going over and over the story material in a dreamlike state, like she used to when preparing for an exam.

She became angry with herself. What the hell's the matter with you? Finally she picked up the receiver and began to dial, but felt a surge of panic and put it down again. She began to scan the notes one more time, but gave up, overwhelmed with confusion, exhaustion. I can't do it, she thought. I'll never be able to do it.

"Is there anything else you want to talk about?"

Phyllis rumpled her hair mischievously. Pat enjoyed the feeling of her hand on her head. She'd come to see Phyllis for her post-partum check-up. Physically, everything was fine, she said.

Phyllis looked her in the eye. "Come on, out with it."

Pat spilled out the whole story—the sleeplessness, the panic, the despair.

"I don't know what to do, Phyllis. Sometimes I feel like I'm going right off the deep end."

"I know," Phyllis said quietly.

On the way out she put her arms around Pat.

"You just remember you're not alone. Call me anytime. I mean that. And Pat," she stood back, looking her full in the face. "I think you're doing a fantastic job."

Pat burst into tears.

"I don't feel that way, Phyllis. I feel like a total failure. How can I be a mother, when I'm still such a baby myself?"

I can't help it, she wrote in the tenth week. *I long for the old days. Before Leueen. Before her endless wants. I long for the freedom to worry about no one but myself. I long to have my breasts back, my body back. I can't help it. I wish I was the way I was before. I wish I could go back.*

Pat did her best to manoeuvre around the slushy puddles. Everywhere around her cars sprayed mud-coloured snow onto the sidewalks. Leueen was sound asleep in the carrier next to her chest. She'd just dropped off the second draft of the story for *Canada Journal.* Sue had said the first draft was fine, just a bit of rewriting here and there, and few more quotes.

She stopped on Queen Street to look at some pottery in a store window. Inside a woman began to wave at her. She strained to see, then realized it was Ruth, from her prenatal class. Yes, of course. This was Ruth's store. She went in. Ruth greeted her warmly.

"Hi. How are you making out?"

"Surviving."

"Tell me about it." Ruth laughed richly. "Let me see the little one." She peered into the carrier at Leueen, who stirred slightly. "Hello, angel. What's her name, Pat?"

"Leueen."

"Oh, that's lovely."

"You had a boy, didn't you?"

Ruth nodded. "His name's Bradley, after his grandfather. We call him Brad. He's at home now. We've got a babysitter three afternoons a week, so I can start putting in time here at the store again."

"How's it going with you?" Pat said, "Phyllis keeps telling me I should get in touch with you."

"Oh, god, she told me the same thing. I've been meaning to call you. I even had it in my date book. 'Call Pat Morrissey.' Some days I count myself lucky if I can get to the bathroom, though."

They both laughed. Ruth's eyes crinkled up and Pat noticed the deep circles around them. She understood why Phyllis had tried to get them together.

"You just don't know what it's like until you've been through it yourself, do you?" said Ruth.

Coming out of the abyss, I think, she wrote in the twelfth week. *Stepping off the roller coaster. Three months. It feels like centuries. Changed, changed utterly. But still myself.*

Everyone keeps telling me it gets easier now. So here I am, waiting for everything to be all right, like magic. I wish they wouldn't say those things.

Mary Meigs

Pandora was a Feminist

Secrets. The origin of secrets—a great puzzle that I'm trying to solve, for it seems to me that there is an urgent need to decide which, if any, are necessary and which spring from the ego's need to protect its truths and its lies, hence, the idea that every self is a sacred place and that all secrets have the same sacred character. Other people's secrets, as we know, beg to be told, make up the fabric of gossip and innuendo even if severe penalties are attached to telling them. As for our own, they are raided, so to speak, by others with their conjectures, their analyses that we so fiercely reject (like ours of them). One's secret self is guarded as closely as spies guard secrets in wartime, not because of a real penalty for telling (unlike the spies), but an imaginary one, because of the feeling that it belongs to oneself, like one's brain, one's heart, and the illusion that it is invisible to others. But, in fact, those others are nibbling away, like fishes around bait, so that it might be better to give them an authentic whole to nibble on. Better still, perhaps, to sit in one of those cages in which one is completely visible but protected from over-eager sharks, the cage of indifference to what other people think. I often wonder if the secret of oneself is worth keeping, if it shouldn't be released like the contents of Pandora's box. That story is a wonderful example of patriarchal ingenuity, which has invented yet another mythical explanation for the woes of *man*kind, i.e. the unbridled curiosity of womankind. Personally, I think of Pandora not as irresponsible and foolish but as a radical feminist, sister of Eve and Bluebeard's wives, of all women who *want to know.* We are all Pandoras, each with her box complete with instructions not to open it, the box of the secret self.

Pandora, according to Zimmerman's *Dictionary of Classical Mythology,* was made with clay by Hephaestus at the request of Zeus, who desired to punish Prometheus for stealing fire from heaven by giving him a wife. "All the gods and goddesses of Olympus vied in giving her gifts:" beauty, eloquence, the art of singing, beautiful clothes, a gold crown, etc., not to mention the famous box, a gift from Zeus himself. But Prometheus saw through Zeus, and Pandora ended by marrying his brother Epimetheus (which means Afterthought). "Don't open the box," said Zeus. Naturally, Pandora opened it. So do I open things: Christmas presents before Christmas, the last page of a book to see how it's going to end (I have to know whether it will have a happy ending, or whether so-and-so will still be alive at the end. I hate suspense, cannot read detective stories, cannot look at movies full of suspense without intolerable anxiety.) But to get back to Pandora. "When the box was opened, a host of plagues escaped to harass hapless man; only Hope remained in the box." Why? It seems to me it would have been much better to let Hope out, too. "Women's curiosity is always punished," I remarked to Paul, a male friend. "Pandora's, Eve's, Bluebeard's wives." "Of course," he says. "Evil is woman's fault. That's part of history." He's making fun of me, of course. I say I think people should be less possessive of their secrets, that Pandora was right to open the box. And then he tells me a fascinating story about himself. He used to dream, he says, to remember his dreams and write them down, until one day a dream told him something about himself that he didn't want to know. So he pushed it back into his subconscious. "And I never remembered another dream!" Pandora couldn't possibly have been more curious about the contents of her box than I am about this dream-truth that he doesn't want to think about. I say to him that nothing in my dreams makes me want to censure them, that there is nothing they tell me that I don't want to think about, that they have helped me to think about the things I don't want to think about. And far from wanting to turn them off, I want to stimulate them, I want them to tell me the worst!

Curiosity, how it can be thought of as either a virtue or a vice, how it is a virtue for men in men's eyes and a vice for women which must be punished, and how the punishment becomes dogma until women, too, feel impatient with Eve, Pandora and Bluebeard's wives for being so foolish, for wanting to know. God or Zeus or Bluebeard loves to tempt them by inventing rules that as high-spirited women, they are bound to break. Don't eat of the fruit of the tree! Don't open that box! Don't look in the closet! Sometimes God, just for good measure, tests a man. Don't ask me *why,* he says to Job. But much more often, men's curiosity is rewarded and women's is punished. And yet when it comes to opening the Pandora's box which is in each of us, men and women are alike. Paul's self-censorship—the Pandora's box of his dreams—he seemed to think it was wrong to know *too much* about himself and called on the Zeus in himself to close the box forever. I wondered how often he had told this story, whether each telling wasn't to reinforce the lock, whether the *thing* he wanted to shut away didn't manage to reach out a paw under the lid like an angry kitten in a basket. He told it smiling, with a kind of excitement, triumph, ha! *it* almost got out! It seemed to me that *it* was amazingly discreet; it could be talked about without betraying what it was even to Paul. Perhaps it had become so tame that it was ready to be let out of the box; perhaps he told it as a way of taming it?

I think about *it,* the beast, silenced but still there in the dreams that are not allowed over the threshold of consciousness, and want to say, "Let it out. It won't hurt you," want to say that secrets, once released, often sheath their claws, stretch, rub against other people's ankles and finally curl up in a comfortable chair and go to sleep. Interestingly, Pandora was not punished (note that the plagues "escaped to harass hapless *man*"). Long after the affair of the box, Zeus sent a deluge to destroy *man*kind and Pandora's daughter, Pyrrha and her husband, Deucalion (Prometheus' son) were the only survivors. They had the foresight to replace "the loss of mankind by throwing stones behind their backs; those Deucalion threw became men; those Pyrrha threw became women." So the sexes, each reproduced by a kind of parthenogenesis (another case of patriarchal wish-fulfillment) were equal for a while, and Pandora was the grandmother of all the women in the world. True, the "host of plagues" was still at large, but Zeus himself had invented them and put them in the box, a cover-up, so to speak, and Pandora had the courage to show everybody what Zeus was up to. It was a tremendous victory over Zeus, just as Eve had won a victory over God by disobeying his senseless edict about eating the fruit of the tree. Confronted by boxes that are not supposed to be opened, we contemporary Pandoras say to ourselves, "Where did this rule come from? Was it Zeus who told me not to open the box, and is he impersonating me so skillfully that I think his commands come from myself?"

Anne-Marie Alonzo

frileuse et seule

frileuse et seule
d'une chaise
unique appartement
à peine lente et lampe
sur pied
d'avance

Marie Cholette

Un autre jour est là . . .

Un autre jour est là, dans la simplicité de sa présence. Il m'appelle sans dire mot, ses paysages mimés créant des gestes autour de son corps. Le mime s'approche, recueille ce silence étendu en rond à mes chevilles: les paysages se reforment sous la douceur de la lumière. Le silence se voit maintenant, vertige océan, à perte de vue. Le jour m'appelle à travers l'aisance, la pureté de ligne de ses mouvements tracés à tire-d'aile. . .

Le jour s'immobilise: un fleuve est en train de naître à l'origine de mon épaule nue jusqu'aux extrémités tremblées de l'horizon de mes doigts.

Ann J. West

Once Upon

It's time we weren't here.
Grenades suspend possibility.

If it matters in the clamour-light,
I've lost a little hand—
Mine or a child's grip.

Fire
and counter point bells
ringing Fire.

Probably, I lost a little
of the hand the child was holding.

Beth Cuthand

Grandmothers Laugh Too

"Do you know what I fear most?"

"What?" she asked. "What do you fear most?" Her heart was thumping.

"I fear that you'll leave. I feel it." He rose resting on one elbow, his fingers touching her face. "You're more than my wife, my lover, my woman. You're my friend. I don't want to ever lose your friendship."

"You're my friend too," she said, her eyes swimming. "But sometimes good friends have to part."

He lay back, his hands over his head, and sighed. The pain was tangible, a physical force in the air. She sat up reaching for something, anything to cover her nakedness. He reached out, stroking her back. She rose abruptly and went to the bathroom, locking the door, taking great gulping gasps of air. She would not give in to the pain. She wouldn't cry. But she did finally. Cried and cried. When she was finished, he had gone out.

The baby was crying—great wails. He must have been crying for a long time. She went to his crib and picked him up, making soft cooing, comforting noises. His diaper was soaked and dirty, a great pool of shit inching its way up his back.

"Mathew needs a bath," she said. "Yucky babes, yucky babes." She tickled his little tummy. Mathew giggled. She looked at her child and the tears came again. He looked like his father—his eyes, his smile, his chin. She bathed him automatically, paying no attention to his happiness.

"This time I have to talk this out with someone else. I need a friend, but who? Laurette would be no good. She was in love, going traditional now. Mary Jane was too busy. Paula had her own problems. Bess—Bess would understand."

She put Mathew on a blanket, surrounded him with toys and placed a few baby cookies in strategic places around him. She dialed the phone. It rang and rang and rang... "She's not home, not home..."

"Yes," said a gravelly voice on the other end.

"Bess, oh I'm so glad you're home." Her voice cracked. The damn tears started again.

"Linda? Linda, where are you?"

"At home."

"I'll come and get you." The phone went dead.

Linda packed the diaper bag. Three pampers, No. 6, pablum, apple juice, one bottle No. 2, toys, extra clothes, wet ones, diaper ointment... sweater? Linda opened the front door and stood on the porch. Definitely sweater weather.

"Mathew, we're going for a car ride." Mathew was delighted. Linda went to the bathroom and looked in the mirror. "God, what a mess!" She ran a brush through her hair and looked at the makeup. "Aw, to hell with it." She didn't have to pretend with Bess.

The doorbell rang and a loud knocking sounded simultaneously. Bess always did that, as if the doorbell couldn't be trusted.

They drove down the street in silence. Linda couldn't trust herself to speak without crying and Bess knew better than to try some inane conversation. Bess maneuvered her RX 7 through the downtown traffic adroitly. They got on the freeway.

"Where are we going, Bess?"

"We're taking Mathew to the babysitter."

"But she doesn't work on Saturdays."

"This one does." The little red sports car stopped beside a big old house.

"But this is your mother's."

"Yes," Bess said definitely. "Come to Aunty Bess, Matt. Ooos just a happy baby, aren't you?" She grabbed Mathew and his bag expertly before Linda had time to protest and returned in less than a minute. "OK kid, we're going out on the town." Linda leaned back into the seat. She felt the tension, or part of it, begin to lift.

"Where are your kids?" asked Linda suddenly.

"They've gone to visit their father."

"Really? Did he finally win big at the race track, or what?"

"Yeah. He won the triactor last Saturday. It paid twelve thousand big ones."

"No kidding. Did the kids fly down, or what?"

"They flew. Connoisseur no less." Bess was laughing. "They've got most of his money spent already. He doesn't know that he's buying them an Atari, the entire set of toys—big ones—from Star Wars and the Empire Strikes Back and E.T. Can you picture that big galoot in a toy store?"

"You like Larry, don't you Bess?"

"Sure. I never stopped liking him. I stopped loving him. There's a big difference between the two."

Linda sighed. She wanted to say something but didn't trust herself to speak.

"You know Linda," said Bess softly. "I've watched you trying, trying, trying to be the good traditionally Indian wife. I did that too, you know."

"You did?" Linda was surprised because Bess seemed to her to be the antithesis of everything that was traditional. But she never knew Bess when she was married.

"Yes I did. I was the traditional Indian woman, wife, mother. I did it all, Linds."

Linda looked over at her friend.

"I don't wear it on the outside any more," said Bess. "I don't wear ribbon dresses, or braid my hair or bead moccasins or stay at home and dutifully make tea and cook unless I feel like it." Bess laughed. Her laughter held no malice, no anger.

"Do you think I'm a fool?" asked Linda as Bess pulled into a posh restaurant, all glass, cedar and hanging plants. Bess turned to her friend.

"You're no fool, Linda. And you're no victim either. Remember that."

The meal was delicious; the wine white, dry and clean. Linda sat by the window looking at the view. She sighed. Bess was quiet, studying her friend, supporting her in some unspoken way.

"You're feeling guilty on two levels. Politically you feel guilty eating in a place like this when thousands of Indian people can't. And on another level you feel guilty that your family is not with you. Right?"

"You're magic Bess."

"No, just an Indian woman," Bess smiled.

"What is an Indian woman? I don't know enough to know any more." Linda looked tense and unhappy.

"Do you want my intellectual analysis, or my straight from the gut stuff?" Bess asked.

Linda didn't answer.

"We all sort of know or talk about the effects of colonialism on the Indian male psyche. But what *we* have trouble dealing with, is the pain and the guilt."

Linda clutched the table suddenly. "I'm leaving, Bess. I can't stand it anymore. I want to fly. I want to use my talents. I want to be free. No more fences, no more walls. I have to see . . . far . . . or I'll go nuts."

"I know, that's how I felt. So confined, so . . . grounded," said Bess. "And so guilty for feeling that way."

"When do you stop giving, giving, giving and start getting?" said Linda fiercely. "I'm tired of giving. I want something in return. Does he give me anything? No, the shithead! If I hear one more reference to his goddamned grandmother I'm going to scream. I'm not his grandmother. I'll never be his long suffering, silent, uncomplaining, salt of the earth grandmother!" Linda pounded the table and threw herself back into the chair.

"He's idealized his grandmother as the epitome of Indian womanhood. And I'm everything that she wasn't. I talk too much. I laugh too loud. I wear makeup. I wear jeans. I like to go out. His grandmother was content to stay at home and raise sixteen children. Hah, his grandmother had no choice. She didn't have birth control and the nearest town was forty miles away. But she had family and friends who helped her, who took the kids while she went out to trap. Her husband hunted and fished and when he was home, he'd make tea, wash dishes, clean up. He forgets that I'm angry, Bess."

"That's good, you've got to get it out. This grandmother stuff reminds me, one time Larry told me, 'Make me some bacon and eggs, babe, like the good traditional woman.' I said, 'You hunt me a bacon and I'll cook it for you.'" Linda laughed and Bess continued. "Larry got real quiet and I got feeling guilty as hell. I thought, 'Why did I say that?' Then I got to thinking there's a lot of truth to that and damn it, men don't have a monopoly on truth. Women were given brains too."

"Oh Bess . . . I'm smart. I've got brains. I think I was wishing that I didn't think so much, that if I could just turn off my brain I could be the woman David wants me to be. But I can't be something phony. I can't pretend. And David isn't strong enough to accept me as I am. That's what hurts. I can't make him strong. I've tried . . ." Linda stopped. The ache in her throat was unbearable.

Bess held her hand across the table. "Do you think it's your responsibility to make him strong?"

"Isn't that what we're supposed to do? Stand behind our men and give them strength?" asked Linda. "That's what the elders say."

"There's nothing wrong with that except for it to work, men have to be open to receive women's strength," Bess said. "There are very few men our age who have that openness, who accept that women are strong. David's basically a decent man. He doesn't beat you or fool around. He works. He loves his child."

"What more could a woman want?" asked Linda cynically.

"But David doesn't understand women's power because he doesn't understand mother earth. The cycle of life, and the woman's place in creation. As long as he doesn't understand, he can't accept women's power. Linda, he's got to *want* to understand before he can become strong. You can't *make* him want that. It's got to come from him."

"That's what's so hard to accept," said Linda. "I guess, deep down inside, I know that it's got to come from him. We're so foolish, both of us. I'm trying to make him into something he's not and he's trying to remake me."

"Larry and I tried that too. It didn't work. Linda, it never works. The question now is: 'What are you going to do with your life?' "

"I want to fly, Bess. I had a dream the other night. I was standing on a mountain top and a great shining eagle flew up to me and said 'Come fly with me.' I jumped off the cliff and turned into an eagle. It felt so good to fly. My wings strong. We flew through the valley catching the wind, soaring, swooping, laughing. Did you know, Bess, that eagles laugh?"

"I'm sure they do. That's a powerful dream."

"It told me something. The eagle *wants* me to fly. I can fly high and see far Bess, if only I take that leap off the cliff."

"There's your answer. A very Indian answer. You're privileged to dream of eagles. The eagle comes to so few."

"You know what else it told me? If eagles laugh then so can we. I've been too serious. I've lived from my head for too long. I've stifled my laughter with pain and guilt and thoughts piled on thoughts. I guess I was really trying to be David's grandmother."

"Grandmothers laugh too," said Bess gently. She paused, then continued. "I told you I don't wear ribbon dresses, or do bead work or all those things associated with the 'traditional Indian woman,' unless I feel like it. I meant that I have to feel it to understand it. And in understanding the act of beading or the act of braiding my hair I can translate that into the actions of my life here and now."

"What do you mean?"

"I tried to be the traditional Indian woman. I did and wore all the things we think are Indian. I did them because that's what I thought being Indian was. You know the more I sought to understand, the more I realized how superficial the external trappings were if there was no knowledge underneath."

Linda sat up suddenly. "Bess, I got to go home. David will be back now. I know what I want to say to him."

"Well, that was quick."

"Hurry, we got to hurry. Or I'll lose my nerve."

Linda was silent throughout the drive home. They picked up Mathew and she greeted him with a quiet hug. When they drove up to the house, David was waiting at the window. A look of relief and fear crossed his face when he spotted her.

"Thanks Bess. You've helped me." Linda smiled, a fleeting smile, and walked into the house.

"Where were you?" he asked. "Where did you go? What did you do? Did you eat?"

"I ate a lot, David." Linda changed Mathew's diaper and snapped up his sleepers quickly, efficiently.

"What's the matter? You look so . . . so mad."

"David, we got to talk. This time I mean *really* talk. Get down to the nitty gritty."

"I kind of expected this. In fact I've been expecting this moment for years."

"You have, eh?" Linda could feel white hot anger rising from her gut. 'Slow down girl,' she thought. 'Count to ten, grit your teeth, don't yell.'

"Yes. I guess I've always known it would come to this. 'Someday,' my grandmother told me, 'that woman will leave you.'"

"Quit fogging the issue David. We're talking about you and me, not your goddamned grandmother!"

"You poor kid. You could never see the wisdom of our elders."

"Don't patronize me, David. I've had enough of that sanctimonious shallow shit from you. If you lived the wisdom of our elders, I could believe it. But you don't live it. You just mouth it. It's all pretty words to you."

"Oh aren't we brave. Did that women's libber friend of yours tell you what to say? Or have you women got some kind of handbook that you read to each other when you're ready to screw up some man's life?"

Linda turned abruptly and walked out of the room. This was not going as it should. She was angry. He was angry. She hadn't meant for this to happen. She went into the bathroom and locked the door. She sat on the edge of the bathtub, trying not to think of anything really. 'I should have put up that magazine rack, a long time ago,' she thought. 'Those curtains are rather tacky too. A hanging plant would be nice over there, and a full-length mirror on that wall.' She studied the bathroom.

The doorknob wiggled. "Linda, come out," he said. "Let's talk. I'll try not to get mad if you don't."

Linda considered the proposition carefully. There was no turning away from it. She couldn't live in the bathroom forever.

She opened the door. David stood there, leaning up against the door jamb. He smiled crookedly. "You'll always be my friend, you old rug," he said. "When we're old, we'll visit together and laugh about this. I'll say, 'Remember the time we were married?' You'll cackle through your toothless gums, and you'll say, 'Yeah honey, I lived in the bathroom.'"

Linda laughed. David reached out to stroke her hair. They walked together into the living room.

"David, I didn't mean all those things I said just now," she said, feeling guilty.

"Oh but you did. Now let me finish. I am a sanctimonious bastard."

"I didn't call you a bastard."

"No, I'm calling myself that. Men got rights too. If I want to call myself a sanctimonious bastard I will. Okay?"

"Okay, okay," she said, sitting down on a chair.

"I've watched us become shallower and shallower," said David. "It's like we've been playing our role. I've been what I thought was the good husband. You've been what you thought was the good wife. But it's not enough. Linda, I don't know how to be more."

"David." His name was like a prayer.

"I've been thinking, thinking, trying to figure out where I went wrong. I get to thinking about my life. I talk about my grandmother all the time because she was the only safety in my life. I never knew my dad. My mother drank. Boarding school didn't teach me how to be a family man. The nuns taught us what not to be, never what to be." David was pacing back and forth, across the darkened room. Suddenly he knelt down beside Linda's chair. He clutched her hand. "I've watched you, Linda. Every day becoming less than you really are. It hurts me that I can't give you more. It hurts." David was crying. Linda held his head in her lap, making soft cooing baby noises, rocking him back and forth, back and forth.

"I appreciate that you tried, David. I really do," she said, rocking. "You're a good guy, a good guy." Linda held David gently, feeling distant, ancient, old beyond her years. She stroked his head like she would stroke Mathew's head to calm him.

"David, I have to leave," she said finally. "There's no room for me here. You take all of me."

David sat up slowly and plucked lint off the rug. His head was downturned, intent on the cleaning job.

"Where are you going to go?" he asked slowly.

"Back home. I talked to our Chief the other day. There's a job coming up at the Band office."

"Can you get a house?"

"Yes. My sister's moving into town. I can stay with mom and dad till then."

"You thought of everything," he said, trying to be sarcastic.

"I had to, David."

"I know, Linda. I know. You're going to do all right. You got brains. It's time you used them kid."

"Don't call me kid," she said playfully, pushing his head. "I feel so old, David, I sometimes feel like a grandmother."

David got up and looked down at her intently. "That's what scares me about you. I see my grandmother in you. I resent that." He was clenching and unclenching his fists. "You're tied to something stronger than me. . . older. . . with your women's secrets." He turned and walked to the kitchen. Linda could hear the kettle being filled for tea.

She looked out, onto the sleeping city, remembering Bess's words 'grandmothers laugh too.' Maybe someday she'd laugh.

She leaned back and waited for her tea.

Janice Williamson

Service

the first time
they dressed me
in hot pink polyester
from neck to ankle
and set me
waiting on tables
of government bureaucrats
and texas oilmen
one of whom
(the latter)
flew me to london
and the ritz
where i bought
black suede boots
and cashmere sweater
where i wandered through
mazes
quoting olson
and ezra's lovesong
where i visited the symphony
where a woman in the washroom
suggested i should
marry her son
and later
on seeing my escort
retracted her invitation
with an eyebrow

The second time
years later
after a marriage
and a dozen moves
they dressed me
in black fishnets
set a tray
on my upturned palm
and turned me into the room
where a gangster's moll
almost put me
out of the picture
with a champagne glass
in flight

Rona Murray

A Stillness in the Air

There are rumours that she's dead and perhaps she is because I haven't seen her again since that night. I haven't really expected her to be there but late every evening, just the same, I've walked down to the point from which I can see her dried up stretch of grass making its way down to the beach. That was where I saw her about a month ago when the chrysanthemums were blooming. Now their leaves are turning brown.

In any case, there's a sign near her gate now, saying the place is for sale. The price is supposed to be over a million, but even so somebody will buy it and subdivide it and tear down the old house and put up dozens of new ones with blank windows and false brick trim. There'll be lawns and flower-beds that are covered in black plastic and wood-chips to keep down the weeds. Everything will be different. That is, of course, if she's dead. If she isn't she might refuse to sell at the last moment (they say she's done that before), and the dance might go on happening when the moon is full as it is now.

She lives across the street from us, but not close because of the fields between. Every day I go into those fields to pick mushrooms now that it's October: October is the month for mushrooms, and they grow where horses have been pastured. They spring up overnight between the clumps of manure, growing quick and thoughtless and dying within a day or two. Each day I go after a trail of white buttons in the early sun.

Beyond the fields and the horses and the mushrooms and all the straw-coloured grass, is the house. On Sundays cars go by—I watch them while I garden—driving slowly, sometimes stopping to look at that house which was once white but is now grey, its wood stripped and peeling with sea salt and weather. It's very large with porticoes and columns: a sort of decayed southern mansion. A long avenue of trees with black-spotted and shriveled apples, which fall and rot in the dead grass, leads up to it. It looks as if the house is deserted and has stood there forever and as if a winter storm would blow it into a heap of tangled toothpicks. But it's not deserted because at night a faint light glows in the darkness at the back. Sometimes I think the light isn't there anymore and sometimes I think it is. It was always only just there, if you know what I mean.

We haven't lived in this neighbourhood long, but long enough to know that nobody visits that house, although everybody talks about it and the woman inside: the children, the plumber and the postman, the women who collect for charities, the real estate people who've been waiting a long time to get their hands on the property.

Once I spoke to the woman. I'd been warned not to, had been told she would scream at me, it was better to keep away. But the soil is poor here, a heavy clay, and I needed fertilizer for my garden. I walked up the long avenue in the hot sun to ask if I could collect manure from her fields. The horses are not hers, are merely pastured there, and often break through the falling fences to run the roads. They've broken some of my shrubs, left deep hoof marks in the lawn during the winter rains. I've been tormented by them and thought of complaining, but haven't known whom to complain to, so I saw no reason why I should not get some compensation. I walked up alone, my husband impatient at my fussing over trampled grass and my daughter amused but not going with me. My husband's name is Richard, and he's a reasonably successful lawyer. My daughter is Isobel. They're not gardeners.

Since then I've imagined her standing at the curtainless window watching me while I cart away manure or pick mushrooms. Perhaps she doesn't stand there now, perhaps never did. Even so, I still feel self-conscious when I go over.

That day I went up to the front door and knocked, because it was before I knew she lived only in the back of the house. There were small, leaded windows on either side of the door, and after some time she came to one of them, which she opened about four inches—enough for voices to go in and out. She was tall, straight, white-haired, and very thin. She reminded me of one of those herons you see perched on a kelp head, looking as if it's standing on water. They're always alone, grey birds without a flock. Do they watch their own reflections, I sometimes wonder?

She held the window open with one hand and stared past me

while we talked. I looked at her hand more than I looked at her, and felt ungainly: a middle-aged woman in old jeans asking a favour.

"Is there any?" she asked.

"It's everywhere," I said.

"I don't mind if you take it."

"We're your neighbours. We live in the white house over there." I pointed across the road.

"I used to know someone who lived there. A long time ago."

"Would you like me to come and visit you?" I asked, groping for words that might bridge the chasm between people who are cut off from each other—who are shy, perhaps, or proud. "I could help in your garden in return for the manure." That was a ridiculous thing to say. There was no garden.

"You should phone first," she said, not looking at me, staring into the distance. Then she added, "Nobody knows what it's like when they're all gone."

"No," I said, shifting my eyes while I took my gardening gloves off and put them on again. Some people can handle these kinds of conversations.

"I take them out and try to get answers from them," she said. "I try to understand."

Take them out of where? I couldn't say anything to that, so I asked her if she had an unlisted phone number.

"No," she answered.

But she was not in the phone book. I had looked.

I did know after that that at least some of the stories about her were not true, or only partly true. The story about the hand must have been exaggerated. It was said she had once been a manicurist and had married a man from a very rich family (you would know the name if I told it to you, but I won't; there has been enough gossip already) which had given him a lump sum to settle far away with a bride they couldn't accept. That would have been a long time ago when people thought differently. In any case, it was hard to believe the story, looking at her.

Perhaps it was started by the woman who said she had gone to the door to collect for the Heart Fund or whatever and had knocked and waited until a faded voice from inside had asked her what she wanted.

She'd explained, and after a time the door had opened a crack (it was the back door) and a hand had come through with fifty cents in it: just a hand with beautifully manicured nails and a couple of diamond rings on the fingers. A voice had said that that was all she had, she was sorry. Just fifty cents.

It was true, they said. She couldn't pay her land taxes, but the municipality wasn't worried because they'd get it all when she died.

After that it was believed she kept hidden because her face was deformed by some hideous disease, or by acid.

Actually, no explanations were needed. One thing or another was believed, the way the children believed, without a doubt, that her husband was buried in the basement.

But her face was not in any way hideous. It was old and thin and her hand was old and thin with no polish on the nails and no rings on the fingers. It was just a frail hand, holding open a window.

When I got home, I went up to Richard and put my arms round his neck and kissed him. He was surprised. I hadn't done that for a long time. He waited patiently for me to go away so he could go on reading the paper.

Issy said, "Well, what happened? Did she scream at you? You didn't actually see her, did you?"

"Yes, I saw her. She said she didn't mind if I took the manure."

"What did she look like? Is she as weird as she's supposed to be?"

"No," I answered, quite sharply.

Issy laughed, but I thought she was grudgingly proud of me. "The kids at school say they wouldn't go up there for a million bucks, at least not alone. But you'll do anything for your garden, won't you, mother? They say she had a daughter once, but she left home and never came back. They say she killed her husband. D'you think she did?"

I shrugged. "How should I know. They say everything, actually."

"Yes, well, anybody who'd live like that must be a bit of a nut."

Issy will be leaving home soon. She wants to go to university in Toronto. I think she should choose a school nearer home, but Richard takes her side. He says it's good for children to stand on their own feet. I suppose he's right, but sometimes I wonder what it will be like with just the two of us here.

Today I took the old rowboat out to collect kelp. This is the time of year it's uprooted and swept onto the beaches by the storms. It lies like a tangle of great snakes and is heavy to lift. I disentangle the pieces and drag them to the boat, thinking of my roses and their glowing colours as they suck in the phosphorous. Then I row back over the beds of living kelp, like tall women whose long hair flows off their heads under water. While I rowed I watched a cormorant ahead of me, twisting its head this way and that as if it were trapped in a hidden snare. It reminded me of that woman. Why can't I forget her? What is she to me?

It's probably true her husband was found shot, a revolver beside him, after a party. It was judged suicide, but nobody believes that. It happened about the end of the war, and soon afterwards her daughter left home. That is true. She did have a daughter. I know that from the postman.

I keep visualizing what happened, but oddly enough it's Richard I see: Richard lying on a carpet in a games' room—which might be quite wrong; perhaps there was no games' room, no carpet—with blood dragging a dark stain across the room. The gun is in her hand—and I still see the hand as exquisitely manicured with scarlet nails—and a young girl is running down the stairs wakened out of her dreams by gunshot and a woman's hysterical screaming. She's delicate, flushed, with long, curling hair and a bone structure that makes you weep to be an artist. She is standing in the doorway in a nightgown, looking at the blood. But that's all too like a bad movie.

On the other hand, I do trust the plumber because plumbers are solid men and don't think of inventing things. When we first moved here, we had trouble with our pipes, and after he had gone through walls and replaced fixtures the plumber had a cup of coffee with me and talked about the woman across the road. He'd worked on her plumbing some years before and said that when he was in her kitchen he'd noticed a pathway leading from the table to the stove. The places where she walked had been etched out from the years of dust and dirt which covered the floors, the way a path is browned into a lawn if people will walk across the grass. He also said that all the window sills in the house were speckled with a trail of mould. Before he died her husband had picked apples and placed them on the ledges to ripen. That's no way to treat apples—he can't have known much about fruit growing. In any case, they'd never been removed. First they must have shrivelled, developed ancient faces like the ones you see on dolls whose heads are apples. Then they must have crumbled into puffs: dark spots would have appeared, then earwigs, wasps, beetles—cross-grained insects, watchers of death. Wouldn't the infection pit into the woodwork, peel the paint off, turn into clumps of furry spiders' webs? But he was a talker, so I didn't ask about that or we would have spent all day over our coffee.

I did ask about the daughter. Yes, he said, there was a daughter all right, but that was before his time. Other people remembered her and the parties they used to give in the big house.

I think of Issy and the day she was born. If you give birth only once it is a memorable occasion. She was not really a beautiful baby, but she had an exquisite forehead, tendrils of hair curling in small, separate circles over her skin.

Issy plays chess and goes fishing with her father. I don't usually go because there's too much to do around here. I'm compulsive, of course, I realize that, but each plant has to be guarded against flooding or drought, caterpillars, fungus, aphids. Weeds shoot up overnight. I don't think Issy and Richard mind; they get on well together. Issy sometimes accuses me of thinking more of my plants than I do of her, but that isn't true. It's just hard for me to tell her I love her.

Maybe it was hard for that woman too? Whether it was or not, I think of her as a kind of Ceres who let everything die as she searched for her daughter. But Ceres found Persephone, and in the end spring returned while across the street there has been no spring. The horses have poor foraging. That's why they like to get into my garden.

When I go out at night, I say I am taking the dog for a walk. That's partly true, but really I like the dark and the night smells and the moon which is so bright now it casts shadows. I always go to the same place, sit on the same log, and look over at the big house, hoping that figure will come out again. While I sit there I imagine what it must have been like in that house forty or so years ago.

You see, it was so different then: a mother and a father and a pretty child, living in a white mansion by the sea. They must have had horses or cows because of the fences, dogs and cats perhaps, friends who came to swim, to have beach parties with steaks and marshmallows. It seems to me, as I sit there, I can hear voices drifting over the water, which is phosphorescent here: if you dive in tiny sparks of light fly in all directions. The voices exclaim to each other about the lights, the moon; perfumes of broom and wild roses hang over the bank. And then I think of dances in that house. In those days bands played at house parties, and people wore long dresses and dinner jackets. I know because I must be about the same age as her daughter and in those days I went to such parties: lighted cigarettes on the verandah, large, soft moths, wisteria hanging over the trellises. And inside a wide staircase coming down into an entrance hall where young girls could sit on the steps, drinking from fragile glasses, their feet tapping to the music, wondering who will ask them to dance.

In the winter they must have had house-guests with evenings sitting in front of the fires, at Christmas a large tree covered with birds and balls and golden coins; and I think of them choosing it, chopping it down, shaking snow off its branches, bringing it into the house, propping presents beneath it in bright paper. What did she give her daughter? And did her daughter like her presents? I'm never sure with Issy. Sometimes she seems to.

It's true I'm obsessed. I feel I could put out my hand and touch that woman, could say, "I remember it all," but of course I wasn't there, and she wouldn't understand.

The postman has been driving this route all his life. That's unusual, isn't it? He'll retire soon. He says that almost every day, in the beginning, she would be down at her gate to give him a letter that he would post for her. Her letters were sent to somewhere in India or China. In any case, to somewhere far away. And she never got any back. He knows that because he used to watch out for foreign stamps and ask for them if the person wasn't a collector. For months and months—a year—she was down. And then she stopped coming. She only gets junk mail anyway, he says, and he doesn't put it in the mailbox because it fills up and won't shut; in the end the paper turns into a soggy mess which the starlings peck out in the spring. He just puts in one or two bills, and they disappear eventually. Perhaps the delivery boy takes them up when he leaves food at the door. At least she still phones for food, or used to, if she has a phone. She must, because I've seen him. He leaves quickly.

I'll go for my walk now. I'll have to take a winter coat as it's growing quite cold. The porch light shines on the climbing roses so I'll take the dead heads off on the way. Then they'll last, unless we have a frost, until Christmas. Soon it will be too cold to sit out there with comfort, so I do hope if she's going to do it again, she'll do it soon.

One can only catch fragments, after all. I caught that fragment, and I think tonight will be the same as then, with a stillness in the air. Awaiting. A night for her to be again on that unkempt lawn, facing the sea which stretches to China, wearing her pale, floating dress and the hat with its long feathers curling down over her shoulder, stepping delicately through the wet grass, making the awkward movements of a heron or cormorant on land. I remember she crooked her arms at the elbows, and they became wings. Sometimes her old body swooped down and then straightened until it stretched tall, her head arched back on her neck. Each movement backward and forward seemed to be balanced by something or somebody I couldn't see.

Perhaps any pain can be borne if a dance is made out of it.

When I reached home that night after watching her I didn't tell Richard or Issy. If she's there tonight, I won't tell them either. If she isn't there this time she must be dead.

Gisele Dominique

The Desaparecidos

Mad women of the Plaza de Mayo
each Thursday you walk
arms linked two by two
amongst the crowd which turns away.

You stand in a silent vigil
for the Desaparecidos of Argentina
your sons, daughters, friends, babies
who disappeared without a trace.

Women of courage
wearing white kerchiefs
alone against a wall of silence
knowing it will be your turn next.
You stay bearing witness
to the Junta de la Muerte.

You know the awful answer
a mass grave of mutilated bodies
faces of children tortured.

Mad women of the Plaza de Mayo
each Thursday I, too, mourn
for the Desaparecidos of Argentina
Chile...Uruguay...San Salvador...

Erin Mouré

Neighbours

They are in the street boiling the sweat out
of their clothes
In their houses scraping paint off the door
to eat it as a meal
They are in the basement sleeping at work-benches
after the tools are sold
They fidget
Social workers come in & out of their doors
Their drawings are suspect
& their lists of groceries
too much love & insufficient macaroni
what is this

Do they think they can get away
Do they think *steal,* do they know the sad night
of hunger after the children are fed
Do they dream of jobs

They are the neighbours
Hello my neighbours
In this age there are more of us than there are soldiers
Still, if we cry out our sadness & break the government
will it turn us into salt
or food

Evelyne Voldeng

De ses chaudes mains humides
A la fragrance de racine
La Mère des herbes
A cueilli parmi les graminées lunaires
Où dansent des soleils rouges
De magiques plantes baumières
Au souffle de sagesse.

Femme-oiseau
Aux veines saignées par de fausses aurores
Je marche et soupire dans la nuit
Mouette rieuse
Je me nourris de paroles de vent
Et gobe les serpents de crachats
Qui étoilent les trottoirs
De mes crépuscules interlopes.

Des langues de flamme
Jaillissent de la vulve rouge du magnolia
Etreinte à mort
De l'oiseau de feu au ventre de soleil
Et du serpent de cendre aux écailles de braise.

L'adolescent
Dans sa parure
D'oiseaux des bois
A rencontré la femme
Au vagin denté
Et son pénis de pierre
A brisé les arêtes
De son fantasme.

L'homme aux femmes-oiseaux
S'est fait un tambour et un pipeau
Sous les pétales de neige
Les yeux clos
Il chante
Au sud un volier d'oies sauvages
S'élance sur la piste du soleil.

Le sang brille
A sa lèvre bleuie
Exsangue
Elle regarde l'arbre mutilé
Encerclé de perles rouges
Un couteau brûle dans les images d'écorce.

Il neige des plumes blanches ébouriffées
L'étoile du matin a accroché le soleil
Dans un saule de givre
L'oiseau bleu est venu dérober
La fleur du sexe
Parfumée de crevette.

J'ai mis ma peau de printemps
Assise dans la pensée d'un colibri
Je chante à l'oreille des feuilles de groseilliers
Les lèvres décloses
Je déguste le soleil jaune
Et le vent à la fragrance de menthe.

L'aile du dernier oiseau
Prend le contour
De l'ultime falaise
Les vagues grises de mes rivages
Lapent le sable
Où pourrit la chair des anémones
Le buisson ardent flamboie dans mes savanes
Les fraises n'ont plus de sens
Et j'essuie aux ronciers du chemin
Le sang de mes poignets.

Il a terrassé mon âme
L'a ensevelie en un cercueil de jais
Sous l'argile veiné de noir
En un pays de minuit
Où les âmes se fanent bleu-nuit.

Melanie Higgs

An Afternoon

I

There is Bron waiting under the tree. Meredith can see already as she approaches her the look on her face. She knows it is the same look she has herself, a tenseness that collects around her mouth, that draws her lips down, and she knows the same look is in her walk, striding and arrogant among the other students over to where Bron is waiting under the tree.

How beautiful she is, Bron watches her sister coming along the path, moving quickly and surely, her cape moving about her, the dark curls moving about her face, a stray hair catching in her lips set tightly in a way that betrays to Bron the quiet, tight effort, a little awesome for the cracks and splints she knows are there because sometimes she finds her sister sitting in bed crying quite quietly and openly, alone. So thinking Bron feels tender and Meredith knows this instinctively as she comes up and puts her bag down in the dry under the tree, and they look at each other united by this feeling of tenderness that Bron gives and Meredith takes, and so together they wait in anticipation of this afternoon with their father.

II

He is driving a different car, on account of the snow, Meredith says matter of factly, and still it is because of this different car that they at first have trouble recognizing him. Meredith hates the snow, so blandly coming down from the flat, grey sky, that so oppressively weighs down her eyelids like a cold unwanted blanket; absolutely hateful she thinks rather unreasonably of the pretty charm of the snow, muffling and quietly blurring everything she knows to be really there.

Hello cockles Daddy says as he opens the door of the strange car and they get in awkwardly because it is small and their briefcases are heavy with books. Meredith sits in the back, Bron leans over to kiss him on the cheek which is tanned and peeling for he has spent the holidays in the Caribbean. Thank you my love, he sounds a little surprised and so answers Bron's affection with something easy to say, and now is happy with the idea that this is going to be a nice afternoon. Meredith in the back sees his glance in the rear-view mirror and looks out the window.

Uncertainly the car moves away, slipping a little on the snow. Did you have a good holiday Bron asks, and Meredith thinking of that morning asking the same question politely of a professor she knows a little, with ten minutes to wait before the bus, of how behind him the posters were coming down from the wall, soaked and rippled, a Christmas Dance Spectacular, a Workshop for Single Parents—make the best of the Holiday Season alone, Xmas Exam blues?

Daddy is saying that yes they had a good restful break although it wasn't always sunny and it rained all Christmas Day, you'd think it was Vancouver he says, it was so dull and grey. Looking in the mirror his one eye is reflected to Meredith watching her mouth there too moving almost as if it was speaking by itself; they went pretty well, I got three A's, and two B's.

Wonderful, that's splendid, the eye looks ahead, intent on the traffic but relief flickers there for a moment and Meredith seeing it feels strangely reassured, thinking how yes, they are both doing marvelously well at school he will tell his friends politely inquiring after his daughters; it has been such a long time since we have seen them they will say, and he will be pleased to report that both are doing so well and all will be thinking there, what's happened isn't so bad after all, three A's.

How far is it to the new house, Bron fills in the holes with words, dropping down loudly on the bottom of a silence they will never fill. There, as they turn slowly, carefully, the corner, is Daddy's car almost unrecognizable, covered in snow except where two young boys had just run their hands along the sides collecting snowballs and were busy putting little stones in them ready to throw.

Little sods Daddy says, there had better not be any scratches on my car. The eye looked quickly, here we are and the small terse mouth moves again by itself, how nice it looks, and then they stop, the engine turns off, the lights and the eye go out, and so they arrive at the house.

III

They move carefully down the drive, Bron slowly behind Daddy who is saying careful, this is dangerous, arms out for balance, hands spread carefully. How ridiculous he looks Meredith thinks, striding ahead of them both. And so up the steps to the door Bron presses Meredith's hand when from behind the gold glass a shadow moves, indistinctly coming from some room inside, moving closer to the door, clearer as the sisters approach up the steps, becoming distinct, an arm reaching into focus to open the door and

Oh please come in, you must all be freezing

Thank you

Here, let me take your coats

Yes I left the car out in the street

Oh it's lovely and warm in here

You don't need to take your boots off really

No it's more comfortable well just leave them by the door
Well says Daddy straightening out, breathing in expansively, coming to the point among the straggle of getting in and the coats; June, my daughters Bron, and Meredith. Everything gathers for an instant in Bron's eyes as she steps forward to shake hands; a look which June accepts like a small stab because she is in love with Daddy, but which cannot last if this is to be a nice afternoon and so is just as instantly gone as Bron reaches out her hand smiling. Meredith is looking at the hole in her stocking, acutely aware of the big toe horribly exposed and so terribly wrong in the tidy, tasteful room. There is nothing in her eyes as she shakes hands and so they move into the den, also very tidy and in good taste. They sit down, the big toe incurring Meredith's resentment that it should be there at all, so unsightly, with its unclipped nail burst so horribly through the stocking, that June should see part of her she does not like herself. It is because of this Meredith asks where the washroom is, and once inside the bathroom turns her attention to the mirror, to the reassurance of her face she knows is beautiful, yet desperately needing to be sure. Alone in the small room she looks intently and is satisfied with her face, so lovely no one need know anything else and then feeling safe goes back to the den looking out straight, armoured, her beauty like a challenge.

There are tea things on the table Bron is helping put the plates out, the napkins, the cheese and biscuits and the table looks very straight and neatly arranged with new blocks of cheese, an untouched pâté with flakes of dried parsley sprinkled on, a new box of biscuits, and Bron being so willing and helpful. She is right to behave so Meredith thinks looking at her sister, to make the best of things.

They eat. June asks Daddy could she spread some pâté on his crackers, does he want another cup of tea, would you like me to do it for you dear, and Daddy sitting back saying yes that would be best to save reaching over the table. Meredith looking straight at June doing Daddy's biscuits thinks how self-conscious that act seems to make her in front of them all, but does not remove her eyes.

This is very good Bron says of the pâté to help June still doing Daddy's biscuits, did you make it yourself. Oh no, I've been so busy with the new house I haven't had time to.

And so the conversation goes nicely along, Bron obliging, Meredith suffering in the talk floating down, as if through a sieve, a nice soft white flour of talk that has no substance and gradually obliterates everything in an impenetrable surface of pale geniality. Meredith looks at Daddy's Sherlock Holmes on the shelf with June's figurines thinking of seeing it with Mummy in the shop in the Empress, how she said oh we must get that for Daddy, it's so perfect, and then the long time she saved for it out of the family allowance so that it would really be a present for him and not out of his money, and how he stood on the table by their bed those years looking always through his magnifying glass, reducing the world to details, to a circle so small his eyes need never move to take it all in, and so he stands now, still looking.

June is saying how much she likes mousetrap cheese. But Daddy likes Stilton best, Meredith thinks smugly how she knows so much from a lifetime June will never have a part of, how all those Christmases in England there were big round Stiltons and Daddy ate so much and all that clotted cream, Nanny laid such beautiful teas, she always spoiled him, he got a carbuncle on his knee. And on the way home in the New Year when we stayed a night in Amsterdam how Daddy showed us the *Night Watch;* this is a masterpiece he said and we remembered it was a masterpiece long after the image had faded and on the way through the dark to the hotel Mummy stopped and bought for us apple dumplings hot and sweet, from an old man; look how beautiful his hands are she whispered as he dusted the dumplings with sugar and gave them to us, and these we never forgot

and on the way back we saw a sign that said cat show and of course once we got in I knew I had taken your father to the wrong place

how of all our dogs Daddy liked Dim-Sum the best, when she had a mad-five and went racing around and around the room, down on his knees, over she goes he would shout when she jumped his outstretched arms, and called her little Biffington-pie Saturday mornings when she'd come on the bed with the rest of us and have a biscuit and tread on his paper and we'd all watch our tea and make room for her. That Christmas when we didn't go away and Mummy had made Daddy a stocking full of his favourites, caviar, pâté, Stilton, roll-mops and dark chocolate and how Dim-Sum kept sniffing at it and gave the surprise away

so that I was very impressed with the photography but I think you'd get more out of it if you've read the book, Ten Days That Shook The

time in Baja, brown and a little fat, Daddy sat in his deck chair, always with his wine glass and his hat and a magazine, how the waiters would wink and laugh at us putting cream on his bald spot and that night Mummy packed us a picnic and we went out, walking miles down the empty beach in the cool blue light, the sand cool between our toes, and spread our blankets to wait for the moon to rise. Slowly, like a huge, heavy oculus, clouded with cataracts, it moved low in the sky, throwing its pale light over the sea, making little flecks in our eyes while Daddy explained about optical illusions and the tides.

No, he's the one I introduced you to last time we were at Bill's who wanted to talk to you about

one summer when we went to Stanley Park for a picnic and Daddy couldn't find a parking spot and there was a terrible row and Mummy said we had to have somewhere to go away from the city, somewhere green and empty and we bought the cottage and so every spring we could watch the whales come down and play in the waters off Gowland Point and the long hot summers, the sweet-smelling forests, how Daddy found the flint arrowhead beneath the cedars and Mummy made the stone fireplace, and one day we were walking in the woods and nearly stepped on that deer skeleton lying under the ferns, giving way slowly to the insidious growth of the plants, creeping through bone, clutching the skull, the tiny tendrils worming through the eye holes

It is time to go now that Daddy has gone upstairs to fetch the cheque and it is dark outside. Moving down the hall with June, Bron is saying yes they will visit again soon, and Meredith behind in the den looking down at the cold tea and half-eaten cheese, the crumbs, suddenly remembers, and so offers to help clean up, but June, getting out the coats doesn't hear, and so she folds her napkin carefully and laying it on her plate leaves the table.

Penny Kemp

Looking For Something To Do?

Because I am home writing or thinking or whatever all day, what does that assume? "Don't think you have to clean up my room," he calls from within, sorting boxes of clothes and tools and shoe shine material. The idea hadn't occured to me until he mentions it, as if at that very moment I was thinking of cleaning up his room. "It hadn't occured to me," I reply from the kitchen, stirring more vigorously the applesauce into millet for his breakfast on the run. "Unless of course," he jokes, sporting mismatched socks over his shoulder, "You have some spare time and are looking for something to do." He need to understand, I need to tell him, that the effect of such a suggestion is a weight on me, though I shrug it off. It's just as powerful and perhaps more difficult to deal with when suggested in a negative framework, like the statement, "Don't think of an apple." You might have spent days not thinking of an apple, but the mere mention of not thinking of an apple necessitates conjuring it up in the mind before trying to cast the thought aside. So subtle a slightening of our overt agreement. I am sure he meant nothing by it, "was only trying to free me," (who, however, up to that point had been quite free) from taking care of him, he who wants to take care of himself and yet is accustomed to other women, his mother, thinking for him. What was it I was planning on doing? It seems to have slipped my mind. "Don't burn the applesauce!"

Melodie Corrigall

How It Was In Winter

By her seventh birthday, Tanya Beardsley had more dolls, of more sizes, that did more things, than all the other dolls of all the other girls on the block together. For those who would visit, she would display them — a parade of tiny mannequins in costumes of every description. Visitors, however, were rare.

When Tanya sat on her pink satin bedspread and looked in the dresser mirror, she saw a pudgy face, a round pink pudgy face, stuck on a round pudgy body. No matter how she stood, how she stretched her neck, how she contorted her body, she was still a fat, pudgy little shape with a round pink face on top. She sighed, wandering from corner to corner, touching her dolls, staring out the window, straightening her bedspread.

And finally she would go to the bedside table and get the chocolates her brother had bought her, and the Movie Star magazine her mother had forbidden her to read, and escape to another country.

One birthday, Tanya's mother bought her an autograph book. Tanya had particularly asked for one. That year everyone wanted one. Everyone. By the time Tanya had hers half the class had a book of one sort or another, some fancy, some the bare rudiments of paper and cardboard cover.

Tanya's book was of red leather, with the words "Autograph Book" printed in gold across the cover and a page with a flowered border in which you filled in all particulars including weight. Tanya ripped out the page and went in search of autographs.

A couple of the kids didn't put anything bad. The Italian boy put "May you slip into heaven," and the girl who never spoke in class put "Yours 'til the USA drinks Canada Dry," but all the other comments were at her expense. At noon Tanya sneaked up to her bedroom and hid the book under her mattress.

And then Tanya's luck changed. On June 16, 1978, after the

regular tedium of a day in his sterile office and a large supper of roast beef, Mr. Beardsley went to bed complaining of indigestion.

Mrs. Beardsley finished the dishes, cleaned up the living room, climbed the stairs. When she spoke to her husband, he did not reply. She went to him lying there on the bed, shook him, and knew. Mrs. Beardsley sunk onto the bed and pulled her arms to her body. She sat there for an hour, for a minute, for an eternity rocking back and forth on the bed. Finally, she went downstairs and phoned the doctor and her brother in Winnipeg.

She called the children. They came into the living room, surprised to be called down when they should be in bed.

"Your father," she began, "Come here, come here," and she took them by the hand and pulled them down on the sofa. "Daddy is gone," she whispered, "He's gone. He died and the doctor is going to come and take him away."

Peter pulled away from his mother in horror. He ran to the stairs. "Daddy," he cried, bounding up the stairs, fumbling over his legs.

"Peter, Peter, don't go in."

But he did and immediately came out again; ran to his room, slammed the door shut and a minute later they could hear the muffled sound of his sobbing.

Tanya sat there and listened. She had been called down like an adult, like Peter. Daddy was dead. It was for sure because she could hear Peter crying and mother was talking on the phone to her friend Mrs. Cramer and she was crying as she talked. It was like a story.

She should be crying too. She would cry, of course. She would wear black and stay off school. Yes, there had been a girl in the grade ahead whose brother had died and she had stayed off school for months. They said she suffered terribly, that she had loved her brother more than life.

I loved Daddy, she thought, loved him and now he's gone. Everyone will be sorry now; she shivered at the picture of her father dead in his bed.

It was a long night. Tanya was sent to bed more than once but didn't go and no one, in the end, seemed to notice. She saw them take the body out, although she had been most definitely told to stay in the kitchen. Later she couldn't remember if she'd really seen an arm fall off the stretcher as if it were grabbing or if she had just imagined it. That first night or maybe it was the next day, the talk seemed to go on forever.

Her mother and Mrs. Cramer sat at the kitchen table drinking coffee and her mother kept saying they would have to go out West to stay with her brother. They couldn't last out in Ottawa, her mother had said.

When Tanya started along the road to school the first day back her classmates from the street came up to her and asked if they could walk with her. It was the first time, the very first time, they had. Soon all the children on the street were clustered around her, all calling her "Tanya" and saying they were sorry and how did it happen. And that morning the teacher announced in a solemn voice that "we must all be nice, especially nice, to Tanya today as her father died on the weekend and Tanya feels very unhappy."

Tanya told all the stories at school. About the body, and how her father had eaten supper that fatal night just as if nothing would happen. She told what the doctor said, and about her mother crying. Told it all to a hushed audience in the girl's washroom, at recess, that first day back.

Later, when Tanya was first out in the spelling bee, nobody groaned, or made jokes behind their fingers; instead there was a hush and everyone nodded as if it were to be expected.

It was exciting for everyone in the class that week. They felt part of a tragedy. A drama. Life. For what could be more grown up, more part of life than to know about death. To know about a man who they had actually seen who was now dead. Dead in bed after eating roast beef. That was something.

Of all the stories about the death, the most popular, the most poignant, was the story of the new suit. For it turned out that Mr. Beardsley had had a new suit made especially. Made to order by a tailor. The first in his life. A very expensive suit in a brown material. And this suit was only delivered to the house the day after Mr. Beardsley died. Imagine Tanya's mother, they would sigh, going to the door. "Suit for Mr. Beardsley," the man would have said. It was terrible. "Isn't it awful," the girls shivered and tsked when they heard the story again. "And it's still sitting in the hall cupboard," Tanya concluded her eyes wide, "Mommy didn't even take it upstairs because well why . . . "

And they all nodded wisely in agreement.

When every detail of the death and every speculation had been discussed until it became stale in the mouth, Tanya noticed her followers were beginning to drift away. As it was almost Easter break, her mother agreed to let Tanya stay home from school until they moved. So Tanya left in glory, still a story to tell and rumours that the family was moving west. To Winnipeg, Manitoba, a place that not one of her classmates had ever been. Her mother would be a model probably, a serious one. Peter might play hockey or something athletic and Tanya would go to a special school. On her last day the whole class agreed to write her a goodbye letter after Easter.

As it turned out, other things came up after the holiday. The letter was never written. The house in Winnipeg, which Tanya had said would have a swimming pool, turned out to be a small apartment in an older building on a noisy street. Mrs. Beardsley found work with her brother's company as a clerk and Peter dropped out of school.

By summer Tanya began to understand that her father was gone. Really gone. Nothing glamourous, just empty. All the dolls and all the stories didn't erase the sad feeling. In the fall, her mother painted a desk for her room, and made her a seat with a quilted pillow. Tanya sat there by the hour staring out the window. She began to write stories about princes and princesses and death by torture and then finally about Winnipeg. How it was in the winter, still and pastel, and the clean line of the snow on a sunny day.

Gay Allison

Transformation in Central Park

She said she lived in Tucson, owned a teepee in Texas,
was born in Montreal, and could communicate with birds.
As a child she wore black leather pants and wrote poetry
in French. Her mother was a stripper and her father
was a writer who had never read a book in his life.
She said she was hooked on heroin in the sixties,
but now she preferred peyote and magic mushrooms,
had even learned to speak English in one night,
hallucinating in the desert under an Arizona sky.
She told me she slept in gardens and studied flowers.
At night she would dance in the moonlight,
wearing a red dress like her mother, and behead the tulips
for their own good. When she left the park, the birds
followed her, and the bench she was sitting on, exploded from a
bomb.
Sirens began to sound and tulips blossomed everywhere.

Brig Anderson

Annual Visit to My Autistic Child

We have both changed this past year;
you're now a tall, graceful young man.
You still spin your mind away by moving
your forefinger sideways.

But I know you can be fierce, you have terrorized.
Today you are happy wearing my Zimbabwe T-shirt.
We go for a long ride, walk in the camper's park.
You toss pebbles into the stream, not quite obedient.

For a short time we love each other.
I have stopped grieving over you,
fighting campaigns for you,
writing briefs, petitions,
talking endlessly about you,
tricking you with medicine,
despairing over your muteness.
I gave up friends, house,
husband, lovers for you—
finally I gave up you, but loss
has not made me feel bitter:
how could I not treasure you?

You are emotion, incorruptible.
You are powerless, but subversive.
Like a guerrilla, you survive with sporadic attacks,
with patient endurance, silent stubborn anarchy.

Valerie Dudoward

We
Brown Women
Women of Colour
Kiss
Good-bye
to our fathers
Hug good-bye
to our brothers
Cry
Good-bye
to our men.
Our men—
The prisons
Are
Stealing our men . . .
Cement walls
They call home,
Laughter
Echoes cold
In the cells.

We
Brown Women
Women of Colour
Kiss
Good-bye
to our fathers
Hug good-bye
to our brothers
Cry good-bye
to our men.

Kids
Know
Daddies
Each Sunday
Daddies always

Cry—
Good-bye good-bye.

We
Brown Women
Women of Colour
Kiss
Good-bye
to our fathers
Hug good-bye
to our brothers

Cry good-bye
to our men.

But
We
Brown Women
Women of Colour
Say
No more!
We say
Work together
Find
the truths—

They'll
Set us free.
Spill
no more
Red Blood
in jails
For
We
Brown Women
Women of Colour
Will
Cry
Good-bye
No more.

Judy Smith

The Jupiter Effect

(March 11, 1982)

(to be read frantically)

Strange how things gel under the surface, underneath all these things happening I know I'm in a rage, off-centre, off-kilter and for every justifiable reason: I work days then, nights yesterday, evenings today, I don't know when to sleep, when to eat, my study's all disorganized, clutter after clutter piled up and my mother had her leg cut off and I bring Polly home from work with me whose bones are slowly being eaten up by cancer and yet between and among all these things happening I find myself being totally obsessed with music. Ma Carter. Kitty Wells. Hazel Dickens. Sarah Oddum Gunning. Songs keep rollin round my brain for no conceivable reason and then suddenly they all come together. Ma Carter's "I'm thinking tonight of my blue eyes" starts out with the same melody as Kitty Wells' "It wasn't God who made honky tonk angels" and Hazel Dickens at the Folk Festival last summer saying, "Well, since this is supposed to be a workshop on women in country music I guess we best start out with this tune . . ." and she looked at me and I knew right away what song she meant, christ I'd forgotten all about Kitty Wells, standing at the window looking out at highway 365/the Red and White grocery store/Tribune Saskatchewan, standing there ironing to the tune of Kitty Wells, "It's a shame that all the blame is on us women . . ." and all of it passed between the look that Hazel gave me, all the embarrassment, the turning away from Kitty Wells because nobody, nobody liked her, oh yes and I too made fun of her nasal twang and turned my back on her. Until that day. That look from Hazel and suddenly I caught up with myself, where I come from, who I am and all of it settled right on down to where I was sitting, smiling for all I was worth: I'd finally come into my own.

And later on the way to the workshop on Music from Appalachia, there was Hazel walking beside me, talking to me like we'd been friends for years, and her saying how I simply have to hear Sarah Oddum Gunning, "Oh she's had such a hard life it most did her in you know, took us all morning to git her outta that ho-tel room and up here on the stage."

And there was Sarah Oddum Gunning, looking for all the world exactly like my mother, with her red patent shoes and polyester pale green pant suit, dyed red hair flying every which way and Hazel standing behind her propping her up and looking at me like, "You see here is your mother and she's had some life, you see her here now." And Sarah singing it all out, all the pain of it in that high quick lilt at the end of a line, her husband who died in the coal mines, her father who died in the coal mines, her kids starving to death in front of her very eyes, and her saying how people said she was a hero, how the coal company chased her out of Kentucky, but "nobody chases Sarah outta no where, I left Ken-tucky cuz my keeds was starvin?"

And I finally dropped off to sleep to the tune of Hazel Dickens' "Old calloused hands don't bring you much cheer," and I was standing on top of a revolving restaurant looking over the Vancouver skyline and there! Oh! There was the big orange full moon and... What? Following it was another one, it wasn't the moon it was Jupiter for chrissake and all the other planets moving into line, 13 of them there were—yes, 13. 3 more we don't know about—and one of the 3, a small one circling Saturn was called "Euthanasia"—they all had their names beside them like a picture from an Astrology textbook but they were moving, shifting into line and the building started trembling

Oh Christ how stupid can I get what the hell am I doing way up here

I ran all the way down the stairs swaying back and forth and when I got to the bottom

I was in full uniform standing in front of Polly with a needle in my hand trying to convince her to take it but Polly wasn't Polly, she was Sarah Oddum Gunning and then she was my mother and none of them would take the needle. They, she, just stared at me, refusing to take it. And Hazel was standing behind me and all of it passed between the look she gave me, the needle dropped down, my shoulders dropped down and I heard a voice inside me say, "Don't take it away. Look at it."

Maguy Duchesne

Les danseurs de Waglisla

(extraits d'un journal)

Masset

neige épaisse
tourbillon blanc
envahissent Masset,
le vent siffle
les lumières se sont éteintes,
seules les bougies
jaunâtres
éclairent les fenêtres noires.
Au bar, les visages
bouffis, endormis,
entassés.
Une femme danseuse triste
au milieu d'êtres déformés
attend,
donne à chacun
l'espoir, l'illusion, le rêve.

Ce matin, à St. Saturnin, terre de Provence sèche, rugueuse où se mélangent citronnelle et lavande, il est à peine dix heures, les oiseaux sont des fous dans les platanes, je me laisse envahir par le printemps. Au Canada j'avais rêvé à cette campagne douce, usée, amie de l'homme. En arrivant sur la côte du Pacifique la nature sauvage m'a attirée et écrasée. Je cherchais des lieux où l'homme avait vécu; c'est dans les réserves indiennes que j'ai trouvé une campagne, un peuple possédant une chorégraphie hallucinante, une race qui combat le désespoir avec le rêve et la danse du rire.

Waglisla, village de 1200 habitants a été mon premier contact avec le monde indien. J'y suis venue enseigner. Après quelques semaines, l'unique camion du village m'a renversée. D'une certaine manière cet accident m'a donné un statut particulier et privilégié auprès de la population indienne. Les femmes venaient me voir, me soignaient avec des potions. Parmi elles, Alice petite femme d'une cinquantaine d'années me parlait souvent; son mari et sa fille étaient morts noyés et elle vivait maintenant avec son plus jeune fils âgé de quinze ans. Elle parlait un peu indien et je lui demandais de me dire quelques mots dans sa langue: "Vous savez je n'ai pas honte de parler indien; si je pouvais dire ce que l'homme blanc nous a fait: enfants nous étions enlevés de nos familles, mis dans des orphelinats, loin de nos villages et battus à chaque fois que nous parlions indien. Toutes nos céré-monies et nos rituels nous étaient interdits, comme une honte, mais moi je n'ai pas honte d'être indienne et je parle ma langue quand je veux."

Alice n'était pas la seule à laisser aller son coeur et après être sortie de l'hôpital, j'avais régulièrement les visites des uns et des autres quelquefois à trois ou quatre heures du matin. Les premières fois j'avais ouvert ma porte, mais par la suite je criais à travers le mur que je devais dormir afin d'enseigner le lendemain et ils repartaient.

D'autres soirs, cependant, ils insistaient, s'asseyaient devant ma maison, me suppliaient et ces nuits-là pendant des heures j'écoutais leur nostalgie.

Un soir, Marc, le grand-père d'un de mes élèves entra, il n'avait pas l'âme gaie, je lui ai offert de s'asseoir et il est resté un long moment en silence. Marc, comme la plupart des hommes dans ce village était pêcheur et sa fille, la mère de William mon élève, était partie pour la ville. "Quand j'étais enfant" commença Marc, "J'allais à l'école ici comme William mon petit-fils. Les affaires indiennes, entièrement dirigées par les blancs s'occupaient de notre éducation. Ma maîtresse, Mrs. Cunningham, venait d'Angleterre; chaque matin elle nous mettait en rang devant la classe et faisait l'inspection de nos mains et de nos cheveux. L'inspection hygiénique de Mrs. Cunningham nous terrifiait; nous sentions sa règle fouiller nos têtes à la recherche de quelques poux, quelle honte! J'avais tellement peur d'être envoyé chez le directeur que le matin avant de partir j'arrangeais du mieux que je pouvais ma tignasse noire; ma mère avait acheté un peigne, mais on ne savait jamais où il était ce peigne, de plus, dormant presque toujours avec mes vêtements, j'avais un air tout fripé le matin à l'école. Mrs. Cunningham nous montrait comment se laver les dents, les oreilles, les cheveux. Je me sentais angoissé, humilié et je n'étais plus heureux. Je n'aimais plus autant la maison de mon père et de ma mère et je ne m'asseyais plus près du poêle à bois où séchaient les algues. De plus en plus souvent je répondais en anglais à mes parents: ma mère se taisait mais mon père furieux me criait que j'étais indien et que je devais le rester... j'aurais tant voulu le croire mais je repartais à l'école et Mrs. Cunningham continuait à nous menacer et à nous interdire de parler cette langue de sauvages. Une seule fois j'ai été pris en flagrant délit et envoyé chez le directeur, celui-ci m'ordonna de baisser mes pantalons, décrocha sa lanière de cuir et me frappa dix fois, à dix il s'arrêta: "Que je ne t'entende plus bafouiller ce charabia ou je t'envoie à la ville en pension."

Je l'ai regardé bien en face, les larmes aux yeux, et ce jour-là j'ai senti monter en moi une haine toute neuve pour lui et ses semblables; après cet incident je parlais anglais à l'école, à la maison, à mes amis."

"Aujourd'hui les blancs semblent s'intéresser à notre culture, mais il est trop tard! Qu'on nous fiche la paix! L'héritage de William, cet héritage que mon père avait reçu de son père et que moi j'ai eu en morceaux détachés, c'est à grands efforts aujourd'hui que j'essaye de le remettre bout à bout, pour lui. Mon petit-fils appartient au groupe de danseurs de Waglisla et quand je le regarde dans son costume, la tête haute je voudrais que mon père et ma mère puissent le voir, mon père qui me disait—parle indien, tu es indien—et ma mère qui dansait si bien avant l'arrivée des blancs."

Trois ans plus tard à Masset, une grande fête indienne rassembla plusieurs tribus de la côte ouest, ils sont arrivés de partout, en bateau, en avion et quand les danseurs de Waglisla sont apparus j'ai reconnu parmi eux William, le petit-fils de Marc. Je suis allée vers lui, émus, nous nous sommes regardés un instant: "Ton grand-père doit être fier de toi."

"Oui, c'est pour lui que je danse." William souriait, il avait l'air d'un prince!

Quelques semaines après la fête, Alice tomba d'un bateau dans le petit port de pêche de Waglisla; on n'a jamais su si elle avait glissé après quelques bières de trop ou si elle s'était laissée glisser, elle a disparu sans bruit.

Devant l'immensité de l'océan je revois sa fragile silhouette et j'entends ses mots: "je suis indienne et je n'ai pas honte de parler indien."

Un jour la justice blanche est arrivée en avion de la ville pour régler tous les différends des deux dernier mois. Ils sont venus à six le juge, l'huissier, les avocats et les secrétaires, tous en citadin la petite mallette de cuir sous les bras. La plupart de nos élèves assistait au procès, les uns comme accusés, les autres comme spectateurs; les familles, les amis, tout le monde était là. . .

Une excitation fébrile règnait ce jour-là à Waglisla. Le procès avait lieu au temple et la foule assise, parlant à voix basse attendait. La cour est entrée en tenue d'apparat sous les regards des indiens amusés et inquiets.

Trois jeunes, un après-midi pour s'occuper avaient déserré le frein de la voiture des policiers placée en haut d'une côte, juste en face du ponton qui mène à l'océan, la fourgonnette n'avait eu qu'à suivre tranquillement sa route avant de disparaître dans la vague. La lecture du crime à peine terminée, les rires éclatent parmi les spectateurs et les trois lurons ravis du succès qu'ils déchaînent se retournent vers la foule tels de bons acteurs reconnaissants. Le juge frappe sur la table plusieurs fois avant d'obtenir le silence et prononce la sentence d'une voix sévère: "Vous laverez la voiture de la police pendant six mois." Les coupables sourient sachant fort bien qu'ils ne s'abaisseront pas à une telle besogne.

Puis vint le tour de jeunes élèves et plusieurs étaient de ma classe ils avaient cassé la porte de l'école, étaient rentrés et avaient renversé des kilos de confettis; même réaction, regards amusés, rires, mais cette fois le juge perd patience, gesticule et crie. Qui sait ce qui déchaîne chez eux cette hilarité? Ils rient aux éclats, non seulement les enfants mais toute l'assistance. Sans aucun doute le sérieux du juge est la cause de leur joie, c'est inconcevable pour eux qu'on prenne au sérieux une telle histoire. Quant aux petits malfaiteurs, ils furent condamnés à ramasser les papiers dans le village.

Ensuite un couple fut jugé. Le mari avait surpris sa femme dans les bras d'un autre; l'amant s'était retrouvé avec un coup de couteau dans le bras et la femme avec des bleus sur le visage. . .

Le mari fut condamné à un mois de prison; la femme adultère ne semblait guère satisfaite du verdict et trouvait que son mari avait bien fait. Tout l'après-midi les cas se succédèrent jugés par des gens qui n'entendaient rien à la vie que menaient les indiens dans leurs réserves. Le soir la cour disparut dans le ciel et plus tard au pub les toasts se lèvent aux héros de la journée, une fois de plus l'alcool leur permet d'oublier la culture des blancs.

Le pub est le lieu où l'on se retrouve, la musique y va bon train et entraîne les couples de tout âge. J'y allais souvent avec des amis pour bavarder. Un soir j'ai refusé une danse, à peine l'homme s'est-il éloigné qu'une forte femme s'est plantée devant moi: "Il ne vous plaît pas mon mari?" et brusquement elle m'a tourné le dos.

On m'expliqua ensuite qu'elle m'avait fait honneur en m'offrant son mari pour une danse ou deux et je l'avais blessée en ne répondant pas à son amitié. Quelques jours plus tard au pub, de ma propre initiative, je suis allée demander à la femme de mon danseur éconduit la permission d'emprunter son mari; elle me toisa d'un air amusé et me répondit: "Il est à vous pour cinq danses," je l'ai remerciée, me suis pliée à ses exigences et ne voulant pas me soumettre complètement, j'ai osé une sixième danse. Contente de mon audace elle m'invita à sa table. Quant au mari, sans impatience aucune, il a souri tout le temps de notre duel. L'atmosphère dans le pub est le plus souvent joyeuse, folle, jamais vulgaire. Soudain, j'ai commencé à aimer cette société matriarcale.

Waglisla est loin maintenant. A St. Saturnin les enfants de l'école viennent de sortir en récréation et leurs cris se mélangent à ceux des oiseaux.

> Je saisis dans la danse
> une odeur
> d'algue et de lavande
> et je crie d'amour pour vous
> terre indienne et
> terre provençale
> racines inquiétantes
> au coeur
> tendre,
> doux,
> trop facile à aimer.

Francine Pellerin

Étrange Ère

J'ai noté une
absence infinie
dans le ciel

J'ai pas fini
de pousser
mes ailes

pour joindre
le vide à mon
propre néant

j'suis pas gai
j'suis pas triste

c'est bizarre
tout le temps
que je passe
sur cette terre

étonnant

La saison des âmes
La saison des âmes
La saison des âmes
La saison des ours
La saison des maures
La saison des mains

La saison des
maints amours morts

Diane Schoemperlen

What We Want

We could be anything.
We could be wives.
We could be terrorists.
We could be artists.
We could be wizards.
We could be women but we're still dressing like boys.

What we want is a change in style.

Penny and Pat are secretaries. There's nothing wrong with that. All week long they're typing and talking on the phone for hours, mostly to other secretaries, sometimes to each other. Evenings they're watching the sit-coms, rinsing out their pantihose, ironing a skirt for tomorrow. Penny and Pat have been friends for years.

One wants kids, the other one doesn't.
One's been married, the other one hasn't.
One wants to get married, the other one doesn't.
Guess which one?
They both live in the mobile home park. They're paying for their trailers, adding on a spare bedroom, a sundeck, what about a greenhouse, trying to make them look like real houses instead of like trains.

Saturday afternoons they get together for pots of drip coffee and a piece of pie at one trailer or the other. All morning they've been grocery shopping, washing clothes, vacuuming, polishing and dusting, and they're sure ready for a break. They deserve it.

They're over at Penny's admiring her new blue linoleum and figuring out how much it'll cost to repaint yellow in the spring. Then they're talking about the summertime, next year, last year, they'll be having barbecues, playing baseball, working on a tan. Winter is no fun. They might take a night course, Chinese cooking, volleyball, or beginners' photography. They're tired of rug hooking. But some of the things that get planned will just never get done. They're like dreams that way, plans, potent at the time but quickly shed.

The men that Penny and Pat live with are truck drivers. They've gone downtown in the 4 x 4 for a beer with the boys. They'll be talking about gravel and unions by now, smelling like diesel fuel. Men.

It's cold and the trailer cracks. White smoke streams straight up from all the other trailers, drawn in together like covered wagons. Penny and Pat assume they're filled too with warm women in clean kitchens, drinking black coffee and spilling their guts, saying, How true, how true, it's all true.

They make perfect sense to each other.

Last week I was ready to throw him out.

Me too.

But things are better now. We have our ups and downs.

Us too. Ups and downs well yes, how true.

You won't believe what he did.

Never mind, listen to this.

Well, he came home drunk again last night.

Him too?

I've never seen him so drunk.

Me neither.

He passed out at the supper table. Put his head right down on his plate. Chicken pot pie all over his face.

Do they ever laugh. Some things are bearable only because you know you've got someone to tell them to later and laugh.

More coffee and the conversation goes like booster cables between them. Sometimes they're saying the same things over and over again, three times, four, just to be sure they're getting through.

He's a good man though.

Yes.

A good man, yes.

Yes.

He's so good to me.

Yes.

He treats me like a queen.

A good man, yes.

When the boys come home with a pizza, the girls are still sitting there putting a little rum in their coffee and laughing their fool heads off. The cat goes smugly from lap to lap.

Sometimes we want what they tell us to want.

We want a gas barbecue and a patio to put it on.

We want younger-looking hairless skin and a mystery man to rub it against.

We want a Hawaiian holiday, sun-drenched, and a terrific tan that lasts all year round.

We want fur and a dishwasher too but we don't expect to ever really get them. This gives us something to dream about, something harmless to hope for.

Promise us anything but give us an American Express card.

We're not as bad as you think.

What we want is original as sin.

Evelyn is a photographer. She's also divorced. So which came first, the chicken or the egg? She wants to be famous and fairly rich. She may be already famous, already rich (fairly), but artists are just never satisfied. She wants to be all the rage in Paris. After dabbling desultorily in landscapes, living rooms and freaks, Evelyn does mostly portraits now, self-portraits, vegetable portraits, some fruit too.

She's living alone in an elegant studio apartment over some old warehouse down by the docks, of course. It's an unsavoury neighbourhood, yes, but the apartment inside is perfect. One big room, high ceiling, green walls all covered with her own work. She's meeting herself every time she turns around, first thing in the morning, last thing at night. Evelyn thinks it may well be the best place in the whole world.

Her first piece in this vein hangs now over the king-size bed. It's called:

The only thing worth caring about is food.

There's Evelyn in bed in a cheap motel room nursing a cracked *watermelon* which has leaked red sticky juice all over her belly. Arranged in piles on the lumpy sheets are *parsnips, celery, zucchini,* and ten copies of *The Joy of Cooking.* Her stretch marks are like slugs. Some people have said this piece is too obvious. What do they know?

Evelyn's best-known piece is called:
I spy with my little eye something that is edible.

It is a series shot in Safeway downtown and it stars Evelyn and six of her friends, life-size. There they are, each curled up in a shopping cart holding up flash cards that say:

> *broccoli*
> *brussels sprouts*
> *cantaloupe*
> *leaf lettuce*
> *california grapefruit*
> *string beans.*

Evelyn's flash card says: *buy me.*
I'm a nutritious
and delicious
little peach.

The critics usually admire Evelyn's courage, her sense of humour, her technical ability, and her vast and brutal talent, quote, unquote. Evelyn has been alone for years and she figures it's probably just as well, saves having to defend herself and decamp. She cuts out the rave reviews and sends them to her ex-husband Gerry, who is still writing a bad novel in Winnipeg and never replies. He has stopped sending her money and Christmas cards. She could care less.

This afternoon Evelyn's working on something wonderful called:
Portrait of a woman wearing metal.

She sets up the camera in the kitchen, takes off all her clothes and climbs into the stainless steel sink which has been polished like a mirror in preparation. She puts the colander on like a helmet, one *carrot* sticking straight out the top. She poses patiently in the hysterical heat, sweat trickling down her sides, back, nose and into her mouth.

Later in the darkroom she will decide that her baggy *sweet potato* breasts are far more expressive than her face which is too pale, too bland, an ordinary old *potato*.

Evelyn knows she's not getting any younger, she's closer to forty than thirty now. She could care less; in fact, she's kind of relieved. Youth, it seems in retrospect, was nothing more than a damp guilty invasion of privacy. And marriage was like when she worked in that bank one year—a misguided attempt at being, if not exactly normal, at least ordinary.

Now she's well-seasoned with furious secrets.

She wants to be admired from afar by those heavenly young curious men who come to her shows and want to buy her a drink or a vegetarian pizza afterwards. They never have enough money to buy her any of the things she really wants. And so sometimes they're all falling in love with her just when she's walking away.

When we can have whatever we want, we want Beaujolais in crystal, good to the very last drop. It makes us feel silky and smart.

When we can have whatever we want, we want rich red food, the kind that's hard to come by:
lobsters with claws
succulent berries and cherries out of season
steak tartare dripping.
It makes us feel bloody and wet.

When we can have whatever we want, we want a crystal chandelier for the dining room. It makes us feel vicious and spoiled and it will cut you when it falls.

Some people say we're already vicious, already spoiled.

Not spoiled enough.

Not vicious enough.

When we can be whatever we want, we want to be exquisite.

What we want is deluxe.

Lillian dreams about surgeons. She used to be a nurse.
She's on the table in the operating room
blinking in the bright light
waiting for the cocktail party to end.
Everybody she knows is there sipping dry martinis
eating little crackers sucking their thumbs.
Her daughters are drinking tequila and swinging.
Somebody plays a piano poorly.
The surgeons come at her from all directions like bees
kissing through their surgical masks
tickling her with feathers or forks
mental as anything.
They take her apart like a puzzle
painless bloodless

pass her thighs around on a plate
bite-size delectable lox.
There's nothing to fear. There's nothing to fear, dear.
She knows there's nothing to fear.
When they put her back together again
she's a new improved model
deluxe lovable wise and her breasts are perfect.
Only trouble is sometimes they get too drunk
forget how the puzzle fits
leave her spread out all over like that
one arm dangling from the door knob
smelling fishy.

Lillian's husband Hank is a half-crooked new and used car salesman. Lillian's twin daughters are half-crazed teenagers but she's not sure how crazy because they're never home anyway. They might be out getting pregnant, addicted, or arrested right now. You never can tell. What the twins say they're doing is visiting the museum, studying at the library, or attending an afternoon of chamber music. Do they really expect her to believe that? They do it on purpose, they want to be unnatural, they want to annoy her, they think they want to be writers or something.

This family lives in a happy beige house with a view, a verandah, three bedrooms, and a two-car garage. Lillian's in the kitchen right now whipping up hundreds of cookies for Christmas, rolling them in finely chopped walnuts, topping each one with a clot of raspberry jam when they're cool. The whole house smells like a TV commercial.

Hank's out in the garage changing the oil or something. Lillian's waiting for the last batch to bake, licking her fingers and flipping through last month's Vogue or the numbers on the television dial. Outside, the wind is coming up grey, bringing snow at last.

Oh good, it'll be a white Christmas after all.

What's wrong with this picture?

They sniff at her all day like dogs, the dreams. She wants them, doesn't, wants them, doesn't, wants them, doesn't, does. It does not seem possible or necessary to tell anyone or do anything about the surgeons. What you don't know won't hurt you.

Lorraine Martinuik

port moody hill

at first they put her in   like   a ward & there were all these
women   alcoholics & ones who were drugged
shuffling around.
      when her husband came to see her
she was saying to him   what weird people
& he looked around at all this & sd   well
you sure don't belong in here
         (for which she was grateful at the time
but as it turned out he never forgave her her breakdown
& threw it back at her every time he got mad—
having to see a psychiatrist
having to be taken to hollywood hospital
& having the depression go on & on

later they put her in like a semi-private
with an old woman who constantly farted

she cd hear screaming from the electric shock room

they wanted to do that to her
it was like an automatic thing they did but she sd no
she wasn't that bad
     but she had to keep insisting against it

anyway it wasn't her fault she ended up there. she found out later
that hospital was for drug cases & alcoholics & people like that
& that was why they took her there—
        she was having a reaction to
all the drugs this guy gave her
        (he put her on valium & an anti-

depressant   & also a pain-killer because of her sciatica
you know her hip was really paining her then
so she takes all these pills   & has a reaction.   like   this one day
the day they took her in she was   like   staggering
around the kitchen.
                              her husband   he got worried   thinking
she might   like   catch fire to things
so he phoned the doctor   & *he* said
take her to hollywood hospital.
                                        (what a name.   god.

what she remembers   she was there five days   thursday to sunday
& on the fifth day she got to go home.
                                                  she was sure glad
the thing was   things weren't much different.   she had different
medication   i guess
                              but she still had no control
she wd just start having tears stream down her face for nothing
     one time it happened in the morning before school
she had to hide under the stairs so the kids wdnt see

sometimes she wd just get on a bus & ride & ride   going nowhere
just   you know   being out of the house
trying to think things out   like   what was wrong
     (she always had it together to get home
make dinner   so no one knew
                                        but meanwhile just riding around
thinking about her children.
they were always on her mind then
especially the two oldest boys because they weren't with her
& she wondered so much—
                              how they were
& when she'd ever get to see them again

she missed them so much

anyway this one day she was on a bus   going up port moody hill
crying & thinking about the boys
                                        & suddenly she thought of death.

it was like a great wave of relief.   when she thought of that
she suddenly felt really calm & quiet

& it wasn't like she wanted to kill herself or anything   it was
just the thought of   you know   peace   & it was like
     oh, to be out of this life

Jane Rule

Slogans

Jessica did not say, "I am dying." She said, "I live from day to day," that cliché of terminal therapy. Some people never did learn to say the word, *cancer,* but nearly everyone could master a slogan.

Already divorced before her first bout, the children all away at school or college, Jessica bought a wig, took a lover, and in the first remission went with him to Europe.

"Serious about him? Of course not," she explained to a friend they visited. "I'm not serious about anything."

After the second bout, she put a pool in at her summer place and then nearly regretted it.

"The children come home not only with lovers but with pets. I am being overrun with dogs and budgies and a bobtailed cat."

"It's given her permission to be selfish," her critical sister observed.

"She's finally doing what she pleases," explained an admiring friend.

"I live from day to day," was Jessica's only answer.

For some that obviously meant doing what they'd always done, going to work every day or not dropping out of the bridge club or still having everyone for Christmas. For Jessica it meant something quite different, lovers, trips and swimming pools. Finally, at the end of her second remission, when she discovered it was not arthritis in her back but cancer of the spine, she took a trip across the continent to see her birthplace, to attend her twenty-fifth reunion at college, to resurrect old friends who had not been much more than signatures on Christmas cards for years.

"If I'd known you were planning to go to the reunion," Nancy wrote, "I would have planned to go myself," a lie, for not having married, given birth or divorced, Nancy was uncertain what she might say to friends of twenty-five years ago, even if it was also to be Jessica's premature wake. "Come and see me on your way home," she added.

When Jessica accepted her invitation, Nancy tried to remember what kind of a friendship theirs had been. They lived in the same dorm, and they both had clownish reputations, teeth too strong, brows too high to be pretty. So they were funny instead, co-operatively so, setting each other up in song or gag or prank, protecting each other, too, from being thought to be just fools. Jessica had been clever as well, good at winning elections, and Nancy was smart. They were never roommates, never a team, but Jessica was in the crowd Nancy took home for a week of spring skiing, and Nancy was among the few friends Jessica took home singly to keep her holiday company in the house of a much younger sister, reclusive father and put-up-with-it mother, both long since dead of wasting diseases. Nancy's parents were still skiing the slopes, and, if she needed a slogan, it was learning how to live forever.

Jessica and Nancy hadn't much confided in each other, but they came to depend on each other in a casual way, more like sisters than like friends but without sisterly intolerance. Nancy knew first hand about what Jessica called, "the gloom of the ancestral mansion," and Jessica knew that Nancy didn't care a fig about the slopes. "Oh God . . ." they were apt to say to each other just before Christmas holidays.

But one evening, toward the end of their senior year, Nancy went to Jessica's room to borrow a book or check an assignment and stayed for a cigarette, then another. Jessica was obviously in a mood she was trying to joke herself out of.

"Mother says I must simply resign myself to a tailored exterior. I don't tell her about my underwear. I give half a dozen pairs of white cotton pants to the Good Will every year and spend my pocket money on black lace and apricot ruffles. Do you believe me?"

Jessica opened a bureau drawer to reveal stacks of what Nancy's mother would have called "whorish" underwear.

"Some people are too rich to worry about being old maids," Jessica said. "I won't even be able to afford to marry a poor man."

Had Jessica actually asked Nancy what she was going to do, or had she, out of embarrassment at Jessica's vulnerability or some moody need of her own, simply offered her confession?

"I'm a lesbian. I don't suppose I will marry."

"Oh God," Jessica said. "What is it about me that people are always telling me such awful things? Why do I have to bear it?"

It was years before Nancy again risked a friendship with that information. It did seem to her that she had taken unfair advantage of Jessica, presumed far too much on her good will. Jessica hadn't dropped her, but they were both careful, in the months before graduation, to avoid being alone together.

They had met only once in the years since by accident on the street in Edinburgh, both there for the festival, Nancy with Ann, her lover, and Jessica with her stiff young husband, George. They were glad to see each other and raucous about it, like the college girls they had recently been.

"Come help my buy a set of bagpipes," Nancy suggested. "I've decided I can't have them unless I can manage to play them."

While an embarrassed Ann and George stood by, Nancy blew mightily into the instrument they found without being able to make a sound over Jessica's laughter. Only when Nancy had left the bagpipes on the counter and crossed the shop to consider the kilts, did there come a soft groan of air like a creature expiring.

"That doesn't count," Jessica said firmly.

When they were back in the street, taking their leave of each other, Jessica explained, "We're having to cut our trip short. My father's dying."

Faithfully over the years, they wrote their Christmas notes to each other, Jessica reporting the progress of her children, the success of her husband's business, the move to a city apartment when the last child went to boarding school, Nancy describing her work, the house she and Ann had bought together, the progress of nieces and nephews, the health of parents.

They had nothing in common really. What held them to their ritual was the shadow of guilt that one evening had cast over their otherwise easy friendship, Nancy's for her burdensome indiscretion, Jessica's probably for her lack of sympathy. That they had both aged into a more permissive climate made that guilt nothing more than a seasoning for their yearly good will. Yet without it, there would have been no reason for putting a good face on year after year.

Then Jessica divorced, apparently with great relief. She asked Nancy some practical questions about getting a job, and Nancy gave what advice she could, but across a continent and the years, Nancy could not easily imagine with Jessica what she might do. It became obvious that Jessica entertained the idea of a job only to be entertained. When the children weren't at home, she found cruises, courses in art history, and shopping for new clothes enough to occupy her. Probably the post-cancer lover had not been the first. Remembering the underwear, Nancy speculated that he might have been one of many over the years.

Now with a spine of fast multiplying cells which would this time surely kill her, Jessica was crossing the continent and coming for dinner and the night.

Ann was fixing the guest room, twin-bedded now that Nancy's parents preferred it when they were away from their own king-sized. It was an arrangement that suited an increasing number of their friends, a less melodramatic symbol of decline than a visit from a dying friend, but it saddened Nancy simply. She had decided, she wasn't sure why, to bake cookies. Motherly gestures, whatever the occasion, occurred to her more and more often these days. She wondered if she'd ever said, in one of her Christmas notes, that she was white-haired now.

"Are you going to smoke in front of her?" Ann asked.

"I hadn't thought about it," Nancy said, handing Ann a cookie to sample.

Nancy got out the large cookie tin, brought to them once by a would-be lover neither of them had liked, partly for that reason. They had kept the tin because they did like it, a wreath of old fashioned flowers stenciled on the lid, in the center of which was the motto:

To the house
of a friend
The Road is
Never long.

It reminded Nancy of the petitpointed mottos of her greatgrand-mother and her great-aunts which used to hang in the stairwell of an old summer house. In childhood, Nancy had been surrounded by protective, promising slogans and superstitions, making wishes on everything from a load of hay to the first raspberries of the season, crossing fingers against her own white lies, wearing a small cache of herbs around her neck to ward off germs.

The tin was too large to put on the table unless they had a crowd.

Then always someone began to read the verses stenciled on its four sides.

Monday's Child is
Fair of Face
Tuesday's child is
Full of Grace

Nancy could never remember the day she was born. She knew it was one of the hard ones, either "Thursday's child has far to go," or "Saturday's child works hard for a living." It was easy to remember that Ann was Friday's child.

Friends usually didn't know their own days either. Nancy didn't always tell them to look in the back of the phone book where the years were blocked out, in silly dread that someone would discover a Wednesday birthday and be "full of woe."

"I'd better put the cookies on a plate," Nancy decided.

"Doesn't Jessica know?" Ann asked surprised.

"Oh, that, sure, I told her years ago when we were still in college."

The tin was also, of course, an "in" joke, which was why it had been given them:

The child that is born
On the Sabbath Day
Is bonny, blythe, good
And gay.

It was Wednesday, not Sunday, from which Nancy wished she could protect Jessica.

Coming toward Nancy through the clutter of people at the baggage claim area, Jessica didn't look as if she needed protection. Though her hair was short and the flesh had begun to fall away from her jaw line, she looked very much like herself. Only when they embraced, a gesture that startled Nancy, could she feel Jessica's thinness under her disguising clothes. Then Jessica was standing her off to look at her.

"I've decided there are two categories of classmates: totally unrecognizable or made up to play the part of forty-six-year-old woman. You're in category two. That hair's fantastic. Is it a wig?"

"No, my very own."

"So's mine," Jessica said proudly, taking a handful to demonstrate. "But not as distinguished as yours. And mine's a suspicious length. I look like a man recently out of the army or prison."

"You look elegant," Nancy said and meant it.

Jessica hadn't rejected her mother's advice. But the suit she wore, a combination of suede and cashmere, was expensively soft and becoming.

"Do you like it?" Jessica asked, looking down at herself. "It's even more important to divorce a rich man once you've married him. I bought it at Carmel last week."

Claiming her bag, walking to the car, driving home, they talked in their old casual easiness. There were, after all, all those people and those four years they had in common, a larger store than Nancy had imagined, not coming directly from a reunion.

"Vera, do you remember Vera?" Jessica asked. "Sure you do. She was that little blonde who was funny *and* pretty. Well, she's still the belle of the ball. She divorced her husband, got a huge settlement, the house, alimony, and now he's moved back in and wants to marry her again. Nothing doing! She likes him better as a star boarder. She says it's much more romantic and practical, because now she's the only woman he can afford."

"Was Larsen there?" Nancy asked.

"Oh, no. The really colourful ones, the really interesting ones, like Larsen, like you, don't go to reunions."

"Like me?" Nancy asked surprised.

"Being a lesbian by now, even in those conservative circles is, well, admirably scandalous. And then you have a career . . . "

"I call it a job," Nancy answered.

"Well, we weren't trained to have jobs, were we? Not like girls today. Even mine. The college is a different place, you know. No curfew, men in the rooms. Some of our classmates were shocked about that. But I said the only thing that shocked me was how stupid we were to put up with all those rules."

"Do you remember," Nancy said, "when we got campused for a week-end for opening a side door after six o'clock?"

"We'd probably be expelled now. There are locks everywhere, even on the rooms. If you want to go out, even to the library, after dark, you have to call the campus escort," Jessica said.

"What about Dr. Ryan?" Nancy asked.

"She gave the dinner speech. She retires next year. She's *old,* Nancy, doddery."

Once they arrived at the house and Nancy could look directly at Jessica, she saw the sudden death's head strain in Jessica's face.

"Rest?" she asked.

"Yes," Jessica agreed simply.

Jessica was still in the guest room when Ann got home from work.

"How is she?"

"Just the same . . . and dying," Nancy answered. "I don't know." How are you?"

"Very glad she's come," Nancy said, "and frightened for her."

"Can she talk about it?"

"She hasn't."

They began to prepare dinner together without exchanging the ordinary bits of their separate days.

By the time Jessica joined them, she had refreshed herself. She embraced Ann as warmly as she had Nancy, as if to include her in that old friendship though they had met only once.

"No drink, thanks. Do go ahead," she encouraged. "And if you smoke, please smoke. I can't stand the role of Hamlet's ghost."

" 'Swear,' " Nancy intoned dramatically, remembering that they used to say that, not remembering why.

"I also hate to waste time resting," Jessica said. "They'll have to put me in again and do something about me when I get home."

"It must be awful," Nancy said.

"It is," Jessica answered. "Do you know what I hate the most? All those articles about the 'cancer personality,' trying to make you feel guilty as well as sick."

"It's the medical profession, passing the buck," Ann said.

"And the friends and relatives. My daughter thinks it's God's wrath for my wicked ways. I said to her, 'Ducky, the only reason I have to die is that we all do. You find me a survivor, and I'll repent.' "

"Why is everyone so stuck on cause and effect, I wonder?" Ann asked.

"A combination of Newtonian physics and Christianity," Nancy suggested, "when we need Einstein and possibly Zen."

"Nobody said anything remotely like that at the reunion," Jessica said, laughing. "Nancy, you don't disappoint me."

Nancy remembered how little anyone at college had ever talked about what interested her, how Jessica had always covered for her accidents of seriousness and turned them into a joke.

"Well, as one of our gallant classmates put it, if divorce makes you a high risk for cancer, at least it lowers the risk of being found chopped in pieces."

"What a ghoulish way of putting it!" Nancy said.

"But Josie Enright (she was in one of the hill halls, do you remember?) had that distinction, haven't you heard, and her 'widower' got off scot free," Jessica said.

"It's not the sort of thing that gets into the class newsletter," Nancy said.

"She was in the obits. in the *Quarterly,* not with the gory details. 'Suddenly,' I think it said," Jessica said.

"Is the general consensus against marriage by now?" Ann asked.

"Oh, I don't suppose so. Sore heads tend to congregate. Ninety percent of us were really majoring in marriage after all. The awards go to those getting ready for their silver wedding anniversaries with one pregnant child or child-in-law. On some, smugness is even becoming. Do you remember Judy Framton?"

Nancy nodded as she got up to clear the table.

"Well she's proto-grandmother of the first category, totally unrecognizable."

"I wouldn't have the courage to go back," Ann said.

"It was fun," Jessica said. "I haven't laughed that much in a long time."

Nancy brought the plate of cookies to the table.

"Home made?" Jessica asked.

"It's what lesbians do when they're alone together," Nancy said.

"Now I wish I'd known *that* before the reunion," Jessica said. "There are still sheltered lives among us. Gosh, I haven't baked cookies in years. Do you remember the enormous chocolate chip cookies they used to make at college? They still do."

Nancy remembered the short-and-thicks, milkshakes you had to eat with a spoon, and fresh orange juice at the college shop.

"I had to buy the whole pitcher of it once," Jessica remembered, "because Donna (she was my roommate) was so hungover she couldn't write her exam without it."

The remembering went on over coffee, which Jessica didn't drink. She and Nancy apologized to Ann, who said she knew some of the stories as well as they did and could even join in on a punch line or two. But Jessica was tiring.

"You have a long trip tomorrow," Nancy said.

"Oh, I know," Jessica said.

Ann and Nancy went into the kitchen to finish loading the dishwasher.

"What about Einstein and Zen?" Ann asked.

"We have to accept the random. We know all the leaves are going to fall, but we have no way of knowing when any particular one..."

They heard Jessica coming down the hall to the bathroom. She stopped at the kitchen door.

"I forgot to say about the flowers in my room. They're lovely. Goodnight."

For a few moments they moved around the kitchen without speaking.

Then Nancy said, "Zen masters write death poems. Odd things like:

Seventy-seven long years
I've reviled the Scriptures,
Zen itself. A failure through
And through, I piss on Brahma"

Ann gave a startled laugh and then said, "Maybe you should have..."

Nancy shook her head, "It's just another slogan."

Marie-Louise Sorensen

Mabel Dons a Diving Suit

I

Mabel's father a lawyer
and instrumental

national geographical
society and a school for the deaf

While mother Gertrude kept her talking
Mabel suffered the scarlet fever

at five years two months
totally and permanently deaf:

No explanation
A black curtain falls simply

in the first act
And those who can afford to

whisper make signals
while Mabel

one foot in a memory
speech articulates

the other
forever in a metaphor

II

1876 the telephone is patented. Mabel lets Alexander know he should
exhibit the piece. Too much work he puts her off with students and

exams and besides it needs more tinkering etc.

The closing registration day for electrical exhibits passes finally. Mr.
B seems relieved almost pleased.
Mabel thinks not to give up.

She has of course instructed the driver to make it to the railway
station and they arrive and Alec realizes what is happening protests
bitterly but Mabel who is by then engaged informs him if he does
not get on that train right there and then she won't marry him and
so off he goes of course and Mabel—

he would have been tinkering with that telephone forever if I hadn't
taken it from him.

A. states
you my dear constitute the chief link between myself and
the outside

M. writes
he demanding the utmost of my strength from the first
refusing to admit any greater claim to my consideration
than his own

Provider of a Refuge for the Husband Mabel came back
to Baddeck knowing the need for women to discuss matters
of current fascination organized the Young Ladies Club
of Baddeck (not the Baddeck Club at the risk of offending
the men). The Club soon focused on literary matters
countless long descriptive letters
sent back from foreign
lantern slide shows but nothing quite as
the real thing

Of course Mabel carried on experiments of her own.
Growing things   vegetables in sunshine and in shade
dried food in WWI   took photographs + developed

negatives volunteered for the Man-lifting Experiment
with the Frost King as all thought she was the best
available subject.

received reports daily from all managers filed patents
research notebooks   sacrificed her new venetian blinds
for flight (Alec working late again)

And this thing with the sheep. Alexander's sheep
breeding experiments producing ewes with twins with no
success and selling the whole lot and Mabel really
worried this time for his work motivation buying it back
by proxy and Alec once again involved with his sheep.
He did carry on with this work until the end of his life
but always referred to them as Mabel's Flock.

August 2 1922   Beinn Bhreagh   Alexander dies.
Mabel dies shortly after

not certain of what she believed as far as religion

Marion Bell Fairchild remembers when she and Elsie
were young their mother thinking fresh air healthy
thinking their clothes dreadfully confining for summer
setting out to find more suitable apparel purchasing
boys clothing in spite of the scandalous nature of her
solution

the Young Ladies Club of Baddeck still meets regularly
and is now called the Alexander Graham Bell Club.

Helene Rosenthal

Women and Word-Stones: Reflections

for M.M., who also loves them

"Before the mind is ready to admit new ideas, it is fixed in its shape. . ., the thoughts we live with in psychic comfort. The weapons that defend these thoughts are our reactions, which we keep stored in handy piles, like a pile of small stones. . "

—Mary Meigs, *Women and Words/Les Femmes et les Mots* Conference,
U.B.C., June 30-July 3, 1983

O
    O
        O

Bouncing
        bounding
meteoric   stones
sisters
of the forward luminous
stream in which our heavenly
bodies shine
reflection of our spiritual
contours

        among us

Mary   you
who handed us a silver
net that first night
jewel eye one
naming
thought-stones:
impediments to the stream

spelling us
to turn our fault to facet
of a common dazzling
mirror
            let me offer this:
stones
        that glow
        in the dark

        that are fireworks
        held forever
        in mid-air

            that are merely
            stones   peacefully
            absorbing sun
            and starlight

        that *are*
        moons pulling tides
        and women
        all over the world

Nicole Gagné

Je suis femme aux yeux de jade mouillé
Je porte en moi des pluies d'incertitude
Des neiges éternelles
Et des embruns d'infinie tristesse

Sur la pierre gravée à mon nom
Je dessine mes angoisses
Je peins mes impatiences
Je sculpte mes déchirures
Et colore mes désirs

Je suis femme au coeur de porcelaine
Je porte en moi des rêves impossibles aux glaçures abîmées
Des misères patentes
Des amours mortels
Et des deuils accumulés

Je suis île baillonnée
Perdue dans d'insondables silences
Peuplée de serviles discours
Je suis asile de mes impuissances

Mon corps tout entier se fige
Mes seins sont de marbre
Mon ventre de plomb
Tant il y a d'effroi dedans

La vie est mortifère
L'azur ne se perçoit plus des sommets du coeur
Le creux du désir se remplit d'aliénants discours
Seule une fenêtre laissée entrouverte
Purifie l'air et l'imprègne de douceur

Je sens un vertige m'atteindre
Je sens la terre trembler sous mes pieds
 Pour avoir confondu l'autre et le même

Je suis une amoureuse triste
Un puits, un antre
Je gratte le sol jusqu'au centre de la terre
 Et mon cri se perd du fond de cet abîme

Avec mon cri agonise ma détresse
Je me surprends à rêver
Je me surprends à aimer
Et la fête rejaillit
Et avec elle je refais surface

Il me vient à la bouche un goût aigre et âpre
Comme le relent d'une souffrance passée
Il me vient aux lèvres une chanson triste
Comme l'écho d'une couleur du coeur un peu oubliée

Et retirée en moi comme marée basse
J'attends que revienne le retour des lames sur elles-mêmes
Et qu'elles viennent briser et recouvrir bientôt
La souffrance d'hier trop grande
Et le blues au coeur de l'enfant blessée qui je suis

Il n'y a de clair
De vraiment clair
Que l'opacité de nos leurres
Que cette mer d'illusions
Qui nous berce

Il n'y a de vrai
De vraiment vrai
Que ces liens fragiles
Qui nous échappent toujours
Que ces liens fragiles qui nous nourrissent d'amour
Un temps
L'espace d'un court instant
Où sonne du même coup
L'heure de l'abandon
L'heurre/leurre de mourir d'inanition

Je baigne dans la lucidité parfois
Je m'y baigne je m'y noie des fois
Je m'en suis fait un lit
Je m'y couche et m'y endors
Je m'en suis fait un berceau
Un berceau plein d'épines
Qui me déchirent la peau
Et je saigne

Dale Colleen Hamilton

Children of Fire

dedicated to the Rice Family and to the memory of Paul Jr. and Paula

The wind kept us awake most of the night, calling out like a child disturbed by nightmares. Around midnight, we climbed out of the bunk in the aft cabin and pulled on raincoats over top of our pyjamas. I stuck my head above deck; the wind slapped me fully awake, taking my breath away momentarily. A group of our neighbours, fellow "liveaboards" here in the Inner Harbour, were huddled in a tight circle on the dock, watching their homes convulse in a feverish dance.

As we retied the straining lines and checked our tarps, Hank recalled a snatch of a dream from which he had just awakened: his dream was of our mattress on fire, totally engulfed in flames: two feathers, both an unearthly colour of blue, soared up from the blaze, apparently unscathed. I dreamed of riding a unicorn in a parade: ahead of me was a buffalo, and behind me, a dinosaur.

By the next morning, storm warnings were still in effect. We stumbled around making breakfast, like drunken sailors, the boat swinging to the beat of jazz music. I suggested we go visiting for the day, preferably on dry solid land. I checked my calendar to see if there was anything I couldn't put off until tomorrow: that was when I realized that exactly a year had passed since The Fire.

That decided it: we would visit David and Suzanne, Hank's brother and sister-in-law. We knew this date would summon up their own painful memories of The Fire and The Funeral: we have come to measure the passage of time by these events.

David and Suzanne were home alone. Hank and I took a long bath together, a luxury for anyone living aboard a boat. By the time we emerged, David had the fireplace going. I took a cushion and sat at the hearth, brushing my wet hair. Suzanne offered to braid my hair for me, and as she did, the words of the Elder who had given me my Indian name came back to me: "When you braid your hair, you are weaving together the three elements of your being: Mind, Body and Soul." I repeated those three words to myself, in turn, as each strand of hair was woven into the braid. Each pull grew stronger than the last. Then three other words added themselves to my chant: "Past, Present, Future". . . and as my eyes were drawn to the fire in front of me, so my mind was drawn into the past. . .

Hank was in college at the time, and I was working across the harbour, at the Natural Healing Centre on Wharf Street. I often spent the mornings refilling the dozens of amber-tinted jars which line the shelves. The label on each jar, printed in graceful calligraphy, gives the name of the herb contained within: False Unicorn, Life Everlasting, Eyebright, Squaw Vine, Devil's Claw Root. When I fill the jars, I often repeat the name of the herb and its medicinal properties. . . but today my chant was interrupted by a telephone call. I recall being taken aback by the way he said hello. His voice seemed to be travelling through a tunnel, the last reverberation of an echo before it dies. The voice on the other end was David, Hank's older brother. It was unusual for him to call; it's long distance from Duncan and they have no phone at the house. Probably the last time he'd called had been to announce another birth in the family. This time I knew that birth was not on his mind. His words confirmed it:

"There's been death in the family. We should all be together. Can you and Hank come to Ladysmith right away? We'll be at Mom and Dad's." They say that when the owl calls your name you will be taken to the spirit world. My voice was like an owl:

"Who. . . David, tell me who. . . "

"George Jr. and Georgette."

His voice was hollow, and understandably so: this man had just announced the death of his children.

"How?" I asked, though the burning question was "Why?"

"They died early this morning, at about 6 o'clock."

Hank and I were making love, I thought, at 6 o'clock this morning.

"They got up early and found some matches by the fireplace. They set their mattress on fire and watched it burn. I wasn't home."

His voice faltered, then grew stronger.

"I don't know why I didn't go home. I spent the whole night in Duncan, drinking coffee in the 24-hour cafe. I was too restless to go home. Suzanne was sleeping downstairs and didn't smell the smoke until it was too late."

"I had a dream about you, David. It was a few nights ago."

"What was I doing." He said it as a statement, not a question.

"You were doing an eagle dance and right before my eyes your face turned into an old man's face. What do you think it means?" I asked, already knowing his answer.

"It was your dream. You tell me."

"I'll talk to you when we get there."

There was nothing left to say.

"See ya," David whispered, and the line went dead.

We stood with our thumbs up for over an hour. Streams of cars went by, as though we were invisible. Hank fell into a deep silence, so deep that I couldn't follow. He was standing behind me: we seem to have better luck hitchhiking when I stand in front. I looked back at Hank; he was staring somewhere just above my head, his hands thrust deep into his pockets. I realized that my own hands were at my side. I assumed that Hank had his thumb stuck out, and he obviously hadn't noticed that my thumb was not in the air. Once I raised my thumb, we got a ride almost immediately with an unemployed mill worker going as far as Mill Bay.

Only Hank's father, Sam, was home when we arrived. Hank asked the obvious question:

"Where is everybody?" Judging from the number of dirty dishes on the table, it looked as if they had all been here for supper.

"Everybody's down at Kulleet Bay at the Shaker Church. They're having a service for the kids tonight." Sam flipped on the T.V. as if expecting to tune into his grandchildren's funeral service, live over most of these stations.

Sam settled down on the couch to watch the fights. I asked Hank if he thought his father would like to come along with us to the service. Sam must have overheard me because he yelled from the livingroom:

"I'll go to the funeral tomorrow at the Big House, but you won't get me inside that church."

As we entered onto reserve land the pavement was replaced by a rutted gravel road. A heavy fog had rolled in off the ocean and the Shaker Church appeared as an apparition. It was a simple structure. Beside it stood the Big House which seemed to merge into a stand of cedars. Our taxi driver refused to go the last few hundred yards, afraid he wouldn't be able to get turned around. I waited for Hank to pay the driver, and Hank appeared to be waiting for me to pay. I thought he had the money, and he thought I had the money. Hank vaguely knew the driver and promised to pay him the next day. He seemed anxious to be on his way and agreed.

It was drizzling and cold. I pulled a scarf from my pocket and tied it around my head. We ran for the front porch and Hank pulled open the heavy wooden door. The service was already underway. Dark faces turned as we stepped into the candle light.

The interior of the church was stark, so unlike the ornate churches of my childhood. A single white cross hung from the ceiling. On either side of it were two wooden coffins, just big enough for a three and a five year old. All around the edges of the church were wooden benches filled with Indian men and women and children. And there were the singers, with bells and candles, gathered around the coffins, deep in song. It seemed to me that everybody there was dressed in sombre colours: I suddenly grew self-conscious of the bright-coloured scarf on my head and snatched it off. Then I grew self-conscious of my auburn hair, which I imagined to be glowing scarlet in contrast to the dark heads all around me.

A wood burning stove in the back corner radiated warmth, even as far away as I stood. As the lid was lifted to add more wood, I watched a young cousin of the dead children step closer to gaze into the fire, the flames reflected in his chestnut eyes. He tossed a small piece of wood into the blaze, captivated by the power of the flame to consume that which, moments ago, he had held in his arms.

I could see Hank's immediate family, including David and Suzanne, all seated together in the far corner of the room. Hank's eyes darted in their direction, but he remained where he was, leaning against a post just inside the door, a few steps ahead of me. I wanted to step forward and take Hank's hand, but I couldn't move. I thought that maybe he didn't want anybody to see me . . . didn't want the Elders to know that the only non-Indian in attendance was there because of him.

I couldn't read these once-familiar faces: they appeared as death masks all around me. My Grandmother's words came to me: "Sometimes you're respected more for the things you *don't* do, rather than for the things you do." I stole towards the door, opened it in slow motion and crept down the steps into the shadows.

I found myself a relatively dry spot under an arbutus tree and sat motionless in the moonless night. I searched the sky, but found nothing. Then I let my head collapse onto my chest. . . and listened to the voices coming from inside.

We spent the night at Sam and Pearl's, bedded down on a collage of homemade quilts on the spinning room floor. Several Cowichan Indian sweaters, in various stages of completion, hung around us, guardians of our dreams. Between us lay a nephew named Cedar. My body was exhausted, but my mind remained on the threshold. I gazed around the room, finally focusing on a blond wig, perched inside a dusty punch bowl on top of the dresser.

Both Cedar and Hank were gone when I awoke in the morning. Cedar was watching cartoons with his grandfather and Hank was helping his mother, Pearl, with the breakfast. I watched her place a handful of copper-coloured herb on top of the airtight: it erupted into sweet silvery smoke. . . "to keep the spooks happy," she said.

A familiar station wagon pulled into the driveway. Hank's oldest sister Diane emerged and pulled two green garbage bags from the seat beside her. We ran out to help her. She dropped the bags and the three of us hugged. She looked tired to me. Hank noticed too and commented on it.

"I sat up all night with the kids," she sighed. She must have sensed my confusion because she explained:

"Some of us sat up all night with Georgie and Georgette, singing and talking and praying and just sitting."

She motioned towards the garbage bags.

"I brought their clothes. Some of them smell really smoky. I'm going to take them to the laundromat. But right now, I want to lay down for a couple of hours."

I hesitated for only a moment.

"I'll do the laundry, Diane." She smiled slowly and handed my a roll of quarters.

The Pink Elephant Laundromat is just around the corner from the funeral home. It was deserted when I arrived. I opened the first bag of laundry: it contained Georgie's clothes, and the other, Georgette's. Both smelled heavily of smoke, and inside each bag, I found a pair of pyjamas, blackened with soot and slightly damp to the touch. I put these pyjamas into a separate washing machine and set the dial for the hottest wash.

I paused over each article as I sorted the colours from the whites. If it is possible to do laundry with love and respect, then I did so. Ordinarily, laundry is a mundane task to be put off until no clean socks are to be had, but this was no ordinary act of laundering: this was an act of purification, this was my own private ritual, performed in a public laundromat.

I sat on a bench near the window waiting for the wash cycle to end. My eyes were drawn to a small sign attached to the wall. In bold letters it read: "In Case Of Fire..." The rest of the message was in fine print and I moved closer to decipher it, as if the message was intended especially for me, just at this moment. I read that sign over and over, half-expecting to find some bit of wisdom printed on a sign in a laundromat in Ladysmith. Soon I had the words memorized and could repeat them by heart, only my lips moving, my eyes closed. I was in this same state when Diane touched me on the shoulder. The clothes in the machine were spinning.

"Diane, I thought you were going to get some sleep?"

"I tried, but the phone rang." Her eyes no longer looked tired: she was beyond sleep. "It was Thomas on the phone. Two more people have died. Mom's cousin Fred Winter died in the Big House last night and John Martin shot himself early this morning." Diane let out an old woman sigh; the only time I've ever heard such a sigh is at the height of a sweat lodge ceremony when the steam from the sweltering rocks is almost unbearable.

We embraced there in the laundromat while people all around us came and went, folding laundry, reading *The National Enquirer,* smoking cigarettes; just another Tuesday afternoon. I felt Diane go limp in my arms for a moment; then she straightened her back, pushed the hair out of her eyes and stood up taller than before.

Before Diane left, we discussed other arrangements to be made before the ceremony, the multitude of details designed to keep those still alive somewhat grounded at the time of death. I was left watching a show of chaotic colours tumbling behind the window of the clothes dryer.

A gust of wind made me look towards the door. An Indian family entered, a mother, father, and their two teenagers. Although I didn't know them well, I recognized them as the family of John Martin, the young man who had shot himself; the one of whom Diane had brought news.

John's father unloaded the duffle bag. John's brother and sister stood behind him, their faces clouded over. Emile Martin, who I know is related to Hank's mother, studied each article of her dead son's clothing, as if searching for clues. Just before she closed the lid of the machine, she lifted a blue sweatshirt from the top of the pile and buried her face in it, smelling the essence of her son's body one last time. Then she let go of it, closed the lid gently and chose a setting on the dial.

By the time I began folding the children's clothes, The Pink Elephant had grown busy. There were very few machines not in use. I was shaking sparks of static electricity from a violet-coloured sweater when a voice with a slight English accent startled me:

"Excuse me, do you have change for a dollar bill?"

I gave her four quarters and accepted the dollar bill, hoping that would be the end of our exchange, but she continued:

"It looks like I'll have to wait for a machine again. I swear that every time there's Indians in here doing laundry, they use up half the machines in the whole laundromat. They must only do laundry once a month." She paused for emphasis, then continued.

"And they never wipe out the machines when they're finished." She paused again, expecting me to agree with her, I suppose. I said nothing; I simply stuck her dollar bill in the breast pocket of her shirt and took back my quarters.

John's mother finished unloading the washer. The woman who had asked me for change was hovering about them and dove for the empty machine. As she passed me on her way to the soap dispenser, she snapped:

"You see? I told you she wouldn't clean out the washer." I moved directly behind the woman, breathing down her neck as I whispered:

"That woman is washing the clothes that belonged to her dead son. If you're so concerned about your clean white wash, maybe you should do it at home and stop complaining about the bloody washing machines." I prepared myself to meet with hostility, but received no such response. The lines in the woman's face seemed to deepen as she spoke.

"Oh, dear. I heard about her son from my son; they went to school together."

Both my anger and hers had dissolved and, in silence, I helped her with the floral-patterned blanket she was folding.

At the ceremony, I sat between Hank and his Auntie Emma. Most of the service was in the Salish language. Some people watched Emma to see when she sat and when she stood because they know she speaks their language fluently and knows the traditional ways: she was chosen by her grandmother, at the age of nine, to begin her training as a midwife and medicine woman.

It was all like a half-remembered dream. Long chains of people circled around the coffins, each person stopping to take a last look at those ageless faces. Just before the coffin lids were closed, Suzanne approached Emma and, in the faintest of whispers, asked if it would be alright to take a picture of the children. Emma gave a slight nod. The coffins were closed in a flash of blinding light.

The drummer, having warmed his drum by the fire, set up a thunderous beat that seemed to control the rhythm of my heart. A song arose, from whose throat I couldn't tell. That same chain of people began shuffle-dancing in a wide circle. I caught Hank's eye across the room and he motioned for me to join, but I hesitated, wondering where I should break into the chain. Diane intercepted the look that passed between Hank and me; she broke from the chain and pulled me into the dance.

The graveyard was just down the road from the Big House. A steady rain pulsated on the caskets as they were hoisted upon the shoulders of brothers and uncles and cousins. Family and friends followed behind, dodging some puddles and walking straight through others, as children playing in the rain will often do.

One of Hank's sisters, Jean, was in the last weeks of pregnancy. She walked with the rest, holding her belly with one hand and her daughter with the other. Children's faces appeared at the windows of the houses and from behind skeleton of abandoned cars, peeking at the child-sized coffins as they passed.

The procession wound its way into the graveyard; the graves were alive with blooming narcissus, and on the edge of the forest I could see a growth of Saint John's Wort. An old woman, her head bound in a yellow scarf and an emerald-coloured shawl around her shoulders, passed between the mourners. She carried a basin of water and a towel. She moved so silently that I wondered if her feet were touching the ground. She offered each person the opportunity to bathe their eyes, their faces.

An old man, standing to the rear of the crowd, began to speak in Salish. Emma translated into English—"the borrowed language." He asked the people to wash their faces with this water, to wash away the death, to be cleansed and to get on with living. His voice rose and fell.

"You must learn the lessons of these deaths. You must look inside, and to your Elders, for the answers... even though it is sometimes painful to see."

As he spoke, the old woman offered me the basin and I splashed the water, cold as stone, onto my face, allowing it to cascade down my cheeks like the purifying tears I had been unable to release.

I had brought along two handmade dolls stuffed with herbs, intending to give them to one of Diane's children as a birthday gift. I considered, momentarily, setting them on top of the caskets as they were being lowered into the ground, but I abandoned the idea. The bodies of those children, asleep in the arms of Mother Earth, would have no need for such things: the dolls were stuffed with herbs intended to induce peaceful sleep. Instead, I walked over to Jean and pressed the dolls into her hand, a gift for her unborn baby.

A hot meal awaited the mourners. Long tables had been set up in the back room of the Big House. Women and girls entered from the kitchen, bearing plates laden with smoked salmon, potatoes and fried bread, plus steaming pots of clam chowder and duck soup. Hank was deep in a conversation with an old man. I found myself a seat next to Lenny, Diane's youngest son, who proceeded to throw his arms around my neck, welcoming me with a kiss that smelled of the sea.

After the cake had been served and consumed, I rose to help with the cleanup, but Pearl said no and led me to a table where another ceremony was about to begin. Diane handed small knitted pouches to her parents, her brothers and sisters and their spouses. I fingered my pouch lightly, then opened it to find several coins inside. I had no idea what was expected of me. Hank must have recognized my confusion: he leaned over, and in a hushed voice, translated the ritual into words as it began to unfold. I followed the movements of the ceremony closely, but at a certain point I hesitated too long. An old man with a blanket draped across his shoulders flashed me a child-like smile and waited patiently for me to complete my offering.

It was well after dark when we left the Big House. As we walked towards the car, I was startled by Diane, who appeared unexpectedly from behind a tree.

"Can you two help me for a minute?"

We followed her to the rear of the car: there sat the bags of laundry. We transferred the clothes into wicker baskets and carried them to a clearing, where a bonfire was being stoked by an old woman. A circle of family gathered around the fire. I had seen this old woman around the reserve, but had never heard her speak a single word. Even now, her words were few: the power was in her movements, which seemed not to be her own. The painstakingly laundered clothing was cast into the orange dance before us. . . a final offering of love to the Children of Fire.

Suzanne had finished braiding my hair; at least six tiny braids were wound around my head and fastened with a beaded clip.

Hank and David were staring at each other over a chessboard, and Suzanne was bent over her guitar playing an old children's folk song. I hadn't seen her touch her guitar since before The Fire. The last chords of the lullaby sounded: it seemed like the time to make my announcement.

Aside from Hank, my mother, and my father, Suzanne and David would be the first to hear the news. I moved across the living room and stood behind Hank, my fingers massaging his neck muscles. He turned in his chair and wrapped his arms around my thighs, resting his head on my belly. I leaned down and whispered a few words in his ear. He nodded and held me tighter. I broke the silence: "Suzanne, David: I know you've already got a dozen or so nieces and nephews, but how'd you like to be an aunt and uncle again?" That's all I needed to say.

The child growing inside me was conceived aboard our boat, and if I have my way, that's exactly where all our children will be born. . . as their father had been, in the cabin of an old wooden-hulled fishing boat.

And if we have our way, and I vow that we will, our children will grow up in the country, just like their mother: surrounded by the cycles of birth, growth and change. . . Children of the Earth, Children of the Ocean, Children of the Wind, and Children of Fire.

Helen Potrebenko

Hey, Waitress

If you don't like it here, go somewhere else.
Anywhere else.
Go to another restaurant.
Restaurants are pretty much the same—
you won't like it there either.
Go to another restaurant
where you won't like it either.

Get a job in a bank, if they'll have you.
Work there twenty years
by which time you might be earning enough to live on
and, in the meantime,
walk to work,
get a loan,
make your own clothes,
sacrifice.

Go and be a stewardess.
Straighten your teeth,
do electrolysis on your chin,
get those varicose veins repaired,
lose half your weight.
Don't get wrinkled.
Don't get old.

Take a typing course after work.
Work at it for a year every chance you get
to get your speed up.
Of course, they want you to know something about bookkeeping
nowadays

with some knowledge of dicta and telex
and, of course, previous payroll experience
and it goes without saying that you must have
some knowledge of computer forms
and probably you will be expected to relieve on switchboard
and, naturally, all women know about filing.
So, it will take you about five or ten years
to acquire enough skills for an "unskilled" job
at the same low pay you are now getting.

Go to university.
Work nights; study days.
You get quite strange, of course,
and you get quite sick.
When you graduate you won't get a good job anyway
but by that time you'll have enough seniority as a waitress
that you can switch from night shift to day shift.

Get a job with a firm that promotes women.
Make your own clothes,
copying the styles out of fashion magazines.
Act intelligent but not too intelligent.
Don't have children.
Don't hang around with other women workers.
Work overtime.
Don't cry.
Take night courses.
Have a good address.
Be thin.
Don't socialize with women workers!

But then, maybe it's not worth it.
It's better to have friends.
It's better to have family.
Join the right side.
Join us.

Hey, waitress!
Organize your workplace.
Get a lunch break.
Demand decent pay.
Work collectively.
Win job security.

Hey, teller!
The waitresses are on strike.
Support their strike.
Start your own.

Hey, typist!
Join the tellers' picket line.
Get paid according to your skills.
Get paid enough to live on.

Hey, stewardess!
Bring your children to the picket line.
Get fearless.
Get old.

Hey, everybody!
The economy needs our cheap and unpaid labour.
Let's ruin the economy.
Let's improve our lives.

Lorraine Davies

embracing guide for men

1. some women draw in their breasts
   when you embrace them:
   these are the ones who have been hurt
   by zonal adoration.
2. some women close their eyes:
   these are the ones whose secrets have been
   skimmed and eaten
   like fishes playing in sun-flecked shallows.
3. some women put their lips upon your neck:
   these are the ones who dare not utter
   what they know behind the teeth,
   whose tongues are bruised,
   who still believe—ah, miracles—
   in love and silences.

Karen Romell

Old Woman

I sit in the sun
like a raisin, my
juices drying to a vestigial
trickle, a subtle
twitch of pulses under dust-dry skin,

and one remembering
heart.
It's glory
to sit like a queen in a chair of
warmth; my hands
have varnished air with their expressions;

every word is filial. I covet my foolishness
like a dream.
I have no superstitions;
eclipses and moon-falls, all
delight me.

I
am no fatalist, though my body
sends mercenary pains upon me like dim
shrieks
that exhaust themselves in the dullness of nightfall.

I am no
sparrow; my bird-bone
hands are eloquent still, my eyes are true.
I spin the wind to silence, I stare
at the vagrant sun,
my blood.

Sylvie Sicotte

Cent fois sur le métier

Et des femmes, cent fois sur le métier, remettent leur ouvrage. Et leurs conjoints, affolés devant ces orgasmes qui se multiplient, en perdent littéralement leurs lettres ancestrales.

Vers quel révoltant "isme" les tirent-elles, eux qui viennent tout juste de se faire enseigner... pudiquement (car il est dépassé entre hommes de tomber dans la naïve confidence), eux à qui leur propre père vient tout juste de démontrer... avec un soupir ou petit rire entendu (on n'y peut rien, elles sont si lentes à venir), eux qui ont compris seulement récemment... (mon Fils, la paix de ton ménage est hélas à ce prix) les vertus de la maîtrise!

D'accord pour la maîtrise, et même le doctorat s'il le faut. Mais pour le contrôle d'une jouissance simultanée! Pas pour se voir subitement déclassé! Pas pour regarder bêtement l'autre s'extasier toute seule!

Où s'en irait la littérature?

Lettre à un ami anglophone

Mon cher Bill,

Tu te rappelles, (je sais que tu as souvent des blancs de mémoire) nous avons été présentés l'un à l'autre par une connaissance commune. Oserais-je le dire? Par une entremetteuse. Par la charmante directrice d'une agence de rencontres.

Un jour, j'ai trouvé dans mon courrier une jolie carte blanche discrètement enfouie dans deux enveloppes, la plus petite, pré adressée, devant être renvoyée au cas où ta face, ton corps aussi je suppose, ne me reviendraient pas. Il était écrit: "Nous avons le plaisir de vous présenter (il y avait un espace blanc pour le nom de l'heureux élu) Bill Sanders, 178-1980 ou 234-5678. Nous vous suggérons de communiquer avec cette personne dès que possible. Si par la suite vous désirez rencontrer quelqu'un d'autre, renvoyez-nous cette carte après avoir inscrit vos commentaires au verso."

J'étais toute excitée. Tu serais mon premier. Mon premier homme vraiment libre.

Depuis que j'étais chef de famille monoparentale, j'avais bien rencontré quelques célibataires, mais ils étaient malheureusement encore très attachés à leur enfance, malgré leur âge parfois avancé. Par contre, je manifestais un flair extraordinaire pour m'amouracher d'hommes mariés. A croire qu'il traînait en moi un nostalgique attachement pour l'état conjugal. A croire qu'un jonc brillant de tous ses feux à l'annulaire d'une main virile se transformait pour moi en un fétiche irrésistible. Et même quand la main était nue... Les moines, on le sait, ne portent plus leur habit. Ce qui me séduisait alors, était sûrement ce regard d'autorité conféré automatiquement à celui qui sait mettre la légalité de son côté. Ou peut-être ce regard de prisonnier? J'ai beaucoup pratiqué le bénévolat.

Quoi qu'il en soit, je me félicitais d'avoir vigoureusement réorienté ma vie émotive. Enfin je connaîtrais un homme qui voulait remédier à sa solitude. Pas un aventurier à la sauvette. Pas un affamé des lundis soirs.

Je voyais bien un nom anglophone sur la carte alors que je m'étais adressée à une agence francophone. Mais je me suis dit: C'est probablement un immigrant qui veut s'intégrer à la majorité québécoise et perfectionner l'usage de notre langue nationale. Il a compris le bien fondé de la loi 101.

J'ai toujours eu beaucoup d'affection pour nos minorités. Comme si ça me revalorisait. Je me suis intéressée à la cause amérindienne, je me suis frottée à quelques Africains refaisant leur vie chez nous, mais je n'avais pas eu, jusqu'ici, de contacts très intimes avec nos voisins de Westmount ou de Côte Saint Luc. J'étais fière d'avoir une nouvelle occasion de faire connaître le Québec aux Québécois.

Néanmoins, je décidai d'attendre que tu communiques avec moi le premier. Tu devais avoir reçu une carte similaire à la mienne t'indiquant mon nom et mon numéro de téléphone, alors je me suis dit qu'il valait mieux ne pas avoir l'air trop pressée. Les hommes sont souvent si inquiets de leur virilité. La moindre spontanéité, surtout si elle vient d'une femme, risque de les effaroucher.

J'ai donc laissé passer les derniers jours de la semaine et toute la fin de semaine. (Je déteste dire "week end" en français, je trouve que ça fait emprunté, que ça fait retraité en Floride.) Rendue au lundi soir, à bout d'attente, j'ai empoigné le téléphone et j'ai signalé le premier numéro...Pas de réponse. Le 2è...Ah, on décroche...Hello! ...Bonjour, je suis Anne Lavoie...(Il y a eu un petit silence) Oh oui, euh...glad to hear you. Can I call you back in a few minutes? I have a long distance call on my other line. Okay?...

Tu m'as rappelée une heure plus tard, en t'excusant de m'avoir fait attendre. Mais tu avais plusieurs fois signalé en vain pour comprendre finalement qu'on avait oublié d'inscrire le petit un au début de mon numéro. C'était un interurbain. Je t'ai rassuré tout de suite: It's not far from Montréal.

Toi aussi tu as voulu me rassurer. Même si je t'avais rejoint le soir à ton bureau, tu n'étais pas un intoxiqué de travail. Non simplement, tu avais été malade et tu avais du temps à rattraper. En fait, tu ne venais plus "at the office" que trois jours et demi par semaine et jamais le lundi. Excepté ce soir-là évidemment, où tu rentrais de ton chalet dans le nord. Tu voyageais beaucoup cependant. Tu pratiquais la mobilité pan-canadienne si chère à Trudeau.

J'ai su que tu étais divorcé, que tu avais quatre enfants éparpillés dans le pays et que tu étais originaire des maritimes. Puis, comme je prévoyais, le mercredi suivant, aller porter un texte à Montréal et assister ensuite à un cocktail, nous nous sommes donnés rendez-vous pour ce soir-là.

Cette agence qui nous avait mis en contact, était sobre et discrète. (Elle l'est sûrement toujours si elle existe encore.) Pas de ces appareils-vidéo qui vous permettent de choisir parmi une série de mâles tous plus beaux les uns que les autres, celui qui a le plus de chances de faire tressaillir votre muscle cardiaque. Non, ici vous exposiez tout simplement vos désirs. vos exigences et on les notait.

Par exemple, si vous étiez un célibataire montréalais très près de vos sous et que vous ne vouliez pas augmenter vos dépenses de gazoline, vous pouviez exiger une partenaire habitant dans les limites de l'île. Ou bien si vous étiez une dame à l'oreille particulièrement chatouilleuse, vous pouviez refuser de rencontrer un homme dont le prénom vous rappelait trop celui de votre père ou de votre ex-mari. Mais moi, je n'avais pas formulé d'exigence particulière, ni sur le plan physique, ni sur la condition sociale, ni sur l'état de fortune, sauf ce souhait, oh combien illusoire, que l'on ait réglé ses problèmes.

Alors j'étais malgré tout nerveuse. Allais-je tomber sur un quinquagénaire à l'esprit plus bedonnant que son ventre? Allais-je me retrouver devant un grand sec qui aurait attrapé le torticolis à chaque fois qu'il aurait baissé les yeux sur moi? Je n'avais pas compté avec la perspicacité de mon intervieweuse qui avait appris que le premier coup d'oeil est important et qui savait agencer les physiques sinon les les coeurs.

Oui, j'étais nerveuse ce mercredi-là. Une fois rendue à Montréal, je me suis aperçue que j'avais oublié mon manuscrit chez moi. Mais ce n'était pas dramatique, même si la pièce elle- même prétendait l'être. Personne n'attendait après. C'était pure générosité de ma part d'offrir ainsi, spontanément, de la matière à émission.

Et curieusement, j'y mettais en scène un anglophone et une francophone. Mais tout était imaginaire dans ce texte, ou à peu près. Pas grande chose de vécu. Mon jeune businessman de 33 ans, frais arrivé de Calgary, s'y débrouillait un peu trop bien en français.

Toi, tu avais 49 ans et tu vivais à Montréal depuis 13 ans, depuis l'Expo en fait, mais ton français se limitait à "Bonjour, comment ça va?" Même si tu disais avoir été conquis par le caractère enjoué des "French Canadians." Bien sûr, tu as essayé au début de glisser un mot par ci par là en français, mais à chaque fois je m'y attendais tellement peu et ça sonnait si étrange que tu devais toujours répéter en anglais.

Ça ne me dérangeait pas de devoir parler ta langue. Au contraire. J'aime parler anglais. J'ai l'impression alors de faire des exercices de hata-yoga avec ma bouche, de danser avec mes mâchoires. De sortir de mon ordinaire en quelque sorte, d'apprendre du nouveau, de me perfectionner. J'ai toujours le désir de me perfectionner. J'ai une âme d'étudiante. De pucelle romantique diraient certains de mes accidentels partenaires sexuels. D'intoxiquée de l'amour. De femme qui est toute dans son trip et qui ne pense pas à son vis-à-vis mâle, ajouteraient-ils l'âme froide et sentencieuse.

Toute frémissante, je tournai donc le coin de ta rue. Auparavant j'avais caqueté au coquetel. Je l'avais quitté, toute fière intérieurement, de pouvoir dire à mon tour: "Excusez-moi, je dois partir, on m'attend." Il m'était arrivé si souvent de voir s'éloigner les autres et de me retrouver sous une averse soudaine de solitude, l'âme trempée.

Malgré tout, je me séchais vite après ces averses. Il était plus dur de voir un couple me fermer la porte de son amitié, craignant tout à coup que ma tierce personne ne fasse diverger leurs mutuels regards convergents.

Enroulée dans ma cape d'octobre, les cheveux au vent, je grimpai jusqu'à ton premier étage, un panier de pommes sous le bras. La saison avait été abondante cette année-là, j'apportais vraiment de mon superflu, pas du tout de mon nécessaire.

Toi, tu m'offris de la musique classique parfaitement stéréophonique, du vin et des céleris au fromage. Tu te dépensais pour mon confort.

Nous étions tous les deux satisfaits de notre premier coup d'oeil l'un sur l'autre.

Cette première nuit aussi, nous nous déclarâmes enchantés l'un de l'autre. Tu avais été généreux, jusqu'à t'écorcher la peau des genoux. Car nous l'avions commencée cette nuit, sur la fourrure qui s'étendait paresseusement devant le feu de foyer. En plus, tu ne ronflais pas. C'était vraiment fantastique! Comble de joie, tu m'as demandé si j'étais libre le samedi suivant, seulement deux jours plus tard...

Pourquoi t'es-tu retiré dès que tu as senti de l'émotion chez moi, de l'amour? On m'avait déjà fait le coup mais ça pouvait se comprendre, on était marié. N'avais-tu pas dit que tu étais libre?

Ironiquement, c'est le jour de la Saint-Valentin que tu m'as fait comprendre ton indifférence. Tu avais oublié notre rendez-vous. Ce n'est pourtant pas que j'accorde de l'importance à la Saint-Valentin.

Non, c'est tout bêtement à l'échange, à la communication que j'attache de l'importance, à ce qui peut réunir les gens.

Toi, c'est à quoi? A ta seule efficacité? Une fois le visible appréhendé, n'y a-t-il aucun désir chez toi de l'invisible, de l'inédit?

Et tu me coupes la parole et tu me bouches les pores et tu me coinces l'estomac et tu me mouilles les fesses. Et tu crois m'avoir muselée à jamais alors que tu as débridé en moi vulves et clitoris, bouches et sourires, ventres et songes.

Et je te vois si faible, si blanc, si rigidement occidental dans tes souliers de jogging...

J'ai voulu te revoir. Une fois dans l'exubérance de l'été, une autre fois pour l'anniversaire de notre rencontre. Tu comprends, j'essaie d'être positive. Je veux considérer que mon verre n'est pas à moitié vide, mais à moitié plein. Et n'avais-tu pas écrit, en réponse à une de mes vibrantes lettres, que tu avais beaucoup "d'affection" pour moi, que tu désirais me revoir "occasionnellement?" Mais j'ai dû me rendre à l'évidence. Ton désir pour moi n'excitait même plus ton obsession de la parfaite performance.

Tu m'as dit: "Je n'ai jamais su aimer. Je n'ai jamais pu établir une relation de confiance et d'intimité avec une femme."

Oui, tu étais le premier. Le premier qui osait avouer son insensibilité. Je devrais enfin comprendre, me faire une raison.

Je t'ai donc demandé: "Mais pourquoi t'es-tu inscrit à une agence?" Tu m'as répondu: "To be swept away."

J'avoue que je m'attendais à tout sauf à ça. J'aurais été moins surprise si tu m'avais dit par exemple: "Pour me venger de ma mère" ou "pour vérifier si une femme pouvait encore être amoureuse de moi."

Peut-être soupçonnes-tu que seul un électro-choc pourrait maintenant dégeler tes sens? Peut-être cherches-tu à te précipiter dans l'utérus ultime? Tout seul?

En sept mois, depuis notre simili-rupture, tu ne m'as téléphoné qu'une seule fois de toi-même. Tout récemment. Nous venions de nous revoir, à ma suggestion, j'étais donc étonnée de ton geste. Tu n'avais pas l'habitude d'appeler uniquement pour le plaisir. Tu es un homme sérieux. Il devait y avoir une raison suffisante...

En effet, tu avais souffert de malaises génitaux, très bénins cependant, et tu venais de recevoir un verdict de la clinique indiquant la présence de gonocoques. Est-ce que ce ne serait pas moi qui...

Après examen, il s'est avéré que non, ce n'était pas moi qui... Et tu ne m'avais même pas contaminée.

Qu'est-ce que tu veux? Nous avons au moins cette qualité, nous les Québécois. Nous sommes des résistants.

Bien à toi, en ce morne accord du Canada Bill,
Le 5 novembre 1981.

Phyllis Webb

Leaning

I am half-way up the stairs
of the Leaning Tower of Pisa.

Don't go down. You are in this
with me too.

I am leaning out of the Leaning
Tower heading into the middle distance

where a fur-blue star contracts, becomes
the ice-pond Brueghel's figures are skating on.

North Magnetic pulls me like a flower
out of the perpendicular

angles me into outer space
an inch at a time, the slouch

of the ground, do you hear that?
the hiccup of the sludge about the stone.

(Rodin in Paris, his amanuensis, a torso. . .)
I must change my life or crunch

over in vertigo, hands
bloodying the inside tower walls

lichen and dirt under the fingernails
Parsifal vocalizing in the crazy night

my sick head on the table where I write
slumped one degree from the horizontal

the whole culture leaning. . .

the phalloi of Mies, Columbus returning
stars all shot out—

And now this. Smelly tourists
shuffling around my ears

climbing into the curvature.
They have paid good lira to get in here.

So have I. So did Einstein and Bohr.
Why should we ever come down, ever?

And you, are you still here

tilting in this stranded ark
blind and seeing in the dark.

December 19-20/82

Marian Engel

Banana Flies

Now I want to flap my arms and fly. Something's happening: I am a bird in the shape of a banana peel, going far, but not to the terminus.

Let's play games. Let me tell you a true story and pretend it's unreal. Let me tell you a real story and you make it unreal.

The true story is that we had a dinner party and nothing happened except that skeletons were made of birds. But something did happen: I came home and happy and I didn't mind the banana peel on the coffee table. I am still happy. Something happened.

To make it fiction we have to change the names. I sat beside Almond and across from Pear. I am Apple, because I've always wanted to be Eve. I'm not, but because it is I who push the keys of the typewriter, I can choose to be.

The party was given by Cherry in honour of Almond, who was supposed to be leaving for Figland. In fact she is not: she is having an affair with Lime Ricky and is not upset by the cancellation of her voyage, although she needs a new job.

I have left out Greengage, because I do not know her well. Mirabelle, whom you may prefer to call Victoria Plum, was next to Cherry. She is the only one of us who is still married. I don't see enough of her. She made a wicked birthday punch in baby-days.

It was happy, that evening. We were in full fig. Nothing has been changed but the names.

These are the facts: we talked and talked. Pear talked of her travels. I talked of my desire to travel. Everyone talked about going south to visit Pear on her island; how to rival Pear in parsimony. She is the cleverest of us all, the high-wire dancer among us acrobats. The oldest, too, an empty-nester, while most of us are just beginning to wave goodbye. Almond's boys left this year, Apple is between hope that they will and despair that they might, Mirabelle doesn't know how she feels, Cherry cherishes her five-year-old, dreaming dreams we have outgrown. Greengage moved out, leaving the Independence Party behind, and bought new furniture.

It was Pear who dominated, Pear who all her life had done more with less, and has taught us much: live, fill up the cup, be the cup, shed your leaves when the time comes.

"What movie star did you want to be?"

"Hedy Lamarr," she said.

I confessed to lacquered Merle Oberon, whom my mother-in-law humanised by using the surname Obrien. Longlegged singers and dancers came in, and small blonde fleshpots. We sighed for our stupidity, and laughed at the greasy lovers we had desired. What movie star did you want to sleep with, before you dared to think what that meant?

The past, the future, hope. Pear's first divorce told with exquisite humour: a bunch of pulp magazine writers concocting a story too good for the judge, mission accomplished with bated breath.

Almond's pride in her boys.

Mirabelle's happiness: to have survived a most difficult marriage, to have fine children. She is kind and tolerant.

So are we all, this group of women under the lamplight, the anthropological decorations from other days.

It was the sort of party men might have called, in my day, a hen party. It wasn't a stag.

We ate two birds and a garden of vegetables, grapes and cheese and a pineapple cut to look like a pheasant. The brie abandoned itself. Cherry provided.

Cherry and Almond passed a joint. Pear refused most intoxicants. Apple was at the grape.

There was not a lemon among us.

The divorces, the struggles, the love of children, of irresponsible men, the leaving or staying: the desire for the new. Resignation, hope, search for new places. Give us the country I wanted to say, we outgrew the movie stars, moved into reality, did it. O'erleapt mothers' neuroses, grandmothers' proprieties, fears, madnesses, the strictures of the men in our lives, judges, doctors, mountebanks. Became.

This group of women around this table, who had met misfortune, alienation, fame, success, disgrace, competence, love, hate, disaster, disorientation, fear, the love of children. Learned to raise them, learned to part with them and move on.

Apple to Pear: I became an 'art' writer because I was supported by Potato.

Pear to Apple: He was more of a salmon and you're allergic to fish.

Sense of accomplishment: I am the winged supermarket basket I saw in the performance at the art gallery. The banana, too, the banana I found on the coffee table crouched like a spread spider which instead of annoying me grew wings.

Have you ever noticed a banana peel flying, how its wings flip and soar, five segments in the sky speeding to the garbage can with elegance and eloquence? All fear of loneliness, falling objects, obscenity, falls away.

Apple speaking. Dinner party over. Send flowers to Cherry. Go to bed. Cover yourself up: you are your own child.

Biographies

Jennifer Alley was born and raised in Vancouver. She lives there still with her husband, and dog. She has received two awards for poetry, The Bliss Carmen Award 1978, and the National Norma Epstein Award, 1980. She has had publications in *Waves, Grain, Poetry Canada Review* and in the anthologies *Pomegranate* and *Handouts from the Mountain*. She has given readings at the Surrey Art Gallery, the Literary Storefront and, most recently, with Maggie Shore on Saturna Island. She is currently working on a book of children's stories, adventures which are based on Winnebago Indian stories.

Gay Allison, a Saskatchewan-born Toronto poet and founding editor of *Fireweed,* is currently Poetry Editor of *Waves.* She was co-editor of *Landscape* (1977), co-founder of the Women's Writing Salon and a founding member of the Women's Writing Collective. Her first book of poetry, *Life: Still* (Williams-Wallace), won the 1982 FWTAO Poetry Award. She has just completed *The Unravelling,* a second book of poetry.

Née en 1951 à Alexandrie, Egypte, **Anne-Marie Alonzo** vit au Québec depuis 1963. Détentrice d'un baccalauréat (1976) et d'une maîtrise (1978) en études françaises de l'Université de Montréal, elle y poursuit présentement des études de doctorat. Collaboratrice à *La Nouvelle Barre du Jour,* à *Possibles,* à *Spirale* et à *des femmes en mouvements* et *Fruits* (Paris), Anne-Marie Alonzo a aussi signé de nombreux textes radiophoniques. Critique littéraire à *La Gazette des femmes* et à *La Vie en rose,* elle a dirigé de janvier 82 à janvier 83, la collection fiction aux éditions *Nouvelle Optique* (Montréal).

Oeuvre: *Geste,* fiction, Paris, éditions des femmes, 147 p. 1979; *Veille,* fiction, Paris, éditions des femmes, 99 p. 1982; *Blanc de Thé,* fiction, livre-objet, les Zéditions élastiques, Montréal, 1983.

Brig Anderson. I'm a wandering, lonely but loving her solitude woman, restlessly searching for something to illuminate my days and bless my nights. Sacrificing fifteen years to an autistic child has left me exhausted but determined to dare new challenges and environments, emotional and physical. My child has taught me the meaning of altruism, fearlessness, activism, unconditional love.

Susan Andrews. Lives in Saskatoon. Poems published in *Grain, Event, Network, Antigonish Review, A Room of One's Own, Fiddlehead, Arc* and others. Poems also broadcast on CBC (Sask.) Radio and CHSK-FM Radio (University of Saskatchewan).

Jeannette Armstrong is an accomplished Okanagan Indian artist recognized for her poetry, writing, sculpture and painting. She works in research and development for the Okanagan Indian Learning Institute. Her first book, *Enwhisteetkwa* was published in 1982 by Theytus Books of Penticton, B.C. Other titles available are *Neekna and Chemai,* part of an Okanagan children's series, *Kou-Skelowh; We Are the People* and *Slash,* a contemporary historical novel that follows the experiences of an Okanagan man from 1960 to 1983. Also in production is a collection of her poetry.

Germaine Beaulieu est née à Montréal en 1949. Psychologue et directrice d'un service communautaire, elle poursuit son activité littéraire depuis bientôt six ans. En 1977 elle publie son premier recueil de poèmes intitulé: *Envoie ta foudre jusqu'à la mort, Abracadabra.* En 1979, elle publie un roman avant pour titre: *Sortie d'elle(s) mutante.* Un nouveau recueil de poèmes sortira prochainement sous le titre: *Archives distraites.* Germaine Beaulieu a également publié de nombreux textes dans diverses revues littéraires notamment *La Nouvelle Barre du Jour.*

Louky Bersianik. Née à Montréal. Etudes à l'Université de Montréal et à la Sorbonne. M.A. (Lettres) et scolarité Ph.D. Séjours en France (5 ans) et en Grèce (1 an). A écrit pour la radio, la télévision et le film, et publié des contes pour enfants. Depuis 1972, travaille à un cycle de textes féministes (romans, poèmes, nouvelles, pièce de théâtre, chanson, essais) et participe à un grand nombre de colloques nationaux et internationaux. A fait des tournées de conférences à travers le Canada et les Etats-Unis et donné des ateliers d'écriture dans plusieurs universités canadiennes ainsi qu'à Cerisy-La-Salle (France) en juillet 1983. Ont paru: *L'Euguelionne,* roman triptyque (Montréal 1976, Paris 1978, Victoria/Toronto 1981); *La Page de Garde,* poème, (1978); *Le Pique-Nique Sur L'Acropole,* roman (1979); *Maternative,* poèmes (1980); *Les Agenesies du Vieux Monde,* essai (1982); *Nuclea Epiphane (Au beau milieu de moi),* poèmes (1983); *Frange Dé-Mesure,* poèmes (1983); ainsi que de nombreux textes dans différentes revues et livres.

Ayanna Black was born in Jamaica and lived in England before moving to Canada in 1964. She is now active as writer and publicist who has worked extensively with women and Black artists. She has given many poetry readings including poetry performances of her work. Her poetry has appeared in *One Out of Many,* the first collection of work by 21 Black Women in Canada and *Fireweed,* a feminist Quarterly. She's presently working on a book for publication in 1984.

Michèle Boisvert. Mi-Shelle, Née à Montréal Le 3 mars 1957, Fille de Béatrice, Fille de Caroline, Fille de Cordélia, Fille, depuis des millénaires, La mer est mon berceau. . .

Biotype: amoureuse des sons et de leur graphisme; Origine: radiant point zéro-zéro; Agée de: presqu'un cycle solaire; Hémisphères complémentaires: application des fonctions chiffres- mots en sciences poétiques.

Etudes (officielles): Sciences de la santé, Certificat en créativité à l'Université de Montréal, Ateliers de création littéraire avec Louky Bersianik.

Nicole Brossard est née à Montréal où elle a fait ses études. Elle a publié ses premiers poèmes en 1965 dans *L'Aube à la saison.* Son oeuvre comprend une quinzaine de livres: des recueils de poèmes, des romans, des textes pour le théâtres, et de nombreux articles et textes d'intervention. Elle a régulièrement collaboré à plusieurs revues québécoises, canadiennes et étrangères. Le prix Gouverneur général a été attribué a *Mécanique jongleuse* en 1975.

Pauline Butling teaches at David Thompson University Centre in Nelson, B.C. She has an M.A. from U.B.C., and did doctoral work at S.U.N.Y. at Buffalo. Since 1967 she has lived in South Slocan, B.C. with her husband Fred Wah and two daughters. She has published several reviews and has recently completed a critical essay on Gladys Hindmarch's work.

Née à Québec le 2 octobre 1954, **Marie Cholette** obtient en 1977 un B.sp. en littérature française de l'Université Laval. Elle réalise un film en 16 mm couleur intitulé: *La mer* à la fin d'une mineure en cinéma, qui lui a valu une mention fort louable au Festival canadien international du film d'amateur en 1980. Elle vient d'achever au même établissement d'enseignement un B.sp. en linguistique. Elle a étudié la musique au Conservatoire de Québec et souligne l'importance de la musique dans l'élaboration de son oeuvre.

Lis-moi comme tu m'aimes, poésie. Ill. de l'auteure. Paris, Éd. Saint-Germain-des-Prés, 1975. *Les entourloupettes,* poésie. Montréal, Éd. Echouris M.C., 1979.

Jan E. Conn has had poems published in several Canadian literary magazines, journals, and anthologies. Two books of poems have been accepted for publication: *Road of Smoke,* Colophon Press, Vancouver, and *Red Shoes in the Rain,* Fiddlehead Press, New Brunswick. She has lived in Montreal, Vancouver, and is currently a Ph.D. student in entomology at the University of Toronto.

Melodie Corrigall. Born Ottawa, 1942. Raised in Ottawa Valley, idyllic summers at grandparents' in Quebec. After University lived for two years in Europe. On return to Canada, became active in left politics. Presently B.C. public servant, living in Vancouver with union representative, Hans Brown, and daughters Sarah and Joanna.

Lorna Crozier lives in Regina. Her poems have appeared in many periodicals and anthologies and in five books, of which *The Weather* is the most recent. She has received the Saskatchewan Art Board's Senior Artist's Award.

Beth Cuthand lives in Saskatoon and is a freelance writer and editor. She is actively involved in the struggle for native rights. She has had stories published in *Indian World* and the *Saskatchewan Indian* and is currently involved with a writing group called the Native Writers' Circle.

Milda Danys was born in Montreal in 1950 shortly after her parents came to that city as Lithuanian refugees. Aside from poetry, she writes plays and prose fiction. Recently she published a history of Lithuanian immigrants in Canada after World War II.

Lorraine Davies. Born in 1938. Lives in Vancouver. Born in Saskatchewan, lived thirteen years in Montreal. B.A. in Eng. Lit. from U.B.C. Worked as teacher, community worker and secretary. This is her second published poem. Currently writing short stories.

Gisele Dominique. I was born in France and emigrated to Canada in 1960. I was a dancer until eight years ago, also a singer and actress in summer stock in Quebec, and with John Herbert in Toronto for three years. I became interested in writing in 1977, joining the poet section of the women's writing collective. I write in both languages, but living in Toronto, my work is confined mostly to English. I am a member of a Francophone feminist group and a member of Amnesty International.

Maguy Duchesne/écrivain en herbe/et passionné/professeur émérite/en Colombie Britannique.

Valerie Dudoward is a 27-year-old writer from the Tsimshian Nation. She began her career in communications with C.B.C. Radio CFPR in Prince Rupert as an announcer/operator. She has worked in communications with several indigenous organizations in B.C. Valerie is working at securing creative and commercial markets for her plays, short stories and poetry, and continues to freelance in radio.

Robin Belitsky Endres is a Toronto playwright, feminist and Marxist. She is the founder and artistic director of Pelican Players—a multicultural neighbourhood theatre which produces original plays by, for and about the people in its community.

Marian Engel was born in Toronto in 1933 into a family with the odd tradition of sending women to university. She took up writing as a stripling, winning a prize for her first essay on the Evils of Drink at Sunday School. She sold stories to *Seventeen* as a teenager and then settled in to write and become rich and famous. Fifteen years and four novels later, she sold her first novel and began to freelance for radio. An interlude of cooking for visiting poets led to a divorce: be warned that "I can't do a dinner party I am working on my book" is a dynamite line and gets you the freedom you deserve. Freedom is something of a monster and has given her a lot to write about. She lives in Toronto with her daughter, and is working on a book called *Elizabeth and the Golden City*. She is a member of the Order of Canada and finds this pleasing.

Mona Fertig. Born in Vancouver 1954. Published in many literary mags. Founder and Director of the Literary Storefront '78-'82. Given many readings, singular and collaborative, across the country. Published 5 books. Most recent, *Releasing the Spirit*, Colophon Books, 1982. New poems, Jungian fairy tales, and a poetic journal, *4722 Rue Berri,* in progress. Living in Beach Grove, Tsawwassen, B.C.

Deborah Foulks. I am a refugee from the Vancouver school system, a university drop-out, and an activist in the anti-war movement. I have been a free-lance writer, a typist, a waitress and a singer. I have written songs, plays and poems, and am now in the process of completing my third novel.

Maxine Gadd lives on Galiano Island, British Columbia. Her latest book is *Lost Language,* a collection of poems from fifteen years of writing.

Nicole Gagné. Née à Montréal en 1942. Etudes universitaires en travail social. Occupe un emploi dans ce domaine depuis 1964. Intérêt particulier pour la philosophie, la musique et les arts visuels. Venue à l'écriture alors que s'élaborait la fin d'une psychanalyse personnelle comme un autre lieu pour dire l'urgence de naître.

Jan Gould is author of *Women of B.C.* and *The Boathouse Question and Other Stories,* also of numerous published articles and fiction. An extensive traveller, she finds outer travel matches inner exploration. Interests: human rights, family, nature, mythology, flying. Divides her time between Victoria and a lakeside cabin.

Candis J. Graham was born in 1949, in Kincardine, Ontario. She started taking her writing seriously in 1976 and, since then, has worked part-time in traditionally women's jobs (mostly office work) to allow writing time. Ms Graham lives in Ottawa. She is working on a collection of short stories and a novel.

Kristjana Gunnars. I was born in Iceland, grew up in Iceland and Denmark, did my B.A. in Oregon and then immigrated to Canada in 1969, at 21. I lived in B.C., Ontario, Saskatchewan and Manitoba since, did an M.A. in Saskatchewan and am doing a Ph.D. at the Univ. of Manitoba at the moment. Have published four books of poetry (*Settlement Poems I* and *II* with Turnstone; *One- Eyed Moon Maps* with Porcepic; *Wake-Pick Poems* with Anansi) and one book of short stories (*The Axe's Edge* with Porcepic).

Dale Colleen Hamilton was born near the village of Rockwood, Ontario. For the past eight years, she has made her home base on the Gulf Islands and in Victoria, British Columbia. She has been involved with Native people for approximately five years; first at the Whitedog Reserve in northern Ontario and most recently in the Cowichan Valley on Vancouver Island. Dale has had several articles published and two plays produced. She is pursuing her on-going study of healing and witchcraft and is working as script writer with Potlatch Theatre and Film Society, a Native organization. She has just completed an article on Women's Peace Camps and is in the midst of writing a new play entitled: "Witches, Invalids and Lunatics."

Claire Hélie. Née à Chicoutimi en 1951, j'ai commencé à écrire à dix-huit ans: un journal d'abord, puis des poèmes au "temps du cegep." Depuis, vivant à Québec, la ville est devenue un de mes personnages intérieurs. J'aime me promener, emportant mon petit carnet, c'est ma façon coutumière d'être heureuse lorsque je suis seule.

Melanie Higgs. I was born August 31, 1959, in Vancouver, and have lived here all my life. I graduated from U.B.C. with a first class degree in English Literature (B.A.), in May 1983. Right now I am working at the U.B.C. Library and at U.B.C. Press (as a volunteer doing copy editing). I'm writing more stories and a novel based on my experiences working in mining camps in the Yukon.

Carole Itter, born in 1939 in Vancouver, artist and writer, has stayed on the west coast most of her life. Her writings include *Cloud in My Eye,* 1970; *The Log's Log,* 1972; *Birthday,* 1974; an oral history, 1978 with Daphne Marlatt titled *Opening Doors, Vancouver's East End; Whistle Daughter Whistle,* 1983, a collection of prose and poems.

Smaro Kamboureli, born in 1955 in Thessaloniki, Greece, came to the University of Manitoba in 1978 where she is currently writing her Ph.D. thesis on the contemporary Canadian long poem. She has published reviews and essays on Canadian writers, and she is vice-president of the Manitoba Writers' Guild.

Penny Kemp is a poet, playwright and fiction writer. 1984 will see the publication of four new books, all poetry: *Animus* (Caitlin), *Some Talk Magic* (Ergo), *Eidolons* (White Pine) and *Binding Twine* (Ragweed). Playwrights Canada is reprinting her play, *The Epic of Toad and Heron.* Penny gives readings and workshops across the continent.

Hilda Kirkwood, Toronto based writer and editor. Contributor to *Canadian Forum, Quarry, Waves.* Associate editor *Ethos.* One of four founders of *Fireweed* Magazine. Member Women Writers Co-operative, North York. Hobbies: reading, gardening, listening to music. Married to Toronto businessman.

Maureen Leyland was born in Montreal; she now lives in Vancouver with her son, Ryan Moore. She has had stories published in *event* and *West Coast Review* and is presently working on a series of linked stories dealing with entrapment.

Dorothy Livesay was born in Winnipeg, the daughter of Florence Livesay and J.F.B. Livesay. As well as a poet, she has been a journalist, social worker, teacher, editor, broadcaster and university professor. Her earliest book of poetry, *Green Pitcher,* was published in 1928. Dorothy Livesay was the recipient of the Governor General's medal for poetry in 1944 and 1947; she was awarded the Queen's Canada Medal in 1977. *The Phases of Love,* published by Coach House Press, came out in 1983.

Kate Lushington. born in London England in 1953. emigrated to Canada by choice in 1975. studied architecture Eng Lit and theatre design and production. never graduated. currently based in TO working as freelance theatre artist, mainly directing new Canadian plays, writing and performing collaborative intermedia works. member of the Women's Cultural Building and Fuse editorial board. "Griefkit" was written for a peace show, *Every Mushroom Cloud Has A Silver Lining,* devised by Robin Endres of Pelican Players to take place in a government designed bomb shelter aka church basement.

Daphne Marlatt, a Vancouver writer, has published 11 books of poetry including *Steveston, What Matters, How Hug a Stone,* and most recently *Touch To My Tongue.* She has also edited two oral histories and several little magazines. She is a member of the feminist editorial collective "Tessera" and is currently writing a novel.

Lorraine Martinuik. I have been writing since childhood, being occasionally published in the past ten years. I have been on Denman Island for four years, where I have been writing, making art, and building a house. I will be spending this winter in Vancouver working in a coffee store and attending Emily Carr College of Art.

Kathleen McDonnell is a Toronto writer and mother. She is the author of many articles and has written three plays, the most recent of which, "Body Shop," will be produced in Toronto by Theatre Passe Muraille in its 1984-85 season. She is currently writing a book about abortion, *Not an Easy Choice: A Feminist Re-examines Abortion,* which will be published by Women's Press (Toronto) in the fall of 1984. She is co-editing a Canadian women's health source book, and beginning work on a new play. This is her first published fiction.

Kathleen McHale is a writer who lives in Quebec.

Anne McLean. Born 1951, Montreal. Early prophet of Post-Feminism. Started writing fiction in 1977. Books: *Lil*(1977); *A Nun's Diary* (1984), *Snakebite and other stories* (unpublished). Author of an unpublished novella *(Mona's Latch)* satirizing pornography and the women's movement. Toured the Mediterranean on the tail of a dragon. Currently resting in Montreal, and masterminding a clandestine War on Poetry.

Mary Meigs was born in Philadelphia in 1917. She graduated from Bryn Mawr College in 1939, was an instructor in English there from 1940 to 1942, served in the *WAVES* and studied painting after the war. She came out as a lesbian in her two autobiographical books *Lily Briscoe, a Self-Portrait* and *The Medusa Head* which were published by Talonbooks in 1981 and 1983. She now lives in Québec.

Erin Mouré was born and raised in Calgary, and has lived in Vancouver for the past ten years, where she works on the transcontinental passenger train. Her three books of poetry are *Empire, York Street* (Anansi, 1979), *The Whiskey Vigil* (Harbour, 1981), and *Wanted Alive* (Anansi, 1983).

Rona Murray spent her early childhood in India, coming to Canada in 1932. She has published five volumes of poetry, had four plays produced, and has had short stories accepted across Canada. Presently she is living in Metchosin, B.C., where she is completing a book of short stories for publication.

Suniti Namjoshi was born in Bombay, India in 1941. Her books include *The Jackass and the Lady* (Calcutta: Writers Workshop, 1980), *Feminist Fables* (London, U.K.: Sheba Feminist Publishers, 1981) and *The Authentic Lie* (U. of New Brunswick: Fiddlehead Poetry Books, 1982). *From the Bedside Book of Nightmares* will be published by Fiddlehead in 1984. She teaches English Literature at Scarborough College, University of Toronto.

Francine Pellerin. Je suis originaire d'Ottawa. J'ai étudié trois ans en Beaux-arts à l'Université d'Ottawa et ensuite deux ans en Art graphique au Collège Algonquin (d'Ottawa également), duquel j'ai obtenu mon DEC. Puis j'ai travaillé à la pige et à temps plein comme graphiste à Montréal. Pour autant que je me souvienne, j'ai toujours aimé lire et dessiner. Mes écrits se traduisent en prose depuis mon adolescence et régulièrement en poésie depuis ces huit dernières années.

Maryse Pellerin. Naître d'une femme en 1948, à Ottawa. Tarder et retarder la venue à l'écriture qui s'impose comme passion et nécessité en 1981. Ecrire et enseigner. Enseigner à écrire. Merci Philippe Haeck. Me voir entre les vers d'Adrienne Rich à jamais, ceux de plusieurs poétesses américaines. Du rêve complice, vivre l'émergence simple.

Jacqueline Pelletier réside à Ottawa où elle est née le 4 août 1945. D'abord enseignante, puis animatrice communautaire, elle est consultante en gestion de programmes depuis 1980, et écrit depuis quatre ans. Auteure de plusieurs documents, y compris: "Au-delà des frontières: le rôle communautaire des collèges de l'Ontario" (1982) et "L'avenir se décide maintenant," rapport du colloque 'Les femmes et l'impact de la microélectronique' (1983). A publié dans *Les Cahiers de la femme, Status of Women News* et *Le Tablier déposé,* revue ontaroise dont elle fut longtemps co-productrice. Boursière du Conseil des Arts du Canada et de l'Institut canadien de recherches pour l'avancement de la femme (ICRAF), elle crée des spectacles de poésie et piano, en anglais et en français. Elle produit aussi des textes humoristiques, sur demande.

Annick Perrot-Bishop est née en 1945 au Vietnam. Professeur de musique puis secrétaire juridique à Paris et à Marseille, elle vit actuellement à Victoria (C.B.). Principalement autodidacte, elle a obtenu le Prix du Récit Fantastique 1983 de la Renaissance Aquitaine (France) et publie régulièrement dans la revue *Solaris* (Québec).

Marlene Philip is a New World poet from Trinidad and Tobago, who has lived and worked in Toronto as a lawyer for several years. Her work has appeared in *The Black Scholar, Presence Africaine,* and was selected for The Pushcart Prize VI anthology. She has published one book of poetry, *Thorns,* and has another forthcoming, entitled *Salmon Courage.* A young adult novel, *Margaret,* will be published in 1984.

Leslie Hall Pinder was born in Saskatchewan in 1948. She was educated at the University of Saskatchewan, Dalhousie University, and received her law degree at the University of British Columbia. Her works of fiction have appeared in little magazines in Canada, and her long prose poem, *35 Stones* was published by Lazara Publications in 1982. She practices civil litigation in Vancouver. She is presently working on her first novel.

Murielle Poirer. Besides doing graduate studies at Concordia University, I'm also working on a novel. My work has appeared in various literary journals across Canada. Born somewhere in Québec sometime after WWII, and if I still insist on writing at all, perhaps I almost believe we can talk ourselves out of that 'looming' number three.

Helen Potrebenko is a Vancouver writer who, during the past ten years has had published four books, numerous short stories, poetry and several newspaper articles. She has been laboratory technician, taxi driver, and student (B.A. in Sociology, Simon Fraser University, 1971) and is currently a secretary in an insurance adjusting office.

Gillian Robinson lives in Prince Edward Island. About "Flossie," she says that the piece was written about a woman in a Newfoundland Senior Citizens' Home.

Karen Romell was born in Vancouver, B.C., where she currently resides. She received her honours degree in English literature from U.B.C. in 1983. Her work has appeared in *Event* and *CVII* and won first prize in the U.B.C. Arts Undergraduate Review in 1983. She intends to pursue a career as a poet and journalist.

B.C. poet **Helene Rosenthal** has published three books of poetry (now out of print) and countless poems in a wide variety of journals. She is represented in many anthologies. A member of the League of Canadian Poets, she served as Vice-President for two years. Her current focus is music.

Veronica Ross. Born 1946 in West Germany; now lives in Nova Scotia. Author of *Goodbye Summer* (Oberon 1980) and *Dark Secrets* (Oberon 1983). A novel, *Fisherwoman,* will be published in 1984 (Pottersfield Press). Much of her fiction is set in the Maritimes and surrounds themes of human beings struggling and searching in circumstances they do not understand.

Jane Rule. Born in 1931, author of the books *Desert of the Heart, This Is Not For You, Against the Season, Theme for Diverse Instruments, Lesbian Images, The Young in One Another's Arms, Contract with the World, Outlander.* Resident of Galiano Island in British Columbia.

Diane Schoemperlen. I am 29 years old, originally from Thunder Bay, Ontario and now living in Canmore, Alberta for the past seven years. My work, both poetry and prose, has appeared in numerous Canadian publications including *Event, Room of One's Own, Canadian Woman Studies, Matrix,* and *The Malahat Review,* and has been broadcast on CBC Radio. My first book, a photo/fiction manuscript called *Double Exposures,* will be published by Coach House Press in 1984.

Sandy Shreve. Born: 1950, Quebec; Raised: New Brunswick; Currently living in Burnaby, B.C. and working as a secretary at Simon Fraser University. Poems have appeared in *Event, Going for Coffee, Hysteria, West Coast Review, Raven*, and other magazines.

Sylvie Sicotte. Née à Montréal, je suis tout d'abord comédienne, puis reporter à "La Presse." Ensuite j'accouche de trois enfants et de cinq livres (4 recueils de poèmes, 1 essai), j'obtiens une licence ès lettres et une maîtrise ès arts à l'Université de Montréal. J'écris des dramatiques pour la radio, je fais un stage à U.C.L.A. en "Screenplay writing" et je rédige un téléthéâtre de 90 minutes qui décrochera une mention spéciale aux prix Anik 80 de Radio-Canada. Je prépare maintenant des nouvelles.

Makeda Silvera lives in Toronto and works closely with West Indian domestic workers. Her book *Silenced* was published by Williams-Wallace in the spring of 1983.

Judy Smith. (1945-) RN, BFA, was born on a farm near Tribune, Saskatchewan and has lived the past 13 years in the West Kootenays and Vancouver, BC. Her poetry and prose has appeared in *NMFG, Canadian Short Fiction Anthology, Grain, Melmoth II, Zest, Island, Revue II* and *Kootenai*.

Marie-Louise Sorensen is a poet from Edmonton currently living in Vancouver. Her most recent work revolves around the lives of foreign domestic workers in Canada.

Dawn Star Fire. Of Tsimshian and Norwegian descent, Dawn Marlane Magnussen was born in the autumn of 1953 in Burns Lake, B.C. "Letting Go" was one of several pieces written during 1982 under the pen name of Star Fire.

Danielle Thaler (B.A. Montréal, M.A. PhD Toronto) née à Paris en 1948 vit au Canada depuis 1971. Elle enseigne présentement le français à l'Université de Victoria, B.C. Elle a publié *Poèmes à deux voix* en 1980 et *Peuple. femme, hystérie selon les Goncourt* paraîtra en 1984. Elle travaille également dans le domaine de la littérature enfantine et de la traduction.

Nelia Tierney. Nelia was born in 1940 and grew up on the South African Highveld. She emigrated to Canada in 1965. The mother of two teenage children she has degrees in zoology and psychology. She is working towards a M.F.A. in creative writing and is a Ph.D. candidate. She practices psychotherapy in Vancouver.

Rose-Marie Tremblay. Je suis née en 1944 en Saskatchewan, de parents franco-canadiens: un père québécois et une mère acadienne. En 1948 nous avons déménagé en Colombie Britannique, à Port Alberni, où j'ai vécu jusqu'un 1971. Ensuite, je suis allée vivre quatre ans au Québec et deux ans à Calgary. C'est à Calgary que j'ai décidé de m'inscrire à l'université. En 1978, je suis venue continuer mes études en français à U.B.C. J'enseigne actuellement à temps partiel à S.F.U.

Evelyne Voldeng née en 1943 à Saint-Guénolé (Bretagne). Diplômée de l'Université de Provence (anglais, français). Enseigne au département de français de l'Université Carleton à Ottawa. Principales publications: *Femme Plurielle,* anthologie de femmes-poètes contemporaines, Carleton Press, Ottawa, 1980; deux recueils de poèmes: *Les Plaquebières,* Rougerie, Limoges, 1980; *La Rose épervière,* Rougerie, 1983.

Betsy Warland lives in Vancouver where she was the initiator and co-coordinator of the Women and Words/Les femmes et les mots conference in 1983. She has published two collections of poems: *A Gathering Instinct* (1980) and *open is broken* (1984). Her work has also appeared in anthologies and journals.

Phyllis Webb lives on Salt Spring Island, B.C. and teaches part-time in the creative writing department at the University of Victoria. Her books of poetry include *Wilson's Bowl, The Vision Tree: Selected Poems, Sunday Water: Thirteen Anti Ghazals,* and *Talking* (Prose).

Ann J. West. Born in Vancouver, 1950. Two daughters. Currently living in Victoria. *The Water Book* published by Fiddlehead Books, 1978. Extensive magazine and radio publication. Two poetry manuscripts in progress: *Fire-Drake Occupations* and *Velocities;* children's book *Mulberries and Mice* complete but unpublished. Full time employment as an editor. Actively involved with my children, job and writing.

Janice Williamson is a socialist-feminist active in the peace movement and a member of Women's Press. She lives in Toronto where she is completing her PhD thesis on "The Poetics of Sexual Difference."

Susan Yeates. I am a woman, lesbian, pipe smoking, carpenter, writer. Isolation and wilderness are my teachers. I have a mania to write, it spurs me. I search for the perfect line. Jazz poetry, unwritten, spontaneous flow of words thrills me. poetry is meditation. I draw ancient knowledge via guides in automatic writing. A grizzly bear, and a golden eagle are my animal spirits. My sounder name is *Klungit* meaning churning mighty river.

DATE DUE
DATE DE RETOUR

FEB 2 2 1987			
P.H. JAN 2 8 1998			
FEB 1 1 1998			
APR 2 3 1999			
APR 0 7 1999			